He leaned in toward her. He was much closer than she had realized. His heated stare roamed over every inch of her.

"So lovely," he rasped. "What's your name?"

"M-Maura," she stammered. "L-lady Maura Daventry."

The gentleman froze, every muscle in his body visibly stiffening.

Maura frowned, bewildered. "What is it? What's wrong?"

He was quiet for so long that she began to think he wasn't going to answer.

"It appears that the Lady Grafton was a bit remiss when putting together her guest list," he said at last. "Allow me to introduce myself. I am Hawksley. The Earl of Hawksley."

*Dear God!* Maura stumbled backward as if she had been slapped.

"Yes," he said. "You understand. I believe my father was once . . . well-acquainted with your mother. Before he murdered her."

He swept his gaze over her once again. And she whirled and fled as if the hounds of hell were in pursuit . . .

*Other* **AVON ROMANCES**

# Kimberly Logan

# The Devil's Temptation

**AVON BOOKS**

*An Imprint of HarperCollinsPublishers*

This is a work of fiction. Names, characters, places, and incidents are products of the author's imagination or are used fictitiously and are not to be construed as real. Any resemblance to actual events, locales, organizations, or persons, living or dead, is entirely coincidental.

AVON BOOKS
*An Imprint of* HarperCollins*Publishers*
10 East 53rd Street
New York, New York 10022-5299

Copyright © 2007 by Kimberly Snoke
ISBN: 978–0–06–123919–9
ISBN–10: 0–06–123919–4
www.avonromance.com

First Avon Books paperback printing: May 2007

Avon Trademark Reg. U.S. Pat. Off. and in Other Countries,
Marca Registrada, Hecho en U.S.A.
HarperCollins® is a registered trademark of HarperCollins Publishers.

Printed in the U.S.A.

10  9  8  7  6  5  4  3  2  1

To Connie Kemple, for all of your brainstorming and proofreading help through the years. Your support and encouragement are greatly appreciated and will not be forgotten.

And to Susan Radford, for never doubting I could do it.

# The Devil's Temptation

# Prologue

*"I have finally met the man I am destined
to love for the rest of my life . . ."*

From the diary of Elise Marchand,
April 5, 1794

*London, 1817*

*E*scape.
  The word echoed in Lady Maura Daventry's head in a frantic refrain as she burst through the set of French doors and stumbled out onto the flagstone terrace, desperate to put some distance between herself and the glittering, animated throng of guests that milled about Lady Grafton's ballroom.

Escape. She had to get away. From the condemning stares, the pointing fingers, the cruel whispers.

Even now, snippets of the conversations she

hadn't been able to help overhearing from the moment she had arrived at the ball drifted through her mind in the most taunting manner.

*I say, isn't that one of the Marquis of Albright's chits?*

*By deuce, it is! The middle gel, I think. I had heard she was due for a come-out, but usually the Lady Grafton is much more particular about whom she invites to such affairs.*

*Wasn't her mother once an actress?*

*Yes, and you know what they say. Like mother, like daughter. I expect we shall find her in some dark corner with her skirts tossed up before the evening is over . . .*

Closing her eyes against the sting of tears, Maura took a steadying breath of the cool night air and reached out to wrap her fingers around the balustrade in a tight grip.

How had things gone so terribly wrong? She had dreamed of this for so long, and everything was supposed to be perfect. The very first ball of her first London Season. Her older sister, Jillian, had tried to prepare her, to warn her about the gossipmongers, but she hadn't wanted to hear it. After all, it had been almost four years, and she had convinced herself that tales of her infamous mother would have long ago faded into obscurity, that her own debut into society would cause little more than a few raised eyebrows and some minor speculation.

She had been wrong. Everywhere she had turned tonight, she had found herself the subject of some muffled discussion taking place behind a fluttering fan or gloved hand. And the more she had tried to ignore it, the more insistent their voices had become, battering away at her hard-won defenses until she could barely restrain the urge to scream.

It was beyond enough. After hours of bearing up under every snub and veiled barb, of fending off the not-so-subtle advances of the arrogant young lordlings who had been brave enough to request her aunt Olivia's permission to accompany her onto the dance floor, she had finally reached the limits of her tolerance. Panic had washed over her in an overwhelming tide, and her one thought had been to flee from it all, to make it outside before the walls closed in around her.

With a dismal sigh, Maura tilted her head back, gazing up at the ebony canopy of the sky. In hindsight, she supposed it had been foolish of her to believe that her mother's crimes would be so easily forgotten. *She* certainly hadn't forgotten. The wounds the late Marchioness of Albright had dealt her husband and daughters with her wanton behavior were still just as fresh and painful as if it had all happened only yesterday. And the marchioness's death at the hands of her married lover, the Earl of Hawksley, along with his subsequent suicide, had ensured that the Lady Albright's scandalous end would be whispered about for some time to come.

*But I'm not her*, Maura thought now, her jaw tightening with renewed frustration at the injustice of it all. *I'm not my mother! Why can't they see that?*

At that moment, the French doors opened behind her, and a trill of feminine laughter sent her heart leaping into her throat. She had no idea who was about to join her and no intention of finding out.

Without even glancing back, she lifted the flounced hem of her ball gown and hurried off along the terrace, determined to avoid any further confrontations. She couldn't go far, for she was well aware that Jillian and her aunt Olivia would soon be wondering what had become of her. But she simply wasn't ready to face anyone else. Not yet.

Up ahead, on the far side of the veranda, another set of French doors hung slightly ajar, and she paused before them for a second, uncertain where they led. However, another high-pitched giggle and the sound of approaching footsteps brought a swift end to her hesitation, and she flung them the rest of the way open, darting over the threshold.

The room she found herself in appeared to be a study of some sort. The only light came from a lamp that had been left burning on a sideboard, its pale glow spilling over the heavy oak furnishings. No one seemed to be about, and all was silent

except for the hushed ticking of the ormolu clock
on the fireplace mantel. Even the faint strains of
orchestra music and the hum of cheerful revelry
from the ballroom were muted through the pan-
eled walls.

Safe. She was safe.

Placing one hand over her quivery stomach,
Maura ventured farther into the chamber. She
would stay here for a short while, she decided, and
take advantage of the peace and quiet to compose
herself. If she could just manage to recover a bit
of her usual poise and self-assurance, she might be
able to make it through the rest of this dreadful
evening.

"Didn't your mother ever tell you that it isn't
wise for little girls to go wandering about alone in
the dark?"

The low, indolent drawl drifted to her from out
of the shadows, the unexpectedness of it startling a
cry of alarm from her. Whirling about, she watched
as a tall, broad-shouldered figure unfolded itself
from the depths of an armchair close to the hearth
and stepped forward into the circle of lamplight.

Revealing a face of sheer masculine beauty.

Spellbound, Maura stared up at the gentleman
who loomed over her. Garbed in well-tailored evening clothes that fit his lean, tautly muscled frame
to perfection, he possessed the sort of breathtaking
blond handsomeness and flawlessly carved features
that would have put an angel to shame.

A wicked angel.

High, sculpted cheekbones; a chiseled nose; and a strong, square jaw were offset by the sensuous fullness of a lush and carnal-looking mouth. A passionately seductive mouth that had likely lured more than one unsuspecting female to sin. Eyes of a piercing green peered out from underneath winged brows a shade darker than the golden curls that tumbled over his forehead, their artful disarray no doubt deliberately cultivated to tempt those same unsuspecting females into running their fingers through the tousled strands in hedonistic abandon.

A wicked angel, indeed.

When he spoke again, his deep voice was tinged with the faintest trace of amusement. "The questions only become more difficult as we go."

Maura felt embarrassed heat flood into her cheeks. Good heavens, but she'd been gaping at him like an utter clodpate! What must he think of her?

Swallowing with difficulty, she struggled to regain some semblance of control, to gather her wits about her enough to form a coherent sentence. "I'm sorry. I didn't realize anyone was in here."

"Yes, that was a bit obvious." Those firm lips canted at a wry angle. "And I suppose I should apologize as well. I didn't mean to frighten you."

"You didn't frighten me," she rushed to assure him. But when his eyebrows arched upward in a dubious fashion, she ruefully amended her statement. "At least, only a little."

He tilted his head, studying her with an unreadable expression for what seemed like a small eternity before casting a knowing glance back the way she'd come, toward the French doors. "Hiding?"

"I beg your pardon?"

"I was referring to the way you dashed in here a moment ago. You looked as if the hounds of hell themselves were nipping at your heels."

Yes, well, that was a fairly accurate assessment, Maura mused with an inward grimace. "It rather felt as if they were."

"Ah."

Turning, the man crossed over to the sideboard, his long, lithe strides reminding Maura of the sleek, prowling gait of a jungle cat, and for the first time she noticed that he cradled a snifter of brandy in a manicured hand. As he pulled the stopper out of one of the crystal decanters and dashed another finger of amber-colored liquid into the glass, he looked back at her over his shoulder. "You have me intrigued. Do elucidate."

What on earth was she doing? she wondered dazedly. This was madness, and she should leave at once. Before she was discovered here alone with him, and her already damaged reputation was besmirched beyond repair. But for some reason she couldn't quite bring herself to do so. Never mind the fact that he was a complete stranger, that she knew absolutely nothing about him. Something about this man filled her with an overpowering reluctance to walk away, even when every rational instinct she possessed told her she should do precisely that.

Oh well. It wasn't as if she had anywhere else to go. She certainly had no desire to return to the ball.

With a weary exhalation, she sank down on the edge of a nearby love seat, twining her fingers together nervously in her lap. "It's nothing. I'm being a ninny, I know. It's just that I'm so tired of it all." She leveled a contemptuous glare in the direction of the ballroom. "Tired of being judged by the lot of them and found lacking. And not because of anything I've done, but because of things that someone else did."

Setting aside his snifter, the man crossed his arms over his wide chest and leaned back against the sideboard, regarding her with hooded eyes. "Someone else?" he prompted.

"My mother." The words escaped before she could call them back, but she found she couldn't regret the slip. To her surprise, it felt strangely freeing to confide in him. "It seems like no matter how hard I try to behave as a proper young lady should, to prove to them that I'm different, they insist upon assuming that I'm just like her."

For a fleeting instant, Maura could have sworn the shadow of something bitter and bleak passed over his countenance, but it was gone before she could be certain.

"'The sins of the father are to be laid upon the children,'" he intoned dryly, one corner of his mouth curving upward in a grim caricature of a smile.

"That's a rather pessimistic view."

"But the truth, nonetheless. I learned long ago that the hypocritical members of the ton see only what they want to see, and it does little good to try and persuade them that they are wrong about anything. It's a battle you cannot win."

"You sound as if you speak from personal experience."

"Do I?" With a self-deprecatory shrug, the gentleman reached for his glass and lifted it in sardonic salute. "Let's just say you've come to the right place to commiserate with a fellow outcast."

Maura watched as he tossed back the rest of his drink. The play of muscles in his bronzed throat above his starched white cravat fascinated her, and it took a massive effort to tear her gaze away. Focusing her attention on the polished wood of the floor, she forced herself to concentrate on the conversation at hand. "M-my sister says that they're nothing more than a bunch of empty-headed idiots whose opinions aren't worth a farthing and that I shouldn't worry what they think of me. That it only matters what I think of myself."

His soft chuckle floated across the distance

between them, rising and falling with a velvety smoothness. "Your sister sounds like an intelligent young woman."

"Perhaps," she conceded. "But the ton's approval has never been that important to her." Jillian's stubborn determination to go her own way had long ago alienated her from society, and had only further complicated Maura's quest for acceptance. "She doesn't understand. She doesn't want the same things I want."

"And what do you want?"

It was a question she had spent the last four years contemplating, and the answer came readily to her, spoken with the unwavering confidence of her convictions. "A normal life. A life of comfort and respectability, free from rumor and innuendo, with a good and decent husband who will treat me with kindness and affection."

There was a moment of silence. Then a slight rustle of movement reached Maura's ears, and she looked up in time to see the man push away from the sideboard and start toward her with the same lazy grace she had so admired earlier. He came to a halt before the chair in which she sat, his eyes holding hers with a curious intentness.

"You speak of kindness and affection," he said, his tone quiet, compelling. "But what of love? Passion?"

She lifted her chin resolutely, shoving away the painful memories that the mere mention of such emotions conjured up. Memories of her mother and father that she would rather not dwell on. "I don't expect them, nor do I want them. I have been a witness to the heartache and devastation those emotions can cause, and I have no desire to experience them for myself. In truth, I cannot help but believe that love is nothing more than an illusion, a mask for the less admirable feeling of lust to hide behind."

"A jaded philosophy for such an infant."

The indulgent humor that laced his comment had her lunging to her feet, her hands flying to her hips in indignation. "I'll have you know that I am eighteen, my lord, and far from being an infant," she informed him hotly.

"Eighteen, you say? My, such a great age!"

"And now you are making fun of me."

"A little. But as it happens, I agree with you. It seems we have much in common."

Maura shook her head at the absurdity of his assertion. What could she possibly have in common with someone like him? He was the picture of wealth and elegant sophistication, Apollo in the flesh, while she was the daughter of a former stage actress who had been murdered by her lover. A fact that London's elite would never let her forget. Not even the championship of her mother's good friend, the Dowager Duchess of Maitland, had made any difference in their low opinion of her.

Her Season had just begun and already it was falling apart!

To her consternation, tears once again blurred her vision, and though she tried valiantly to blink them away, one spilled free to trickle down her cheek as she looked up in mute appeal at the man in front of her.

Quite abruptly, his green eyes narrowed and took on an arrested expression, their fierce glitter setting Maura's pulse racing. And when he reached up with one hand to capture the salty, crystalline droplet on the tip of an index finger, his feather-light caress seared her like a brand.

"Come now, little one, don't cry," he told her huskily, his soothing murmur infused with an astonishing tenderness. "It's not as bad as all that."

He leaned in toward her, and she suddenly realized he was much closer than she had thought. So close that she could smell his musky male scent, feel the waft of his breath against her temple. She felt no fear, no trepidation at his nearness. Instead she was aware only of the deliciously thrilling tingle left in the wake of his heated stare as it roamed over every inch of her upturned face, then traveled downward over the dainty curves hinted at by the ivory silk of her gown.

"So lovely," he rasped, his thumb skimming over her lower lip, wringing a shiver from her. "And not quite an infant after all. Who are you, little one? What's your name?"

Her reply was barely audible, strangled by the constriction of her throat and the dryness of her mouth. "M-Maura. L-Lady Maura Daventry."

The gentleman froze, every muscle in his body visibly stiffening as an inscrutable veil descended over that striking visage. His hand fell back to his side, and despite their continued proximity, it was as if a chasm had suddenly opened up between them. A chasm too wide and treacherous to be crossed.

Maura frowned, bewildered and oddly disturbed by his withdrawal. "What is it? What's wrong?"

He was quiet for so long that she had just begun to think he wasn't going to answer when he finally responded, his voice rife with a silky menace that was far from the gentle note he had used with her just moments ago. "It appears that Lady Grafton was a bit remiss when putting together her guest list for this evening."

"What do you mean?"

"Allow me to introduce myself." Taking a step away, he swept her a mocking bow. "I am Hawksley. The Earl of Hawksley."

With a gasp of horror and dismay, Maura stumbled backward as if she had been slapped, all the blood in her body seeming to drain into her toes, leaving her cold and numb.

The man inclined his head stiffly at her reaction. "Yes, I see you understand. I believe my father was once . . . well acquainted with your mother. Before she drove him to murder and he killed himself, of course." He swept his gaze over her once again, but this time there was no warmth at all. Just an icy disdain that chilled her to the bone. "It might be a good idea if you ran away now, little girl."

She didn't have to be told twice. Lifting her skirts, she whirled and fled the room in much the same manner that she had entered it. As if the hounds of hell were in pursuit.

She'd been right all along. She had been chatting intimately with the wickedest of angels.

The devil himself.

# Chapter 1

*"His name is Lord Philip Daventry, and he came backstage to beg an introduction after last night's performance. I cannot explain the connection I felt the moment I looked into his eyes. I only know he is the one . . ."*

From the diary of Elise Marchand,
April 5, 1794

*Essex, 1818*

*What the bloody hell am I doing here?*

Not for the first time that evening, Gabriel Sutcliffe, the tenth Earl of Hawksley, mulled over the answer to that question as he folded his arms across his chest and leaned back against a stone pillar, viewing the bacchanalian scene taking place before him with a curious mixture of detachment and discontent.

15

Masked revelers in various stages of undress frolicked about the Viscount Lanscombe's moonlit garden, indulging in all manner of lascivious activities. In groups of two, three, and sometimes more, naked limbs entwined and gleaming with the sheen of their carnal exertions, they cavorted to the strains of music coming from the gazebo, where a costumed orchestra presided over the goings-on with admirable stoicism.

Those of long-standing acquaintance with Lord and Lady Lanscombe were well aware of what an invitation to one of their "special" affairs entailed, and Gabriel had known what to expect from the moment he had arrived at Lanscombe Manor. But he found he could summon none of his customary interest in the proceedings. A fact that left him more than a trifle bemused.

His forehead furrowing, he pivoted on a booted heel to face the man standing next to him with a frown. "This was a mistake."

At the disgruntlement that laced his words, his companion turned from his own brooding contemplation of the licentious spectacle to eye him askance through the narrow slits of a black demi-mask.

"And you are just now coming to this conclusion? You, who dragged me here to begin with? You, who insisted that I had hidden myself away long enough and needed a night of orgiastic debauchery to take my mind off of—"

Gabriel cut him off with a sharp, impatient gesture. "You can stop there, Stonehurst. I am well aware that I am the one at fault for our presence here. But had I known you were going to stand about like a waxwork with that forbidding expression on your face, I never would have made the suggestion. You've frightened away half the willing females in the vicinity with that fierce scowl of yours."

Royce Grenville, Viscount Stonehurst, shrugged a massive shoulder, his attitude one of careless unconcern. Reaching up, he fingered the long, pale scar that snaked out from underneath the edge of his mask and ran the length of the right side of his face, compliments of a French saber on the battlefield at Waterloo. Its jagged starkness against the bronze of his skin gave him a rather disreputable appearance. "I'm afraid since I came by this that members of the fairer sex tend to avoid me whenever possible."

He paused, then surveyed Gabriel with an arched brow. "But what about you, Hawksley? Those two luscious blond wenches next to the gazebo have been fluttering their lashes and sending you seductive looks for the last hour, yet you behave as if you don't even notice."

Gabriel slanted a glance in the direction of the blondes his friend had indicated. He had most definitely noticed them. Lovely and curvaceous, they looked ripe for just the sort of lusty sport he normally enjoyed. But he felt no desire to join them, or any of the other nubile beauties in attendance, and he was at a loss to explain his utter indifference.

Perhaps this was what those in elitist circles liked to refer to as ennui. Although, at only eight and twenty, he hated to think that he was already starting to lose his taste for such diversions.

After all, he did have a certain reputation to live up to.

In the five years since the late earl's suicide and its resulting scandal, Gabriel had set out with an almost single-minded determination to follow in the footsteps of his notorious sire, and had aptly succeeded. To the ton, he was the Devil's Own, and tales of his rakehell exploits were told in hushed whispers in dimly lit corners of salons and drawing rooms, like bedtime stories meant to frighten small children. Never mind that most of the rumors had been exaggerated to the point of absurdity. He had learned long ago that it was far easier to give people what they expected rather than to try to turn the tide. And what they expected was a man just like his father. An unfaithful drunkard and wastrel.

Not to mention a murderer.

One corner of Gabriel's mouth twisted cynically. It was perhaps a blessing that his poor, beleaguered mother hadn't lived to see what he had become. Always a delicate and fragile woman, the countess had been unable to bear up under the ton's censure and had passed on soon after her husband, leaving her son to face the slings and arrows alone.

Just one more sin he could lay at his father's doorstep.

Shoving away the unwanted emotions of rage and grief that memories of the old earl's transgressions always seemed to stir within him, he forced himself to turn his attention back to the current discussion.

"We are not here for my benefit," he reminded his friend bluntly. "We are here because of you and your refusal to see that you can't keep punishing yourself for things beyond your control. This self-imposed exile of yours has gone on long enough."

The viscount's craggy visage instantly hardened with displeasure, his gray eyes darkening to the color of slate. "Damnation, Hawksley, you know nothing about it."

No, he didn't. Royce had been stubbornly reticent about his time with the British Cavalry, even though it obviously haunted him more than he would ever admit. The war with Napoleon had taken its toll, both physically and emotionally, changing him from the carefree boy he had once been. And when he had returned home, only to discover that his estranged elder brother had died in his absence, leaving him heir to the Stonehurst title and fortune, he had withdrawn even more, isolating himself behind the walls of his family estate in Cornwall.

"I know that no matter what happened between the two of you, Alex wouldn't want this," Gabriel told the younger man now, his voice firm and unequivocal. "He would want you to learn to let the past go and move on. To forgive him. And yourself."

Stonehurst leveled him with a glare. "Are you really going to preach to me about forgiving and forgetting when it's apparent you aren't capable of doing either of those things when it comes to your own life?"

Touché! Gabriel had to acknowledge the accuracy of that accusation, even if only to himself. There was little use in denying it. He hadn't forgiven. Not anyone. Not his father, not the harshly judgmental members of society. And he highly doubted that he would ever forget.

But that didn't mean he had to stand by and watch Royce torture himself in the same way, and he had no intention of doing so. After all, he had a debt to repay. Alexander Grenville had been Gabriel's best boyhood chum, one of the few people who had stood by him even in the midst of his family's disgrace. If nothing else, he owed it to Alex, now that he was gone, to look after his brother.

Even if it sometimes seemed like a monumental task.

Taking a deep breath in an effort to hold on to his rapidly dwindling patience, Gabriel spoke in a slow, measured tone. "I'm certain if you'll simply take the time to consider our respective situations objectively, you'll realize that they are nothing at all alike."

"Aren't they?" The viscount shook his head, his countenance stony. "Face it, Hawksley. The past has left its scars on us both, and the only difference between the two of us is that yours are easier to hide. In my opinion, you are the last person who should be offering me advice on the matter."

Now that remark rubbed Gabriel on the raw, but before he could think of anything to say in his defense, Stonehurst yanked the mask from his face with a stifled curse and tossed it aside.

"That's enough," he growled. "I'm leaving. You're quite welcome to join me if you'd like. But if you'd rather stay, it will be without me. I feel like a bloody fool, and I don't belong here."

Turning, he stalked off across the grass toward the winding path that led back to the house, barely avoiding a collision with a giggling young shepherdess who was being pursued by a leering, half-clothed highwayman.

Aware of an overwhelming sense of frustration, Gabriel stared after his friend, a muscle ticking in his jaw. Christ, this entire evening had turned into a fiasco. Stonehurst was right. It was time to admit that this had been an ill-conceived plan and make good his escape, before things degenerated any further.

He started forward, intent on doing just that, but he hadn't taken more than a step or two when a most decidedly unwelcome feminine voice spoke up from behind him, halting him in his tracks.

"Hawksley! There you are, you naughty boy!"

The cloying sweetness that dripped from each and every syllable was enough to send a shudder of distaste up his spine, but he made a valiant effort to school his features into some semblance of civility as he turned to greet the woman who had appeared at his side.

Full, red lips pursed in a seductive pout, Lydia Stratton, the Viscountess Lanscombe, tucked her arm through his, her pale, tapered fingers digging into his sleeve as if she sensed his urge to recoil and sought to hold him in place.

"I've been wondering where you were," she purred huskily.

"My lady." Barely restraining a wince at the sharp bite of her nails through the material of his coat, Gabriel inclined his head to her in a stiff bow. "You were looking for me?"

"Always, darling. You know that."

Yes, he did. And her rather blatant pursuit of him was turning into more than a bit of an annoyance.

If asked directly, Gabriel would have been hard-pressed to explain why he found the thought of bedding Lady Lanscombe so unpalatable. Several decades younger than her thrice-wed husband, the golden-haired viscountess was just the sort of woman he usually preferred. Experienced, insatiable, and obviously all too willing to welcome him with open arms. But for some reason, her icy blond beauty and almost desperate eagerness left him utterly unmoved.

Peering up at him through a veil of lashes, she gave him a coy little smile. "Why are you hiding here in the shadows?"

Now there was an idea, Gabriel thought with more than a hint of amusement. Why hadn't it occurred to him before? Or better yet, why hadn't he taken Stonehurst's suggestion and departed when he'd had the chance? At least then he might have saved himself the trouble of having to untangle himself from his hostess's clutches. "I never hide, and I am shocked that you would accuse me of such a thing, when I am one of the few guests who didn't even bother with the affectation of a mask."

"That is only because you care very little for what is left of your reputation." Lady Lanscombe's blue eyes glittered with an almost avaricious light as she moved in closer to him, deliberately pressing her ample breasts up against his biceps in a way that had the lush curves overflowing the low-cut neckline of her diaphanous gown. "And I couldn't help but notice that you are also one of the few who is still fully dressed. I could help you to rectify that if you'd like."

Closing his eyes against a sudden painful throbbing in his temples, Gabriel struggled briefly to come up with some polite excuse, then wondered why he bothered. He owed this woman nothing, and it wasn't like him to prevaricate. "I'm sorry, my lady, but as much as I would like to oblige you, my friend and I were just getting ready to leave."

She gave a coolly dismissive wave of her free hand. "I'm sure your . . . friend will understand should you choose to delay your departure for a short while."

"Perhaps he would. But I'm afraid I'm not of a mind to do so. Might I suggest that you try seeking out your husband?"

"My husband?" Lady Lanscombe's laugh was high and trilling and held an almost brittle edge. "Really, Hawksley! How droll. Why on earth would I want to do that?"

He arched a mocking brow. "I allow, it is a rather novel concept. However, you did marry the man."

"Yes, but certainly not for that! Besides, the randy old fool disappeared with some red-haired tart well over an hour ago. I suspect he is far too busy rutting himself into a stupor to concern himself with me."

That was more than likely the truth. Though the man was an old crony of Gabriel's father, Lord Lanscombe's lecherous appetites hadn't lessened with age, as evidenced by his tendency to host such affairs. Knowing the viscount, he had probably retreated to some private corner of the garden to indulge himself to his heart's content, and expected his wife to do the same.

But no matter what was expected, Gabriel drew

the line at cuckolding a man right under his very nose, even with said man's blessing.

His tolerance dissipating more with every second that passed, he was racking his brain for a way to bring the conversation to an end when a swift flash of movement out of the corner of his eye distracted him. He looked up just in time to see a small form dart out from behind a nearby grouping of marble statuary.

And for the first time that evening, his attention was immediately and thoroughly arrested.

He wasn't certain what it was that so captured his interest. Perhaps it was the almost palpable tension that seemed to surround the figure as it came to a stop close to where he and the viscountess stood in the shadows of the faux Greek temple that occupied this section of the garden. Or perhaps it was the fact that amid all the other scantily clad guests, this person was not only still dressed, but was covered from head to toe by a dark cloak with a concealing hood.

In any case, he found that he couldn't look away. There was something familiar in the way the figure tilted its head, a feminine grace that told him this mysterious interloper was a woman. And as she briefly glanced in his direction, the moonlight fell over the opening in the hood, and he caught a fleeting glimpse of a delicate profile and the length of one sable curl.

Surely not! It couldn't be . . .

Stunned, Gabriel watched as the figure moved again, crossing the clearing in a furtive manner before disappearing into the maze of tall hedgerows that lay between the garden and the house beyond.

He didn't even hesitate. Without a moment's thought, he followed after her, his long strides eating up the distance with rapid ease. He was aware of nothing. Not Lady Lanscombe's outraged gasp as he walked away, cutting her off with nary a word. Not the grumbling protests or muttered oaths he left in his wake as he pushed his way through the throng of revelers in pursuit.

Nothing but the overwhelming need he felt to catch up with the cloaked female.

If he was right about her identity, she was bound to get herself into trouble at the first possible opportunity. And though he had no idea why he should care, he nonetheless felt compelled to do something about it.

Just as he always did.

It appeared that the Devil's Own secretly aspired to knighthood, Gabriel mused with a self-deprecatory grimace. At least when it came to Lady Maura Daventry.

# Chapter 2

*"Unlike the other so-called gentlemen who seek my favor, Philip behaves as if he truly cares what I think. He treats me as a person, and not as a mere decorative adornment for his arm."*

From the diary of Elise Marchand,
April 17, 1794

**M**aura entered Lanscombe Manor through a set of French doors that stood ajar on the side of the house facing the garden, breathing a sigh of relief when the sounds of merrymaking from outside were instantly muffled by the red brick of its walls.

With a shaky hand, she adjusted her lace-edged demi-mask, her face heating as she recalled some of the astonishing tableaus she had stumbled across as she navigated the twisting, labyrinthine pathways of the maze. Never in her wildest dreams had she imagined that human beings behaved in such a fashion. Cavorting about in the open, their nearly nude bodies locked together in positions that seemed anatomically impossible to someone of her limited experience.

Perhaps she had been a trifle naïve, but not even Violet's warnings about this affair had prepared her for what she would find. And she had to wonder how many of those taking part in this wanton depravity were the very same members of society who had once pointed their accusing fingers at her, ready to sit in judgment at the slightest indication that she possessed any of the same immoral tendencies as her mother.

Just how many recognizable faces were concealed behind those feathered and sequined masks?

Her pulse gave a fluttering leap as one face in particular sprang to mind. A masculine face of such heart-stopping perfection that it still had the power to rob her of her wits and reason, despite the fact that she was well aware of the unprincipled nature that lurked behind that deceptively handsome façade.

She had noticed him the moment she had slipped onto the grounds through the rear gate and joined the crowd milling about the garden. Standing in a darkened corner of the clearing, he had been engaged in a rather intent discussion with another man. Unlike the other guests, he had made no attempt to hide his identity with a disguise. But even had he worn a mask, she would have known who he was.

The Earl of Hawksley.

His presence here shouldn't have surprised her. In fact, she would wager a guess that this was exactly the sort of salacious gathering he spent most of his evenings attending. But it rattled her nonetheless. He was constantly turning up at the most inopportune times, catching her off guard in embarrassing situations and leaving her feeling like a foolish and recalcitrant child.

As he had on the very first night they had met . . .

But she wouldn't let herself think about that. Not now. She had a more important task to tend to. Though Violet had promised that she would do her best to keep Lord Lanscombe busy, there was still little time to tarry.

Drawing her cloak more closely around her, Maura peered about, straining in the dim light of the few flickering sconces to make out the details of her surroundings. A long, narrow hallway stretched out before her, both sides of the passage lined with closed doors. According to Violet, the viscount's study should be just up ahead on the left, through the archway at the very end.

*You can do this*, she told herself firmly, squaring her shoulders with fresh resolve. After all, she was the daughter of the Marquis of Albright, one of England's foremost experts in the field of criminology and the man who had assisted Bow Street in solving some of London's most difficult cases.

Surely she must have inherited at least some of his sleuthing talents.

She moved forward with quick, cautious steps, taking care to be as quiet as possible and deliberately ignoring the faint noises that drifted from behind a great number of the doors she passed. High, panting moans and deep, rumbling groans that in the last hour had become far too familiar for her own comfort.

Once through the archway, she was gratified to note that the portal to Lord Lanscombe's study stood wide open, and all was still within. The single lamp that had been left burning on the large oak desk in the corner revealed an empty chamber.

Now all she had to do was find something, anything, that contained a sample of the viscount's handwriting. Once she compared it to the note in the pocket of her cloak, she would know for certain whether her newly awakened suspicions were correct.

Crossing the Oriental rug to the desk, she sifted through the items that littered its polished surface. An inkwell, pens and nibs, some pieces of correspondence from the family solicitor, but nothing that looked as if it had been written by the viscount himself.

Drat! There had to be something here! Seconds ticked by like hours as she rifled through the drawers, and she had just begun to panic when her fingers closed around a leather-bound ledger buried under several freshly laundered handkerchiefs in the last drawer she tried.

It was the estate's account book, and she barely stifled a triumphant cry as she removed it from its resting place and opened it on the desk before her. With a rising sense of anticipation, she withdrew a crumpled and much-folded sheet of yellowed stationery from the inside pocket of her cloak and held it close to the page, where the viscount had written several notations, so that she could evaluate the handwriting side by side in the soft glow of the lamp.

*If I can't have you, no one can . . .*

Though Maura had read and reread the note many times in the fortnight since she had first discovered it, tucked into the pages of her mother's diary along with several others, the words still had the power to send a chill of foreboding up her spine, but she forced herself to disregard the implications of it and focus solely on checking for similarities in the two sets of penmanship.

There weren't any.

In dismay, she stared down at the letter she held in her hand, then at the ledger. This couldn't be happening. She'd been so certain. Lanscombe had seemed the obvious choice. But his handwriting was much less cramped, flowing across the page with a looping flourish that was usually foreign in a man's writing.

What was she to do now?

"And what have we here?"

The slurred voice came from the direction of the doorway, and she gave a startled gasp before jerking her head up to find a man standing just inside the room, arms crossed and legs braced wide in a cocky stance as he leered at her knowingly.

Even with a mask covering his features and his lank brown hair coming loose from its queue to fall forward into his face, she knew who it was.

Lord Quincy Stratton, the viscount's son.

When she continued to gape at him in shock and dread, unable to even begin to form an acceptable explanation for her presence in his father's study, he took another step farther into the chamber and spoke again, his mouth curving into a lascivious smirk. "If you're planning on stealing the silver, m'tasty little morsel, I 'gret to inform you that you are in the wrong place. The dining room is in the west wing."

Maura swiftly stuffed the letter back into her pocket, thankful for the concealment of her hooded cloak, despite the heat and discomfort that had plagued her from the second she had donned it. Her only chance now was to stay in the shadows and pray that Stratton wouldn't recognize her as easily as she had him.

For if he realized who she was, there would be hell to pay.

Licking dry lips, she cleared her throat and replied to his comment in a breathy, high-pitched voice that was much more girlish and simpering than her customary tone. "I do apologize, my lord. I was searching for the gentleman friend who accompanied me here this evening, but I'm afraid I got a bit turned around."

"A gen'l'man friend, y'say?" Even in the faint light from the lamp, she could see through the slits in his mask that his eyes were bloodshot, and he was running his words together in a way that told her he was more than slightly inebriated. "Not much of a gen'l'man if he left such a lovely lady alone."

"Yes, well, I suppose I shall have to look elsewhere." Inching around the side of the desk, she darted a glance over his shoulder at the door. It was only a few feet away. If she could just manage to edge by him . . . "Again, I apologize, my lord. If you will excuse me?"

Doing her best to affect a calmness she was far from feeling, she strolled forward, her sights set on the hallway outside and the safety it represented. But just as she began to believe he was actually going to let her go, his hand lashed out to grab her wrist, bringing her to a jarring halt.

"Per'aps I could be of 'sistance. This is a large house and I wouldn't want you to get turned round again." He pulled her in close to him, and his fetid breath brushed against her cheek. The odiferous combination of alcohol and unwashed male was so strong that she had to restrain the urge to retch. "May I suggest we try m'bedchamber first?"

Maura's stomach twisted into a terror-stricken knot, and she shoved at his chest with her palms, trying to put some distance between them. But the man was as immovable as a rock. In fact, he tugged her even closer, letting go of her wrist so he could slide his arms around her waist and mold the curves of her body up against his large frame. The swollen hardness she could feel nudging her abdomen was enough to send her into a panic.

"Please, my lord," she whispered, wriggling in his hold, her mind working with frantic haste as she tried to come up with a way out of this predicament.

"Oh, I'll please you," he crooned, laughing drunkenly. One rough hand found her breast through the material of her cloak and squeezed, wringing a pained moan from her. "Tha's right, love. Tha's what I want to hear. I'll have you screaming m'name before too long."

With that, he began to back her toward a velvet-cushioned settee on the far wall.

And Maura was instantly flung back to last Season, to a darkened alcove with this same man pawing at her, hurting her, just as he was now.

*Are you really going to pretend you're any different than your whore of a mother when we both know better?*

Somewhere inside her a small spark of righteous indignation caught fire and blazed to life, and she brought her slippered heel down as hard as she could on his instep, ramming her elbow into his midsection at the same time.

He released her with an oath and clutched at his stomach, the look of venomous fury that suffused his rapidly reddening countenance enough to send her stumbling backward, out of his reach.

"You right little bitch, I ought to—"

"I don't think so, Stratton."

The fatalistic tingle that raced through Maura's veins at the sound of those deep, rich cadences told her who had spoken, even before she swung around to face the newcomer.

Of course. Of all people to intervene, it would be the one person she wanted most to avoid.

One broad shoulder propped against the frame, the Earl of Hawksley lounged in the doorway, contemplating the scene before him with an unreadable expression.

"I believe the lady has made it clear that she isn't interested," he drawled silkily, those glittering green eyes never wavering from Stratton. Though his posture was relaxed, almost nonchalant, Maura sensed an air of palpable tension that hovered just beneath the surface of that casual demeanor, a subtle indication that he wasn't nearly as detached as he might appear. "Perhaps you would be well advised to brush up on your seduction technique with someone a bit less strong-minded and leave this lass to those of us who know how to handle a more spirited female."

Visibly bristling at the slight, the viscount's son drew himself up with a glare. "Stay out of this, Hawksley," he snapped. "Go find your own woman."

The petulance that laced the older man's voice had the earl arching a golden brow in lazy amusement. "And what if I want this one?"

"That's jolly well too bad! I saw her first, and I won't be handing her over to the likes of you."

Maura bit her lip. Dear God, but the situation was getting worse by the minute. She had to come up with a way to get herself out of this or they were going to tear her apart like two stray dogs fighting over a bone! "Please, this isn't necessary. I—"

But she didn't get the chance to finish her appeal, for Stratton spun on her with a snarl and reached out to grasp her arm, shaking her with such brutal force that her head whipped back and forth on her neck. "Just shut up! Haven't you caused me enough trouble already without yammering on?"

At the man's actions, every trace of mockery fled Hawksley's visage, and he levered himself away from the door, his gaze turning cold and hard. "Let the lady go, Stratton. Now."

"Lady?" Thin lips twisted into a malicious sneer. "What sort of lady would attend an affair such as this? Slut, more like."

As Maura watched in amazement, the earl's fist shot out with a speed and precision that would have made Gentleman Jackson proud, connecting with Stratton's arrogant face and knocking him backward into the settee, where he collapsed among the cushions in a heap.

There was an instant of stunned silence, then Stratton sat up rather woozily, his hands flying to his nose to staunch the sudden flow of blood. "Damn you, Hawksley, I think you broke by dose!"

"If luck is with me."

"Do you doh what by father will say when he finds oud aboud dis?"

"I'm sure I have no idea." Leaning over, Hawksley seized the man by his collar and yanked him to his feet, propelling him the short distance across the room to the door. "Why don't you toddle on your way and tell him all about it?"

"I'll jusd do thad, you hell-born bastard!" Jerking free from the earl's hold and nearly overbalancing himself, Stratton leveled the earl with a look of scathing contempt, the impact of which was lessened somewhat by the blood pouring through his cupped fingers and the fact that his mask had been knocked askew. "And you can have the liddle doxy. Prob'ly pox-ridden anyway."

When Hawksley advanced on him in a menacing manner, the lordling beat a hasty retreat, and Maura winced when his exit from the chamber was immediately punctuated by a loud crash and a muttered curse. Similar noises accompanied his unsteady progress down the corridor until he finally passed through the archway at the end, and all fell silent once again.

And she was alone with her rescuer. A man who was quite likely an even worse threat than the one he had saved her from.

The Devil's Own.

Lunging for the desk, she snatched up the closest thing to a weapon she came across among the clutter—an engraved letter opener—and whirled to brandish it at Hawksley just as he turned back to face her.

"I'd stay where you are if I were you, my lord," she advised him, hoping against hope that her mask and the hood of her cloak would continue to shield her identity from that piercing stare. "Though I thank you for your intervention, I'm obliged to warn you that you are much mistaken if you believe you'll be brushing up on your seduction techniques with me."

To her consternation, Hawksley didn't seem at all disturbed by the fact that she held the pointed tip of the office implement only a hair breadth from his throat. Instead she could have sworn she saw a gleam of humor in the depths of those green eyes as he observed her. "Ah, the lady is armed and prepared to defend herself by any means necessary."

"Precisely. Now, if you wouldn't mind stepping aside . . . ?"

"Actually, I'm afraid I do mind."

And in a move too swift for her to anticipate, he plucked the opener from her trembling fingers, tossed it onto the desk, and caught her in his arms, spinning her about so that he held her back pinned against his front.

"You know," he said huskily close to her ear, "little girls really shouldn't play with sharp objects."

Unable to believe he had disarmed her so easily, Maura let out an outraged cry and began to fight him like a woman possessed, kicking, screaming, and clawing in a desperate bid to free herself. She would not let this happen. She refused to be this man's helpless victim.

"By all that's holy, woman! Will you hold still! I promise you, I have no designs upon your person."

His peremptory and exasperated tone cut across the sound of her struggles and she froze abruptly, aware all the while of the heat of that muscled body pressed against her spine. Unlike Stratton's, the scent that emanated from him was musky and pleasant, saturating her senses. "Y-you don't?"

"I'd have to be bloody mad, wouldn't I?"

For some reason, that stung. But before she could even begin to think of a suitably caustic retort, her hood was gently tugged from her head, and a warm palm cupped her chin, tilting her face upward for his perusal. "Now, why don't you try telling me just exactly what it is you're up to, Lady Maura Daventry?"

# Chapter 3

*"Today Philip surprised me with a picnic in Hyde Park. We had a blissful time, and he confided in me about his current studies in the field of criminology and his desire to use his intellect to do something worthwhile for his fellow man. I cannot help but think what a truly good and noble person he is. Far too good for the likes of me."*

From the diary of Elise Marchand,
May 2, 1794

**M**aura gaped up at Hawksley, horrified by the ease with which he had recognized her despite cloak, mask, and the layers of heavy stage makeup Violet had so skillfully applied earlier that evening. The former actress had sworn that not even the members of Maura's own family would know her if they saw her, but apparently the earl had a far more discerning eye than most.

"Well?" he prompted after several long seconds had passed and she had failed to respond. "I'm waiting, and I am fast running out of patience."

The condescending note that laced his voice was enough to spark Maura's temper, and she jerked her chin from his grasp. "That is none of your business!"

"On the contrary. As I am the one who once again stepped in to save you from the folly of your actions, I would say an explanation for your presence here is the least I am owed."

"The folly of—" She sputtered to a halt, unable to finish her sentence for the fury that washed over her. "How dare you presume to judge my actions? For all you know, I could have a perfectly acceptable reason for being here."

To her surprise, Hawksley loosened his hold enough for her to step out of the circle of his arms, and she whirled to confront him. But he didn't release her completely. One strong hand still manacled her wrist, letting her know in no uncertain terms that he wasn't finished with her yet.

He acknowledged her words with a nod. "You're right. Which is why I have asked you for an explanation. Would you care to enlighten me?"

The sardonic quirk of those chiseled lips roused Maura's ire even more. "I owe you nothing except my thanks, which I have already given you," she spat. "Now let me go!"

His expression darkened, and for a moment she was certain he was going to refuse. But instead he merely offered her a stilted bow and dropped her wrist, crossing his arms over his muscular chest as he surveyed her with icy superiority.

"Gladly. But I must say, my lady, you appear to be making a habit of this. Every time I turn around, you are being accosted in some dark corner and I am forced to come to your rescue. In fact, I believe it was just a little less than a year ago that I found you in remarkably similar circumstances, fighting off the attentions of the exact same man. At the Hayworth ball, wasn't it?"

Maura's face flamed at the reminder, and memories of her previous encounter with Lord Stratton once again flashed through her mind. It was true. This wasn't the first time she had been assaulted in such a fashion, and it was just her appalling luck that it always seemed to be Hawksley who intervened.

Straightening her shoulders, she returned his chilly glare with a haughty one of her own. "I have never asked for your help, and I can assure you that you are the last person I would turn to if I were ever in need of assistance."

The earl's golden brows shot skyward. "If?"

"Yes, if. I'll have you know that I am perfectly capable of taking care of myself. And I resent your insinuation that I am somehow to blame for Lord Stratton's reprehensible behavior. I offered him no encouragement. Nor any of the other so-called gentlemen who have deluded themselves into thinking that I would welcome such treatment."

"That may be. But perhaps if you weren't always wandering off alone, you could avoid these situations."

"I'm sure I don't know why you should care."

"I'm sure I don't know either." Hawksley shrugged, his attitude one of curt dismissal, as if he found the entire matter too taxing to even discuss. "You're the most troublesome wench it has ever been my misfortune to come across."

Maura shook her head. If she had any sense, she would be running for the door while she had the chance instead of continuing to argue with him. After all, just a short while ago the only thing she had been able to think about was fleeing this place as quickly as possible. But something inside her wouldn't allow him to brush her off so carelessly. "You know that's not what I meant."

A familiar shadow passed over his features, but it was gone in an instant, replaced by his usual mask of dispassionate reserve. "I am aware of that. However, I have no desire to talk about my father or your mother or all of the reasons we have to despise, loathe, and otherwise abominate each other. Frankly, the subject has been belabored to the point that I find it tedious."

His gaze locked with hers, and he leaned in toward her until he was so close she could feel the warmth of his breath brushing against her cheek, stirring the loose curls at her temple. "And just so you know, I have no intention of letting you walk away until I have an answer to my question, so I shall ask you again. What are you up to?"

A palpable tension arced between them, and Maura placed a hand against her fluttering stomach, dazed by the mesmerizing intensity of those green eyes. With the lamplight turning his blond hair into a golden halo about his head and illuminating his striking countenance with an almost otherworldly glow, he had never looked more like the fallen angel she had once compared him to. Lucifer come to earth to tempt her to the side of the wicked.

Exerting every bit of self-control she possessed, she took a step back, away from his disorienting nearness, as she fought to rein in her scattered wits. It was obvious from his unyielding expression that he wasn't going to make it easy for her to evade his queries. Perhaps she shouldn't even try. There could be no denying that he had a right to know, particularly if the revelations in her mother's diary proved to be true.

But could she bring herself to confide in him? And if she did, how would he react? How could she even begin to explain not only that his father might be innocent of the crimes he had been accused of, but that his death might not have been a suicide at all? That he had been murdered. Murdered by the same person who had killed her mother.

Somehow it seemed unlikely that Hawksley would allow her to leave it at that. He would want answers. Answers that she wasn't prepared to give. And when she refused to cooperate, she had little doubt he would soon be demanding to see her father. Given the marquis's recent illness and her own need for secrecy when it came to her self-imposed mission, that was something she simply couldn't permit.

The mere thought of Lord Albright lying frail and weak in his bedchamber, his body ravaged by the fever that had plagued him for almost a fortnight, was enough to make her blink back tears and to send a fresh wave of resolve coursing through her.

No, she concluded. There was too much at stake. She couldn't tell Hawksley. Not now.

Taking a deep breath to shore up her flagging courage, she lifted her chin and met that penetrating stare with an air of blatant defiance. "I have nothing else to say."

Her unequivocal statement had the earl's mouth tightening into a grim line, and a muscle began to flex in his jaw. When he finally spoke, his coldly controlled tone betrayed more than a hint of his displeasure. "I see. Then I suppose I shall have to assume that you are here for the same reason as all of the other guests. Perhaps I did you a disservice by routing Stratton and you were enjoying his rather heavy-handed attempts at seduction." He indicated the door with a mocking flourish. "It's not too late to call him back, you know. Or if you would prefer, I could endeavor to seek out the Viscount Lanscombe himself for you. I'm quite certain the old codger wouldn't be adverse to an assignation with such a pretty young thing. After all, everyone knows how close he was to your mother."

Maura flinched, once again caught off guard by the power he held to wound her. Why did she care what he thought? In the greater scheme of things, his opinion should have been of little consequence. Yet the scornful cruelty of his words cut her with the sharpness of a well-honed knife blade.

Determined not to let him see how much his derision affected her, she took a step toward him, her hands balling into fists at her sides. "I will thank you not to bring my mother into this conversation, Lord Hawksley."

"Come now, my lady. It isn't as if her association with the viscount was a secret, is it? Just how many men did the late Lady Albright have dangling on her hook? Two? Three? Ten? Do you even know? It must be confusing to try and keep them all straight."

That did it. His taunts more than she could bear, Maura lashed out at him, ready to wipe the smirk off his arrogant visage with a ringing slap. But he caught her hand within inches of his face.

Shaking his head reprovingly, he made a faint tsking sound. "Ah, ah, ah. None of that. Surely you can't blame me for my assumptions? This isn't exactly the type of affair that most unmarried misses would know anything about, much less attend. One could be forgiven for coming to the conclusion that you are not quite as innocent as you appear." He paused, his narrowed gaze burning a searing path along the length of her delicately curved form in a way that left her feeling naked and vulnerable. "Is that it, Lady Maura? Did you finally tire of your prim and proper charade? Have you discovered that underneath it all you are every bit the wanton your mother was?"

Fuming at his colossal nerve, she drew herself up in indignation, prepared to deliver a scathing set-down he wouldn't soon forget. But before she could say a thing, he wound his arms about her waist and hauled her up against his warm, tautly muscled frame in a move so unexpected that it caused the words to die in her throat.

"If I were you," he warned silkily, "I would give whatever it was you were about to say a great deal of serious consideration." His predatory gaze held hers for a heart-pounding instant before moving downward to linger on her trembling mouth. "In fact, it might be best if you didn't talk at all."

She caught only a glimpse of the intent in those glittering eyes before he bent his head and captured her lips with his own in a ruthless kiss.

And instantly every bit of rationality Maura possessed seemed to go flying right out the window.

It was a bold conquering, a masterful invasion that robbed her of breath and left her head reeling, giving her little chance to fight or protest, even if she could have found the strength to do so. His mouth moved over hers expertly, his velvety tongue flicking the satiny surfaces of her lips before spearing deep, claiming the damp recesses of her mouth with a thoroughness that wrung a shiver from her.

*This can't be happening!* some small, sane corner of her mind cried out. He was the last man who should be kissing and touching her in such a manner, and she knew that she should be pushing him away, berating him for his effrontery. But a strange sort of lethargy had stolen over her, fogging her senses and invading every inch of her body until her limbs felt leaden and all but useless.

And when she finally did manage to cast off the clinging tendrils of her lassitude long enough to raise her arms, intending to shove him from her, they somehow ended up around his neck instead, her fingers tangling in the strands of silky blond hair that curled at his nape.

This was madness! Sheer madness! But the spicy taste of him on her tongue was so undeniably delicious . . .

It was the last lucid thought she was aware of before her reluctant and ever growing desire for him took over, sweeping her completely away.

\* \* \*

This was a mistake.

Gabriel knew it. But as hard as he tried to summon the will to release her, to set her from him and walk away, something even stronger than his certainty that this shouldn't be happening kept him from doing so. It was as if some force beyond his control was governing his actions, clouding his thought processes until logical reasoning was impossible and he was aware of nothing but the Lady Maura Daventry and this maddening need to possess her.

True, the kiss had started out as a punishment, stemming from his anger and seething frustration at her stubborn intractability. But it had very quickly become something more. Something he found he had no desire to examine too closely. All he knew was that he wanted her. No other female had ever felt like this in his arms. Soft and delicate and so . . . so . . .

Right.

And that had to be the most laughable part of this entire debacle. No one could be less right. This was the daughter of the temptress who had seduced his father and lured him to his doom! She should inspire nothing within him except scorn and distaste. None of that seemed to matter now, however. Not when he held her nestled against him with her lush, honeyed mouth moving so sweetly under his own.

Why couldn't he have stayed away? he wondered dimly, even as he deepened the kiss, entwining his tongue with hers and reveling in the tiny, whimpering moan she gave in response. He couldn't understand this damnable compulsion that constantly drove him to seek her out, to come between her and anyone who meant her harm. From the moment he had met her and looked into those bright blue eyes full of wariness and vulnerability, he had been intrigued by this captivating miss, drawn to her in spite of himself, and it made no sense.

Perhaps it was the fleeting instant of mutual accord they had shared that long-ago night at Lord and Lady Grafton's ball. Or perhaps it was the fact that part of him felt responsible for all that she had lost. After all, it had been his father who had robbed Maura of her mother, who had changed her life and the lives of her father and sisters forever.

But whatever the reason, none of the beautiful and more experienced women he had wooed and bedded over the years had ever come close to affecting him as powerfully as she did.

Finally tearing his mouth from hers, he gazed down into her upturned, heart-shaped face, aware of a fierce sense of satisfaction at her flushed cheeks and dazed expression. Unable to stop himself, he lifted a shaking hand to loosen the ties of her cloak, then pushed it from her shoulders so that it pooled on the floor at her feet. Clad in a full-skirted, off-the-shoulder evening gown of amethyst silk that hugged her curves and bared the delectable upper slopes of her breasts, she looked more ripe and womanly than he had ever seen her look. In fact, with her ebony curls spilling about her face in tousled disarray and her rosebud lips swollen from his attentions, she resembled a replete and well-pleasured lady who had just been thoroughly tumbled by a most ardent lover.

The observation was enough to have his cock stirring to rigid, aching life, and he stifled a groan. Sweet Christ, but he was as stiff as a pike. Why couldn't he have had this reaction to Lady Lanscombe or the two blondes who had eyed him so suggestively out in the garden? Why did it have to be she?

Seizing her waist, he pulled her forward, fitting her snugly against the steel-hard bulge that tented the front of his breeches. When he rocked his hips, nudging the apex of her thighs, she gave a little gasp, her blue eyes widening behind the slits of her lace-edged demi-mask.

"Do you feel that, my lady?" he murmured huskily. "That's what you do to a man when you dress and behave in such a wanton manner. I'm afraid the members of my gender have a certain weakness of the flesh that tends to make us forget ourselves whenever we are confronted with such temptation."

He raised his hand, brushing the backs of his fingers over the exposed mound of one creamy breast in a deliberate caress, savoring the silken texture of her skin and the way her nipples visibly tightened beneath the bodice of her gown, poking through the layers of material as if begging for his touch. "But perhaps that's what you want. Is that it, Lady Maura? Is that why you are here? Did you want some man to force you down onto the nearest available surface, toss up those skirts, and plow you until you plead with him to make you come so hard and so deep that it seems it will never end?"

Gabriel barely restrained a wince at his own words. He knew he was being crude, but he couldn't seem to help it. The more she aroused him, the more his anger with himself and his inability to resist her sharpened, making him determined to goad a reaction from her.

When she said nothing, merely shook her head and gaped at him in befuddlement, he jerked his head in the direction of the settee, giving her a knowing smile. "I'm willing to oblige, my lady, if that is the case. Come. Why don't you show me what tricks your mother taught you?"

That did it. Her blue eyes suddenly lit with fury, and this time he made no move to stop her when she slapped him. Her palm connected with his cheek with a resounding crack, and she pulled free from his grasp, her face pale and her kiss-bruised lips quivering.

"You dare to judge me?" she hissed, reaching

down to retrieve her cloak and holding it protectively in front of her, using it as a shield to ward him off. "To accuse me of being no better than my mother when you are called the Devil's Own because of the wickedness and depravity of your own activities? You are beneath contempt, my lord, and you are never to come near me again! Do you hear me? Never!"

With one last look of pure disdain, she picked up her skirts, turned, and fled the room.

And he let her go, staring after her in resignation. She was right. His behavior had been inexcusable, and he deserved every bit of her hatred. From now on he would avoid her like the plague, he decided. It was quite obvious that being anywhere in her vicinity was dangerous to his peace of mind, for she brought out a softness, a protectiveness in him that was utterly foreign to his nature. Bloody hell, but if his usual circle of cohorts ever saw him behaving like such a nursemaid, they would never let him hear the end of it.

So that was it. He wouldn't worry about her anymore.

Attempting to ignore the nagging voice in his head that warned him that might be easier said than done, he straightened his shoulders and started toward the door. He had taken only a few steps, however, when a folded piece of paper lying on the polished wood floor caught his attention.

Curious, he picked it up and unfolded it, squinting his eyes to make out the cramped handwriting in the dim glow of the chamber.

*If I can't have you, no one can . . .*

His heart gave a jolt, and with a chilling sense of foreboding, he glanced back at the spot where Lady Maura had been standing just minutes ago.

What in blazes had the little minx gotten herself into now?

# Chapter 4

"*I know what I long for can never be. Philip is the son of a marquis and will be expected to marry well. But when he makes love to me as fervently as he did last night, I so want to believe there is hope.*"

From the diary of Elise Marchand,
June 8, 1794

It was long after midnight when Maura, dressed in her nightclothes and with her face scrubbed clean of makeup, tiptoed into her father's chamber and seated herself in the chair next to his bed, taking great care not to make any noise that might wake him from his healing slumber.

The journey back to London from the Lanscombe estate, which lay just to the east of the city in the rolling pastureland of Essex, had taken far longer than she had expected, and less than an hour had passed since the hackney she and Violet had hired had dropped her off around the corner from her family's residence. The town house had been dark and silent upon her return, and she'd been able to steal up the back stairs to her second-floor bedchamber without encountering anyone on the way.

Once she had readied herself for bed and settled under the cool, crisp sheets, however, she discovered that she was far too jittery to sleep. Images of everything she had seen and experienced while in the Viscount Lanscombe's home flashed repeatedly behind her closed eyes, allowing her no respite, and she had finally decided to rise and check on her father in hopes that it would help to take her mind off things.

But even here, in the dim glow of the marquis's chamber, the events of that evening played over and over in her head. And to her consternation, the memory that taunted her the most was that of her unexpected meeting with the Earl of Hawksley. The brazen way the rogue had seized her in his arms and kissed her, for all the world as if he had every right to do so, had left her more than a trifle shaken.

*How could I have let such a thing happen?* she wondered, shamed heat flooding into her cheeks. Regardless of his father's guilt or innocence when it came to her mother's murder, the man was a morally deficient cad who had turned seducing women into an art form, and if she knew what was good for her, she would take whatever precautions were necessary to ensure that their paths didn't cross again.

And try to forget the fact that some small, wicked part of her had enjoyed his touch more than she would ever admit.

Firmly shoving thoughts of the infuriating earl from her mind, she reached for her father's hand, clasping it in hers while her anxious gaze measured the slow rise and fall of his chest. According to the physician, Lord Albright's fever had finally broken earlier that day, but it had left him drained and listless, too weak even to lift his head from the pillow or to stay awake for more than short periods of time. Full recovery was still a long way off, and there was little doubt that he would be bedridden for days and possibly even weeks to come.

Maura nibbled worriedly at her lower lip. Perhaps if the marquis hadn't already exhausted himself when the illness had seized hold of him, he might have been better prepared to battle its effects. But with so many questions left dangling regarding his wife's death, and his own search for answers at a frustrating standstill, he had occupied himself by spending the past several months traveling from one end of England to the other, assisting his friend, Bow Street Runner Morton Tolliver, in some of his current cases. It had been during a recent trip to Brighton that he had ultimately succumbed to the inflammation of the lungs that had caused him to collapse upon his return home.

Even now, a fortnight later, Maura could still feel the combination of shock and fear that had washed over her on that rainy, miserable afternoon when Mr. Tolliver had half carried the ghost-white and shivering form of the marquis into the town house foyer. As her aunt Olivia had screeched for someone to send for the physician and the servants had rushed to prepare the master bedchamber, she had been paralyzed, frozen with the utter certainty that she was about to lose her father. The mere possibility had filled her with a panic and a dread that she never, ever wanted to feel again.

"Maura?"

The voice that brought her back to the present was barely audible, little more than a whisper in the silence of the room, but she heard it nonetheless. Looking back over her shoulder, she squinted her eyes against the dimness and managed to make out the shadowed outline of a person hovering in the doorway. A fragile, waiflike figure clad in a white nightgown.

Her younger sister, fourteen-year-old Aimee.

Unable to quell a sudden rush of concern, Maura released her father's hand and turned in her chair to face the girl. "Darling, what is it? What are you doing up?"

The youngest Daventry sister linked her fingers

together in front of her and entered the chamber, moving toward the bed with hesitant footsteps. As she drew closer, the pool of light from a nearby lamp fell over her elfin countenance, illuminating wide amber eyes rife with apprehension. "I wanted to see Papa."

"It's late. You should be asleep."

"So should you."

There was no arguing with that, so Maura didn't even try. Instead she patted the footstool next to her, and Aimee sank down on its plump cushion, her gaze focused on the marquis.

A comfortable hush enshrouded the two sisters as they watched over their father together, and several long minutes passed before Aimee spoke again. "He seems better."

"He is, I think. He's resting more peacefully at least."

"Yes." There was another pause, then the girl tilted her head to peer up at Maura through a veil of lashes. "You know, you disappeared after dinner. Aunt Olivia seemed quite put out when Phoebe informed her that you had retired early."

Maura's heart skipped a beat. She had tried so hard to go about her day as usual, to keep any hint of the trepidation she had felt over her plans for the evening from showing in her demeanor, but there was always a chance that she had somehow given herself away. Or perhaps her lady's maid, Phoebe, had suspected she was up to something and had gone to Lady Olivia. There were any number of scenarios, and none of them boded well.

Attempting to project an air of nonchalance she was far from feeling, she smoothed an invisible wrinkle from her father's coverlet and gave a careless shrug. "Aunt Olivia is always put out for one reason or another."

And that was nothing but the truth. Their father's spinster sister, Lady Olivia Daventry, had come to live with the family soon after the marchioness's death to help raise her motherless nieces. And while Maura was grateful to her aunt, she had to admit that the woman's starchy and critical manner made her rather difficult to get along with.

She cleared her throat and glanced over at Aimee again, praying that her sense of disquiet wasn't reflected in her expression. "Did she say what she wanted?"

"No. But then she never tells me anything. When she questioned me, I simply informed her that you had the megrims and had asked not be disturbed."

Maura had to stifle an exhalation of relief. So she was safe. For now. "Thank you for that. I'm afraid I just wasn't in the mood to listen to her go on and on about the attributes of this gentleman or that gentleman for another interminable evening. It truly is enough to make my head ache."

"It's all right. I don't blame you for needing to escape from her every once in while." Her sister gave her a look full of sympathy. "She has a tendency to be a bit demanding, and I think she expects more from you than any of us."

And sometimes those very expectations weighed her down like a millstone about her neck, Maura thought now with a slump of her shoulders. She knew it often appeared to others that she and her aunt got along rather well, but that was mostly because she had long ago learned to conform to the woman's rather rigid ideas of how a proper young lady should conduct herself. While Jillian's obstinate and independent nature roused their aunt's wrath and Aimee's timidity seemed only to irritate her, Maura had always been the "good" sister. The one that Olivia had pinned all her hopes on. The one who would salvage the family name by making a successful match on the marriage mart.

Once that had been Maura's single-minded goal as well. By being the dutiful daughter, she had believed that in some small way she could make up to her father for the pain he had suffered at the hands of her mother. But in the last few weeks, things had changed. The heartfelt words written in a leatherbound book had so altered the way she looked at life that she wasn't certain what she wanted anymore.

"What's wrong, Maura?"

Once again it was Aimee's voice that yanked her from her ruminations, and she carefully schooled her features into a mask of unruffled composure before meeting the younger girl's far too perceptive gaze. "What makes you think anything is wrong?"

But Aimee was having none of it. Her pointed little chin rose at a pugnacious angle, and with her long, golden-brown hair coming loose from its braid to tumble about her face, she resembled a rather disgruntled kitten whose fur had been rubbed the wrong way.

"Really, Maura," she said severely. "I know you and Jilly still think of me as a child, but I'm not quite as oblivious as the two of you would like to believe. You've been so quiet lately, so pale and worried, even though you've been very good at hiding it from everyone else. And please don't try and tell me it's merely concern for Papa. I'm not blind, and I'm well aware this all started before he even became ill."

Maura blinked in bemusement. It never failed to catch her off guard when her normally shy little sister displayed her more assertive side.

Five years ago, on that fateful night that had forever altered their lives, Aimee had been the lone witness to the murder of the Marchioness of Albright, but the resulting shock had driven all memory of the traumatic incident from her mind, including the identity of her mother's killer. It had left her changed in ways that could not be denied, and the affectionate and trusting child they had all once known had become a frightened, withdrawn shadow of her former self.

In recent weeks, however, Maura had noticed that a subtle transformation had begun to take place. While still quiet and guarded, her younger sister no longer flinched at loud noises or raised voices. She had become more confident, more willing to interact with those around her. To smile and laugh and even speak her mind on occasion.

Perhaps the time had finally come to cease being so overprotective where Aimee was concerned, Maura mused. Surely it couldn't hurt to share at least part of what had been troubling her? She was so very tired of carrying the burden alone . . .

"It's just . . . I've been thinking of Mama quite a bit lately," she ventured, her voice a low murmur in deference to their still sleeping father. "I suppose Jillian's insistence that she wasn't leaving us that night, that there was more to the story than meets the eye, has made me view things from a fresh perspective."

She paused, and for an instant she was flung back in time to the terrible moment when she and Jillian had discovered the lifeless body of the marchioness lying on the library floor. Sometimes she didn't think she would ever be able to forget the brassy smell of blood that had tainted the air, or the fear and horror that had claimed her as she had looked into those blank, staring eyes and realized that her mother was gone forever.

"I've been so angry with her for so long, Aimee," she continued, unable to stifle a sharp jab of guilt.

"I believed everything that was said. All the whispers and rumors. All I could see was how badly she hurt Papa, and I let it affect my judgment. I was truly convinced that she had chosen Lord Hawksley over us."

"But what else could you think?" The younger girl reached up to lay a hand on Maura's shoulder. "Hawksley was here that night. That alone lent credence to the note Papa found asking Mama to run away with him. A note supposedly written by Hawksley himself."

"A note that could have been forged in order to cast blame upon him. And you never doubted her. Neither did Jillian."

"That's different. I was too young to truly understand what had happened or what she was being accused of. And Jilly is . . . Jilly. Once she gets an idea into that head of hers, nothing can persuade her to change it." A wistful light entered Aimee's amber eyes, visible even in the gloom. "I wish she was here now."

Once that statement might have sparked Maura's jealousy, but no longer. "I know."

Looking back on her relationship with her older sister, Maura realized it perhaps wasn't surprising that the two of them had often been at odds. Jillian's secretive work with Bow Street, as well as her stubborn determination to disprove the law's version of events on the night their mother had been killed, had only further contributed to the rumors that had plagued the Daventry family. And her interest in criminology had led to a closeness with their father that Maura had long resented and envied.

In the year since the eldest Daventry had wed shipping magnate Connor Monroe, however, the tension that had once existed between the two sisters had eased, and an honest affection had begun to grow in place of their previous antagonism.

If Jilly were here, she would know exactly what to do, Maura thought now, closing her eyes against the wave of inadequacy that threatened to overwhelm her. After all, it had been Jillian's discovery that someone besides the late Lord Hawksley might have been lurking about the Albright town house on the night of the marchioness's murder—along with the refusal of the authorities to take that discovery seriously—that had set the marquis on his current path. But after working nonstop for well over a year to rebuild Grayson and Monroe Shipping following the loss of Connor's partner and the fire that had devastated the company offices, Jillian and her husband had departed London several weeks ago on a belated wedding trip to the north of England. Maura could only hope that the urgent missive she had posted had caught up with them by now and that they were on their way home with all due speed.

In the meantime, she would have to muddle through the best she could on her own.

With a weary sigh, she leaned forward to press a soft kiss to her father's pale cheek, then rose from her chair to look down at her younger sister.

"It's time we were both abed, sweetheart," she said quietly, wrapping an arm around the girl's thin shoulders and drawing her to her feet. "Papa needs his rest and so do we."

Aimee nodded, her reluctance obvious as she sent one last troubled look in her father's direction before allowing herself to be led from the room.

A quarter of an hour later, after tucking her sister in and bidding her good night, Maura returned to her own chamber and sank down on the edge of her bed, feeling both mentally and physically spent. But despite her utter exhaustion, she hesitated to even attempt to close her eyes. At the very edges of her consciousness, the nightmares that had haunted her for the last two weeks hovered ominously, ready to descend upon her the moment she fell asleep. Nightmares in which her mother came to stand by her bed and stare down at her with wide, beseeching eyes full of wounded accusation. And even though the marchioness's mouth never appeared to move, her voice always echoed in Maura's head as clearly as if she had spoken aloud.

*Why, my sweet girl? Why couldn't you see that I was hurting too?*

Unable to hold back the feelings of guilt and remorse that recollections of the dream always stirred within her, Maura choked on a sob.

*I'm sorry, Mama. So sorry.*

Almost of its own volition, her hand crept forward and slid underneath the pile of ruffled pillows stacked against the headboard, her fingers groping until they closed around the cracked leather binding of the book hidden there.

Her mother's journal.

Drawing it from its concealment, she stared down at the scarred cover, picturing in her mind the neat, feminine handwriting that filled its pages. She had accidentally stumbled upon the journal two days before her father had returned home, hidden in a secret compartment of Lady Albright's old writing desk, and she had been anxious to place it in his hands the second he had stepped in the door. But his sudden illness had prevented her from doing so.

Tears blurred her vision as she clasped the book against her chest and bowed her head. Papa deserved to read the words his wife had written, to know the truth about what had transpired in the months before her death, but he was certainly in no shape to deal with such revelations now. Once he was well and back on his feet, she would gladly hand over the diary and all its secrets. Until then, however, she would have to investigate matters on her own.

The mere thought of the task ahead of her was daunting. Unlike her father and Jillian, she had no interest or experience in criminology, and she had no one to turn to for advice apart from her mother's old friend Violet. She was well aware that what she was doing could turn out to be dangerous. Not just to her reputation and her search for a suitable husband, but to her own life.

A shiver coursed through her as her fingers brushed against the packet of letters that stuck out from the pages of the diary. The very letters that she was sure held the key to the mystery of her mother's death. It was obvious that whoever had written them had been deeply troubled, as well as enamored of the Lady Albright to the point of obsession. And because of their numerous references to her time on the stage, it seemed logical to deduce that the marchioness's secret admirer had to be one of the men she had been intimately involved with during her years as an actress, before she had fallen in love with Philip Daventry.

The hoity-toity members of society would have been shocked by the lack of names on that list. In fact, it consisted of only three: the Marquis of Cunnington, the Viscount Lanscombe, and the Baron Bedford.

Driven by her need for answers, Maura had diligently applied herself to determining once and for all which of these men had been responsible for writing the letters. And thanks to her snooping tonight, she had managed to eliminate Lord Lanscombe as a possible suspect. Now all she had to do was figure out a way to get close enough to Lord

Cunnington and Lord Bedford to do the same.

Weary beyond bearing, Maura finally divested herself of her dressing gown and climbed under the covers, though she didn't bother to douse the bedside light. Instead she relaxed back against her propped-up pillows and opened her mother's journal to one of the pages she had marked, reading once more the words the marchioness had written so long ago.

*Today, while Philip was busy attending to preparations for our departure, I took the girls for a walk down by the lake. It is more than likely the last chance we shall have to enjoy some quiet time alone together for quite a while.*

*Tomorrow we leave for London. For twelve years we have been happy here in our little cottage in Dorset. There has been no one to judge us or the way we choose to live our lives, and I have been content with our peaceful existence. With the death of Lord Albright, however, I cannot help but be afraid. When Philip and I were first wed, it was easy to dismiss all of the naysayers. We were young and in love and cared about nothing more than each other. But now he shall be the marquis, and we have a family to think of. A family that will have to contend with those same naysayers.*

*I worry far more for the girls than myself.
I love them dearly, and the thought of them
being shunned is more than I can bear. God,
please, please don't let my daughters be hurt
because of me . . .*

The tears that had been threatening all evening
finally spilled over, and Maura gave another strangled sob. She had been angry for so long, so ready
to cast blame on her mother for all their family had
suffered, that she had let herself forget the special
bond they had once shared.

Lady Albright had never been the wanton temptress that society had believed. Her diary had revealed the truth. About her abiding love for her
family. Her relationship with Lord Hawksley. All
of it. Yes, pain and disillusionment had led the
marchioness to make some selfish mistakes, but she
had been striking back at a world that had treated
her cruelly. All she had wanted was the affection
and attention of a husband who had drifted away
from her, and instead she had wound up alienating
him even further.

The least Maura owed the woman who had
borne her was an answer to the mystery of who
was responsible for her murder. It was worth the
risk to her future, to her name and reputation, if
she could somehow make amends for all the years
that she had remembered her mother with derision
and scorn.

She would get to the bottom of this. And she would let nothing and no one stand in her way.

For a fleeting instant, a mental picture of the handsome face of the Earl of Hawksley danced before her eyes, but she once more shoved it away. She might not be the investigator Jillian was, but it was all up to her now, and she would not allow herself to be distracted or dissuaded.

Not by her own doubts. And not by her very inconvenient attraction for the most unsuitable and disreputable rake she had ever met.

# Chapter 5

*"The Marquis of Albright paid me an unexpected visit this evening. It seems he had heard of my relationship with his son and wanted to make sure that I was aware I could never be more to Philip than a mistress. I had him thrown from my dressing room."*

From the diary of Elise Marchand,
June 21, 1794

Gabriel reined in and drew his mount to a halt on the sandy shoulder of the bridle path, taking care to remain in the shadows cast by a nearby stand of sheltering trees. Grateful for their concealment, he reached up with a gloved hand to tilt his curly-brimmed beaver back from his forehead before surveying with narrowed eyes the bustling scene that surrounded him.

It was well after five o'clock on an unusually sunny Saturday afternoon, and the stylish set had converged on Hyde Park in droves, anxious to see and be seen. A multitude of elegant equipages carrying the cream of London society traversed the length of Rotten Row, jostling for pride of place. And on the fringes of the crowd, the arrogant and well-heeled gentlemen of the ton trotted along on some of the most impressive examples of breeding stock their stables had to offer, each attempting to outdo the other with his expert display of horsemanship.

Watching as two high-perch phaetons narrowly avoided a collision, Gabriel couldn't help but shake his head in disgust as the reckless young bucks who drove them shook their fists at each other and continued to jockey for position. It had been quite some time since he had made an appearance in such a public arena at the height of the fashionable hour, and with every minute that passed he was reminded of the reasons why. The parade of self-important pomposity was enough to turn even the strongest of stomachs.

Which begged the question. What on earth had possessed him to show up here today?

But even as he let his gaze travel over the carriages that lined the South Drive, searching for a small, familiar figure with a head of ebony curls, he knew the answer to that.

Lady Maura Daventry.

Despite his resolve to put the maddening female

out of his mind, he had spent last night pacing his Grosvenor Square town house, restless and aching, reliving every minute detail of their shared kiss. From the feel of her lush curves pressed against him, to the softness of her lips moving so exquisitely under his own, every nuance of their encounter had imprinted itself on his senses in a most disquieting fashion.

The woman was enough to drive a man mad. And now it seemed that she had managed to attract a demanding and rather proprietary admirer.

Too proprietary, in his estimation.

Gabriel lifted a hand to briefly touch his breast pocket, where he had tucked the note he had found on the Viscount Lanscombe's study floor. The tone of the missive disturbed him more than he cared to admit. This wasn't a typical love letter written by a besotted swain. If one were to read between the lines, it could almost be perceived as a threat.

*If I can't have you, no one can . . .*

The ominous words echoed in his head, and his hands tightened into white-knuckled fists on the reins, causing his big, black gelding to dance skittishly beneath him. Calming the animal with a comforting murmur, he fought to bring his own wildly seething emotions back under control.

He couldn't understand what the bloody hell was wrong with him. The mere thought of the Lady Maura indulging in some sort of illicit liaison with a possessive and overly aggressive suitor filled him with a sudden, overwhelming urge to throttle someone, and the violence of his reaction caught him off guard. Why should he care who the foolish chit chose to involve herself with? It was of no consequence to him.

But no matter how hard he tried to convince himself of that, something wouldn't allow him to so sanguinely brush aside his concerns. Every instinct he possessed was screaming at him that she was in trouble. Why else would she risk her hard-won reputation by doing something as foolish as sneaking into one of Lord and Lady Lanscombe's notorious masquerades? Had she arranged some sort of rendezvous with the writer of the letter, or was something even more nefarious afoot?

His need for the answers to these questions had prodded him into coming here, to the one place where any self-respecting, marriage-minded miss was practically guaranteed to make an appearance before the afternoon was out. Once again, it seemed that he just couldn't resist playing the knight errant to Lady Maura's damsel in distress.

Now all he had to do was find the damsel.

At that moment, as if conjured by the power of his thoughts, an open-seated landau rolled into view at the end of the ostentatious procession that proceeded along the Row. Black with gold trim and pulled by a pair of matching white mares, it was instantly recognizable to him as belonging to the Dowager Duchess of Maitland.

Ensconced regally within its luxurious confines was the plump, white-haired dowager herself. And even from this distance, Gabriel knew without a doubt that the lavender-garbed figure by her side was the very person he sought.

Her delicate profile cast in shadow by the lace edge of her parasol, Lady Maura was leaning forward, speaking rather intently to the thin, dour-looking woman seated across from her and the elderly duchess. Their discussion was interrupted, however, when two gentlemen rode up on horseback and doffed their hats before engaging the trio of females in conversation.

The Duke of Maitland and the Baron Bedford.

Shifting in his saddle, Gabriel observed the little group with a brooding frown. He wasn't quite certain what he was hoping to accomplish with this ill-conceived plan. Though most of the aristocratic members of the ton still treated him with a certain amount of civility due to his wealth and title, there were those who wouldn't hesitate to spit in his face. To approach the daughter of the woman his father had been accused of murdering—in front of half of London society, no less—would be foolhardy, at best. He would be lucky if the masses didn't stone him for his effrontery.

But the menacing tone of the letter burning a hole in his pocket weighed too heavily upon him to ignore. Perhaps if he could just get close enough to speak to her briefly, to let slip a subtle clue that he had the note she had dropped, he might be able to read her expression, to tell from her face whether his instincts were correct and she was hiding something.

But did he dare take a chance on creating a spectacle by approaching her now?

His mouth curved into a grimly sardonic smile. Of course he dared! He was the Devil's Own, wasn't he? He refused to let a few appalled looks and lofty snubs keep him from doing precisely as he wished.

With a clicking of his tongue and a nudge of his boot heel, he spurred his mount and started up the slight incline toward the waiting carriage, his pulse thrumming with anticipation.

"Maura, is everything all right?"

The underlying hint of concern in the softly voiced query effectively cut across the hypnotic rumble of carriage wheels and the clip-clop of horses' hooves to jolt Maura from her musings. Blinking as she came back to the present, she glanced up to meet the watchful gaze of Theodosia Rosemont, Dowager Duchess of Maitland.

A stout, matronly woman with a no-nonsense nature, the dowager had been a good friend to the late Lady Albright and was one of the few people who hadn't ostracized the marchioness because of her background as an actress. Upon their mother's death, she had insisted upon taking the Daventry sisters under her wing, using her considerable in-

fluence to ensure their acceptance by the ton and
to help smooth their way with the more harshly
judgmental members of society.

Her kind brown eyes narrowed; she was studying
Maura now with a perception that was unnerving.
"You've been very quiet ever since we left Maitland
House, my dear."

Maura tightened her grip on the handle of her
lace-trimmed parasol, hoping that its shadow
would hide any betraying signs of her disquiet.
How she longed to confide all her troubles, but
it simply wouldn't do. She had never shared the
same sort of bond with the duchess that Jilly did,
and she had no idea how the elderly lady would
react. If the duchess found out where Maura had
ventured the evening before, it was highly possible
that she would feel compelled to put a stop to any
further search for answers until Connor and Jillian
returned to town.

"I'm fine, Your Grace," she finally replied, managing to force a fleeting smile to her lips. "A bit
tired perhaps."

A scornful sniff came from the woman sitting so
stiffly across from them.

"I'm sure I don't see how that could be possible."
As usual, Lady Olivia Daventry's tone was stern
and reproving as she sent her niece a displeased
frown. "You retired last evening directly after dinner, and not even your maid was capable of rousing
you this morning. I do hope that such laziness isn't

going to become a habit. Why, if I hadn't sent Mrs. Bellows in at teatime to insist that you arise and join us, you would have slept the clock round!"

That might have been due to the fact that she hadn't drifted off until well after the rosy light of dawn had painted the horizon, Maura thought wryly. But she certainly couldn't admit that to anyone. She had no desire to try to explain the reasons behind her insomnia. "I'm sorry, Aunt Olivia, but my head ached so that I could hardly think. I'm afraid I tossed and turned for most of the night."

Her lined face anxious, the duchess placed a beringed hand on Maura's arm. "Child, you should have told me you were unwell. We could have postponed our drive for another day. I shall have the coachman turn around at once and—"

"No, please don't trouble yourself. I feel better now."

Theodosia didn't appear to be convinced by Maura's reassurances, but before the dowager could press her further on the matter, Lady Olivia spoke up.

"That is good, for we have much to talk about. Things I had hoped to discuss with you last night."

Oh dear. Maura had to bite the inside of her cheek to keep from groaning aloud. She very much feared she knew what was coming. Another reminder of her duty to choose an appropriate husband with all due speed. After two Seasons, she was well aware of the role she was expected to play in the salvation of her family, but her aunt still seemed to believe that she needed daily prodding. "Oh?"

"Yes, I have been meaning to speak with you for the past several days regarding Lord Waldron. I do believe he is quite taken with you, you know. I wouldn't be at all surprised should he decide to make an offer for your hand soon."

Maura watched as the duchess's eyebrows shot skyward at this revelation. "The Marquis of Waldron?"

"Indeed." Lady Olivia gave an affirmative nod, her ice-blue eyes alight with satisfaction. "He stood up with Maura twice at Lord and Lady Jessup's ball the other night, and he has requested permission to call on her once Philip has fully recovered from his indisposition."

"He is a widower and old enough to be the gel's father!"

"True. But he is also titled, wealthy, and well respected. It would be a most advantageous match. One that could do a great deal to restore our family's standing among the ton. I'm sure Philip will be delighted."

Theodosia gave an irritated huff and faced Maura, her chin lifted at an imperious angle. "My dear, what do you think of this? Your aunt seems intent on pairing you off with a man twice your age and you have no opinion on the matter?"

At a loss for words, Maura winced at the dowager's obvious disapproval. But she was saved the awkwardness of attempting to stumble and stammer her way through some sort of response when her aunt answered the question for her.

"I am certain she is just as pleased at the possibility as I am, Your Grace. After all, she can't afford to be too particular, what with the scandal her mother created."

"We are discussing your niece, Olivia, not Elise."

"I am aware of that," Lady Olivia acknowledged with haughty aplomb. "But we cannot simply ignore the damage that has been done to our family name and reputation. Elise's past behavior has made finding husbands for her daughters a difficult—if not impossible—task. Why, just look at how Jillian has ended up. Wed to a tradesman, of all things. How Philip could have given his blessing to such a union is beyond me."

"Perhaps, unlike you, he is a bit more concerned with his daughters' future contentment rather than with appearances," Theodosia snapped, spots of angry color decorating her cheekbones as she leveled the other woman with a glare.

Olivia lifted one shoulder in an indifferent shrug, the gesture a clear indication of how little the happiness of her nieces mattered to her in the greater scheme of things. "Be that as it may, it will be different for Maura. She has the potential to rise above her mother's disgrace, though we must act quickly." She sent Maura a gimlet-eyed stare.

"Perhaps if it wasn't already her second Season, she could take the time to be a bit more selective. But her twentieth birthday is drawing nigh, and if she continues in this manner, her prospects will soon disappear."

Maura sank her teeth into her lower lip and bowed her head at the less than subtle rebuke. She supposed she couldn't blame her aunt for being frustrated with her. It was entirely her own fault that a second Season had even been necessary, for her first Season had been a modest success, and she had acquired her fair share of interested suitors.

However, she had determined that she would not be rushed into choosing her future husband. She would take great care, and she would use her mind and not her heart to make the decision. There would be no passionate or melodramatic vows of undying love. Her parents had wed for love, and look what heartache it had brought them. Such strong emotions could only lead to tragedy, and she had no intention of ever hurting anyone or of allowing herself to be hurt the way her mother and father had hurt each other.

"Maura?"

At Theodosia's gentle prompting, Maura took a deep breath and reached out to pat the dowager's hand soothingly, struggling to come up with something to say that would put the elderly lady's mind at ease.

"I get along well with Lord Waldron, Your

Grace," she ventured. "Yes, he is older, but I see that as a mark in his favor. He is more prepared to settle down and start a family than someone of younger years. I'm sure he will be good to me."

The dowager shook her head and released a weary sigh. "My child, you must know I want only the best for you, and I would feel remiss in my responsibility as your mother's dear friend if I did not make sure you are happy with this arrangement." She paused, searching Maura's gaze with a probing intensity. "Is marriage to Lord Waldron truly what you desire?"

A vision of the tall, distinguished, silver-haired Lord Waldron flashed before Maura's eyes. With him, she would be safe. There was no passion between them, but there were also no unrealistic expectations on either part. No danger of anyone getting hurt.

For a split second, another face transposed itself over the marquis's, this one much younger and possessing an almost unearthly sort of handsomeness. The recollection of those chiseled features, those flashing green eyes, had Maura's pulse speeding up even as she forced the image away.

"Yes," she said, attempting to infuse her statement with a certainty she was suddenly far from feeling. "It is."

"Ladies! Good afternoon!"

The voice was masculine and cheerful, hailing them from a short distance away. Grateful for the excuse it gave her to avoid the duchess's piercing stare, Maura glanced up and spotted two gentlemen trotting toward them on horseback, weaving in and out among the carriages that lined the South Drive.

It was Theodosia's stepson, Warren Rosemont, the current Duke of Maitland, and his good friend, the Baron Bedford.

Maura felt her heart skip a beat at the sight of them. Baron Bedford, a charming and debonair gent of middle years with a notorious weakness for a well-turned ankle, was one of the men on her short list of possible letter writers. Though she had her doubts that he could actually be the culprit, she still believed that he merited investigation. His dalliances with women had once been legendary, and his fascination with the late marchioness had been a secret to no one.

"Maitland, Bedford," Theodosia greeted them with a nod, even as the carriage rolled to a halt and the men drew abreast.

Bedford offered the women an elegant bow from the waist, doffing his hat to reveal immaculately trimmed salt-and-pepper hair. "Your Grace. As always, it is a pleasure to see you. And Lady Olivia, Lady Maura, may I say that you are both looking particularly radiant this fine day?"

He flashed a smile that encompassed all three females, but his gaze lingered for a noticeable length of time on Olivia.

The duke, a large and imposing man with a barrel chest, thinning blond hair, and a jovial manner, added his felicitations to Bedford's. "Yes, indeed. It is always a joy to pass the time of day in such lovely company."

Her aunt's reaction to the compliments intrigued Maura. Instead of rapping out a chilly rejoinder, she stiffened, a ruddy flush staining her cheeks, and reached up in a self-conscious gesture to tuck a few strands of graying light brown hair back into the confines of her bonnet. "Thank you, sirs. You are too kind."

Maura's jaw dropped. Seeing Lady Olivia so flustered was a rare occurrence indeed, and it caught her more than a trifle off guard. She had always been curious as to why her aunt had remained a spinster. A handsome woman in her late fifties, she had never seemed interested in men or marriage. But there could be little doubt that the gentlemen's flattering attentions had rattled her.

Bedford's eyes were sparkling with good humor. "Never say so!" he exclaimed gallantly, sketching another bow. "In truth, I find mere words inadequate to express my sincere appreciation of your loveliness."

From beside Maura, the duchess made no attempt to muffle her exasperated snort. "Really, Bedford, I have never known you to be at a loss for words. Since you spout that sort of drivel on a regular basis, one can only assume that you have a ready supply of such hogwash."

Lady Olivia gasped, and Maura stifled a laugh behind her gloved hand as the dowager turned to address her stepson. "Maitland, I must say I am rather surprised to see you. I was under the impression that you were rusticating at Rosemont Hall."

He gave a booming chuckle. "The wife has been in a dither for weeks over the preparations for the house party we are hosting Saturday next, don't you know. She has the servants rushing about hither and yon, making ready, and things are in such a state that a man can hardly think. I finally decided I would get more peace here in town."

"I'm certain in the end it will be worth all of the furor, Your Grace," Lady Olivia interjected, once more the picture of composure. "Your wife does host the most splendid affairs. My niece and I are honored to be included on the guest list and are very much looking forward to it."

The duke peered down at Maura's aunt from under lowered brows. "Indeed. Felicia was a bit uncertain whether you would be able to attend, as Albright has been doing so poorly."

"Oh, but his condition is much improved. He was even able to sit up and take breakfast this morning with only a minimal amount of help from the nurse we have hired, and the physician is most optimistic for a speedy recovery."

"Ah. That is good to hear." He faced Maura with a warm and sympathetic expression. "I'm certain you must be relieved, my dear. I wish him well."

Maura inclined her head to him with a grateful smile. Though Theodosia had never seemed overly fond of her stepson, he had always been kind to the Daventry sisters, treating them as if he were an indulgent uncle. "Thank you, Your Grace."

Olivia cast a hooded glance in Maura's direction, then leaned toward the duke in a conspiratorial fashion. "I had heard that the Marquis of Waldron has accepted an invitation?"

Maitland nodded. "So I have been informed, yes."

At this point, Lord Bedford reentered the conversation. "As it happens, dear lady, I shall be in attendance as well. I do hope we will have the chance to further our acquaintance. I can't think of anything I would like more."

Lady Olivia eyed him askance. "You flatter me, my lord. But I'm afraid I would be very dull company indeed as compared to your usual choice of companion."

"Nonsense. You wound me to suggest that I could ever find you anything less than fascinating, and I can assure you that I shall hang upon your every word." The baron slanted her a practiced grin. "You share your secrets and I'll share mine."

"Really, Lord Bedford, what makes you believe I have any secrets to share?"

"Bah! Everyone has secrets, my lady. In fact, I have discovered that lovely ladies such as yourself tend to keep the most interesting ones."

"I couldn't agree more."

The deep, velvety drawl came from somewhere behind Maura, and at the tingling familiarity of it, a frisson of awareness skated up her spine.

Whipping about in her seat, she felt her breath seize in her lungs at the sight that greeted her. There, just a few feet away and seated on the back of a large and powerful-looking black steed—an altogether appropriate mount for the devil—was the last man she wished to encounter.

Hawksley.

# Chapter 6

◠◞◠

*"Philip has asked me to marry him. I am stunned. Despite the strength of our love, I never expected that he would ever ask me to be his wife. Though part of me wants to throw my arms around his neck and accept his proposal without hesitation, I know how impossible that is. There is so much about my past that he doesn't know."*

From the diary of Elise Marchand,
August 2, 1794

**H**er heart in her throat, Maura gaped up at Hawksley in swiftly mounting alarm.

What on earth was he doing here? This had to be some sort of nightmare or a bizarre figment of her worst imaginings. Though why her subconscious would manufacture such a horrifying scenario was beyond her.

She squeezed her eyes shut and mentally counted to ten, willing him away with every fiber of her being. If her prayers were answered, he would be gone when she looked again. But she knew even before she lifted her lashes that it hadn't worked.

He was still there, sitting tall and straight in his saddle. Clad in a bottle-green coat that hugged his broad shoulders and a pair of buff breeches that delineated every muscle in his strong thighs, he looked far too devastatingly handsome for her peace of mind, and his gaze burned into her with an intensity that left her feeling singed.

"Hawksley, my good man! This is an unexpected pleasure."

The greeting came from Lord Bedford, sounding loud and grating in the hush that had descended over the carriage, and Maura gave a start, glancing back at her companions. The baron was smiling in welcome, seeming oblivious to the sudden tension that hovered in the air, but the rest were staring at Hawksley as if stunned by his brazenness. While the duke simply looked befuddled, Lady Olivia's previously reddened cheeks had paled to a ghost-white, and her mouth worked soundlessly, opening and closing like a hooked fish gasping for breath. Maura had little doubt that if her aunt had been capable of speech, they all would have gotten quite an earful.

The dowager duchess's reaction, however, was much more difficult to read. Head tilted, she was studying the earl with lips pursed, her countenance every bit as inscrutable as his.

What could she possibly be thinking?

"I haven't seen you out and about for quite some time, Hawksley," the baron was saying, still unaware of the pall that had settled over the group. "I suppose if anyone would know about lovely ladies and their secrets, it would be you."

Hawksley lifted a shoulder in an indolent shrug, his disconcerting stare never wavering from Maura. "You might say that."

Now there was an understatement, Maura thought wildly. Her stomach fluttered as the heat of his regard brought back memories of being held in his arms, his chiseled lips exploring hers with a thoroughness that made her pulse race at the recollection of it. But with a supreme effort of will, she pushed those disturbing images away, forcing herself to focus on remaining calm, though that was far easier said than done.

What did he want? Did he dislike her so much that he merely enjoyed torturing her, or did he plan on exposing her furtive activities of the night before in front of her aunt and half the ton?

After what seemed like a small eternity, Hawksley severed eye contact with her, and she breathed an inner sigh of relief as he faced the others, his enigmatic mask still in place despite the smile that curved his lips.

"Good day, ladies. Your Grace." Sweeping off

his hat, he bowed from the waist, acknowledging Theodosia, Olivia, and Maitland. "A beautiful day for a drive. I do hope you don't mind the intrusion."

No one bothered to reply. Maura suspected they were all too flabbergasted to do so. The world around them had gone very quiet. So quiet that she could hear the soft chirping of birds from the trees that lined the parallel bridle path, and she was certain that every eye in the park must be firmly fixed on them.

At that moment, as if to reinforce that impression, a carriage rolled by carrying the Countess of Leeds and her recently wed daughter, the Viscountess Shipton. The two of them had their heads together, whispering animatedly as they gawked at the little assemblage gathered around the duchess's landau with avid curiosity.

Maura stifled a groan.

The man was mad! This was bound to set the tongues of every gossip in town wagging. But of course it would matter little to him if he were the subject of rumor and speculation. In fact, he reveled in the notoriety. Never mind that Maura would suffer the slings and arrows right along with him, that all the work she had done in the past year to try to make society forget the sins of her mother would be for naught.

He was going to ruin everything.

Out of her peripheral vision, Maura saw her

aunt make an abrupt motion, surging forward in her seat as if she planned on flinging herself from the landau and physically accosting the earl. But Theodosia lifted a staying hand, freezing Olivia in place.

There was another short span of silence as the dowager turned to take stock of Hawksley, her narrow-eyed appraisal traveling over him from the top of his head to the tips of his riding boots. Such an examination might have unnerved anyone else, but not the Devil's Own. He endured it with an uplifted brow and an amused half smile.

When she finally chose to address him, her voice was coolly civil, though Maura detected a measure of respect at his refusal to squirm under her intent regard. "Lord Hawksley. How kind of you to grace us with your presence. Is there something we can do for you?"

"Not at all, Your Grace. I apologize for interrupting." Hawksley inclined his head to her courteously before glancing over at Bedford. "I was just passing by and couldn't help but overhear your conversation. Were you discussing anyone's secrets in particular?"

Having at last noticed the strain that marked the faces of those around him, the baron looked confused and distinctly uncomfortable, but he managed to respond to the earl's query with a good-natured if awkward laugh. "The Lady Olivia was just informing me that she does not keep secrets, and I was telling her what a rarity that is. I hate to disbelieve a lady, but in this instance I'm afraid I must."

Crossing her arms, Olivia transferred her resentful glower from Hawksley to him. "And just why is that?"

Instead of Bedford, however, it was Hawksley who answered. "Because we all have at least one thing we'd rather others not know about. Even those closest to us."

"That's a rather sweeping statement, Hawksley." This came from the Duke of Maitland, who furrowed his brow and peered down his long nose at the earl, as if trying to decide whether he should take offense at the man's confident assertion.

"But a true one. It's just that some of us have deeper and darker secrets than others." Leaving that statement hanging suggestively in the air, Hawksley swung his piercing green eyes back to Maura, skimming them over every inch of her features, as if searching for something in her expression. Their knowing glitter sent another jolt of fear and awareness zinging through her, and goose bumps rippled over her flesh as if he had caressed her physically.

He was playing with her, Maura realized dazedly. Toying with her like a cat with a mouse. But why?

She could only be grateful when her aunt spoke up in a querulous tone, breaking the spell that held her in the earl's thrall. "Could we please change the subject?

I fail to see how this has any bearing on anything."

"Er . . . uh, yes," Lord Bedford muttered, reaching up to scrub at the back of his neck in a rather disgruntled fashion. "This has become a far weightier conversation that I intended for it to be."

Hawksley gathered his reins in one gloved hand. "Of course. Please excuse me. As I said, I didn't mean to intrude." Sidestepping his horse closer to the landau, he tipped his hat once again to Maura and her female companions and offered them a devilish grin. The afternoon breeze stirred his blond locks, sending a curl tumbling over his brow and adding to his roguish appearance. "Enjoy the rest of your drive."

"It was good to see you, Hawksley." To the baron's credit, he managed not to flinch at the seething glare Lady Olivia leveled upon him at his jovial words, though he did shift a bit uneasily in his saddle. "I plan on doing the rounds of the clubs this evening. Perhaps you could pop in."

"Perhaps." Hawksley paused, giving Maura one last veiled glance from over his shoulder, then lifted a hand in farewell. "Good afternoon."

Wheeling his horse about, he cantered off toward the adjacent bridle path, and they all stared after him until he had disappeared from sight behind a grove of trees.

Several long seconds of stillness ticked by before the Duke of Maitland finally cleared his throat. "Well, I do believe it's time for Bedford and me to take our leave as well," he announced, his eagerness to escape the discomfort the earl had left in his wake all too obvious under his air of forced cheer. "Theodosia. Ladies. It's been a pleasure."

The group exchanged polite adieus and parted ways, but the gentlemen had no sooner trotted out of earshot than Olivia expelled an outraged hiss and planted her hands on her hips. "The nerve of that . . . that blackguard! How dare he even deign to speak to us? And in such a public venue!"

Theodosia motioned to her driver to proceed, then tapped her lower lip with her index finger in thought as the landau rolled forward. "Yes. It wasn't well done of him, and not at all like Hawksley," she mused.

"It is precisely like Hawksley! He is a rake and a libertine who cares nothing for the scandal he creates with his reprehensible behavior. But then, it's not surprising he has such a disgraceful lack of morals. He is just like his father, and I have little doubt that he is equally as capable of murder in the right circumstances."

At the barely restrained fury that vibrated just beneath the surface of Lady Olivia's tirade, Maura drew back in her seat in astonishment. Her aunt's displays of anger were usually deadly calm and icily controlled, and such a violent outburst was completely out of character. It seemed that the Earl of Hawksley brought out the savagery in more than one person.

The duchess shot the other woman a reproving look. "Really, Olivia, if what Jillian discovered during her investigation last year is correct and someone else was present in the house on the night of Elise's death, it is quite possible that the late earl was innocent of any wrongdoing. In which case Lord Hawksley would be just as much a victim of all of this as your family."

Lady Olivia threw up her hands. "Must we go through this again? Regardless of what Jillian claims, I do not believe the earl was innocent. Obviously, Philip isn't entirely convinced either, otherwise he would have shared the information with the man's family long ago. And Hawksley's son is far from being a victim. He has brought his shame upon himself, if you ask me." She focused her attention on her niece, her blue eyes glinting with unmistakable suspicion. "I must say, I did not like the way he was looking at Maura at all."

Angling her parasol so that it once again shaded her face, Maura mentally cursed the betraying tide of color she was certain had flooded into her cheeks. She had been so busy giving thanks that the earl had departed without causing any major spectacle that it hadn't even occurred to her that one of the others might have noticed his bold appraisal of her.

"I'm sure I don't know what you mean, Aunt Olivia," she demurred, struggling to keep her voice steady in the face of her aunt's scrutiny.

"I mean that he seemed entirely too interested in you. That scoundrel is not at all the sort of gentleman a young lady should associate with, and I certainly hope you haven't offered him any encouragement."

Maura shook her head, at a loss for words to even begin to defend herself. She was afraid that if she opened her mouth, she would erupt in hysterical laughter. Would her aunt consider kissing the man to be encouragement?

It was at this point that the duchess intervened, earning Maura's everlasting gratitude.

"I saw no indication that the gel encouraged Hawksley's attentions," Theodosia pointed out with asperity. "But I must say, Lord Bedford seems to like him well enough."

Lady Olivia appeared momentarily flustered by the dowager's comment, but quickly recovered. "Perhaps Lord Bedford was unaware—"

"Or perhaps the man is a horse's arse." As usual, Theodosia made no attempt to sugarcoat her blunt assessment. "The baron's only concern is his single-minded pursuit of the next skirt or hand of whist. He is no better than Hawksley in his own way, and if you believe differently, then I must seriously question whether or not you should be advising Maura on who is or is not appropriate."

Having delivered that scathing set-down, she then faced Maura, who was struggling to contain her amusement at Olivia's angry sputters.

"I cannot tell you how much I have wanted to believe that the late earl wasn't responsible for your mother's death," the duchess told her, her lined face rife with obvious compassion. "He was always a pleasant and agreeable sort when he was part of my stepson's circle of acquaintances. Before the drink took over. And I knew his wife from the time she was a young girl. She was very sweet, if a bit shy and retiring, and she didn't deserve the censure and recrimination that society heaped upon her after what happened."

Never before had Maura given much thought to what Hawksley's family must have gone through in the aftermath of the scandal, but now that she had learned from reading her mother's journal that the late earl's relationship with the marchioness hadn't been quite what it had appeared to be, she couldn't help but wonder just what the man's wife and heir had suffered.

"I had heard that the countess had passed away," she ventured, taking care to keep her tone only mildly questioning.

"Yes, I'm afraid so." Theodosia gave a sorrowful shake of her head. "Soon after her husband, I believe. I can't help but think that the scandal was simply too much for her. It's a shame. She and her son were very close, and there were no other family members to help him through the ordeal once she was gone. I imagine it must have been difficult for him."

Lady Olivia sniffed. "You behave as if we should feel sorry for him," she said curtly. "I hardly think so. He is accountable for his own reputation."

"And are you accountable for yours, or Maura and her sisters theirs?" the duchess asked, eyeing her with disdain. "Just as the ton assumed that Elise's daughters would follow in her footsteps, society tarred Hawksley with the same brush as his father long before he ever acquired the name Devil's Own."

As her aunt and the dowager duchess continued to debate Hawksley's character—or lack of one— Maura turned her back on the exchange and stared off into the distance, mulling over Theodosia's last statement. She had to acknowledge that in his own way, Lord Hawksley had been just as trapped by the ton's view of him as she and her sisters had been, and she couldn't help but feel a brief surge of sympathy.

However, that didn't mean that she trusted him. Whether or not he had earned the name, he had certainly lived up to it. And she couldn't let herself forget that. Not for a minute.

In any case, she had far more important things to concentrate on. She still had two possible suspects on her list that she needed to find some way to eliminate. And one of them had just ridden away in the company of Theodosia's stepson.

She still had her doubts that a man as inept and ineffectual as Lord Bedford could have had anything to do with Lady Albright's death, regardless of his absorption with her. But she had to be sure. And as she went over the earlier conversation, she remembered that he had mentioned doing the rounds of the clubs that evening. Perhaps there was a way she could use that to her advantage . . .

And as her companions' voices faded away to a soft buzzing in the background, she began to formulate a plan.

# Chapter 7

*"Even now that he knows everything, Philip insists that he still wants me as his wife. He assures me that he does not care that I know nothing of my background or that there have been men in my past. Our love, he says, is all that matters. I only pray he never regrets marrying me, for I do not think I could bear it."*

From the diary of Elise Marchand,
August 10, 1794

**"D**o you mind telling me just exactly what it is we are doing here?"

At the less than patient growl, Gabriel drew his gaze away from the carriage window, turning his head to meet the brooding regard of the man who sat across from him.

Arms folded over his wide chest, the Viscount

Stonehurst sprawled in the opposite seat, long legs stretched out before him and his forehead furrowed in a fierce scowl.

"Correct me if I'm wrong," he continued, his voice a low and irritated grumble, "but I could swear that the reason you dragged me away from my comfortable chair in front of the fire and a good glass of port was so we could spend an evening of hedonistic bliss at Madame Desiree's." One eyebrow arched upward in question. "I know it has been a while since I availed myself of Madame's services, but unless she has moved her establishment from Covent Garden to Mayfair in the interim, this doesn't appear to be the right address."

Gabriel cast another glance out the window at the quiet, night-darkened landscape as he mentally debated with himself over how much of his dilemma to reveal to the viscount. The sad truth was, he wasn't certain what they were doing here himself.

After his earlier encounter with Lady Maura and her entourage at Hyde Park, he was more convinced than ever that she was up to something. Though she hadn't uttered a word during the entire exchange, she hadn't needed to. The mute panic swimming in the depths of her captivating blue eyes had given her away.

He had spent the rest of the afternoon and evening pondering the question of what to do with that information. By the time dusk had finally fallen, he had been no closer to an answer, not to mention ready to go mad from frustration. Determined to put it all from his mind, he had slammed out of his town house with every intention of rousting Stonehurst from his doldrums and spending the next few hours wrapped in the warm and willing arms of one of Madame Desiree's doxies.

But it hadn't worked out that way. As it happened, the viscount's London residence was only a few doors down from the Albright town house on Belgrave Square, and as they had passed by, Gabriel had been unable to resist the urge to ask his driver to pull over and stop.

Now here they sat, drawn up to the curb under the pale glow of the streetlamps while he gawked up at the elegant brick edifice of Lady Maura's home like some lovesick swain hoping to catch a glimpse of the object of his affections.

Gabriel's hands clenched into fists on his thighs. By God, the chit was like an addiction that he couldn't seem to muster the will to try to battle against. Such behavior was completely foreign to him, and it rubbed him on the raw that he had no control over it.

Was this what his father had felt for the Lady Albright? he wondered grimly. This obsessive, all-consuming fascination? If so, perhaps he could finally find it within himself to feel a slight bit of empathy for the man. He had always blamed the late earl for choosing the marchioness over him and his mother, for loving her more than them. And he had always told himself that he would never allow any female to wield that sort of power over him. Yet here he was, behaving like an infatuated schoolboy!

Several more seconds of silence ticked by before the viscount drew Gabriel's attention by shifting his large frame in the close confines of the carriage in obvious discomfort and muttering an imprecation.

"Bloody hell, Hawksley, we've been sitting here for almost a quarter of an hour. At this rate, I could crawl to Madame Desiree's and still arrive before you. If you will remember, I had no wish to go to begin with. So if you plan to continue gaping at that house like a bloody lackwit, I would appreciate it if you would allow me out of this blasted cramped vehicle so I can walk home."

Gabriel released a pent-up breath. Stonehurst was right. Enough was enough. It was obvious from the darkened windows of the house that the Daventry family had either gone out for the evening or had already retired. There was nothing to see, and this was simply a waste of his time.

But somewhere between here and his friend's home, he had lost his desire to visit Madame Desiree. Suddenly all he could think about was Lady Maura as she had looked the night before, her lush curves hugged by the revealing amethyst gown, her raven-black hair tousled about her creamy shoulders.

It had been a stark contrast to how she had looked that afternoon in her modest lavender carriage dress, with every curl smoothed ruthlessly into place. All he had wanted to do was sweep her up into his arms and see how long it took him to have her pale countenance turning flushed and rosy from his kisses, to have her moaning and clinging to him in surrender . . .

Barely suppressing a groan, Gabriel pushed the tempting image away and forced himself to face the viscount with a carefully blank expression. "I fear I am not good company this evening, my friend. I apologize for pulling you away from your port for nothing, but it might be best if we postpone our visit to Madame Desiree's until another time."

Surprisingly, instead of expressing annoyance at the abrupt turnaround, Stonehurst tilted his head and examined Gabriel with an intentness that was unnerving.

"Far be it from me to point out the obvious," the man mused aloud, "but there's clearly something rather weighty troubling you if you cannot even summon the interest in spending the evening with an accommodating female. And this is the second night in a row that you have passed up such an opportunity. Rather out of character, wouldn't you say?"

Gabriel couldn't deny the truth of that statement. But then he hadn't been behaving like himself for months. And now that he had given it some serious consideration, he could put his finger on the precise moment when his dissatisfaction with his rakehell existence had begun.

On the night almost a year ago when a young miss had wandered into a darkened study and proceeded to turn his world upside down with her loveliness and candor.

But no more. Starting now, he was taking back his life.

"You're right, Stonehurst," he acknowledged, lifting his chin with renewed purpose. "I'm done. This ends here."

The Lady Maura's problems were no longer his concern. Let her arrange assignations with half the men in London and attend every orgiastic gathering she could manage to wangle an invitation to. It only proved that he had misjudged her from the beginning and that she was every inch her mother's daughter.

Firm in his decision, he had just started to reach up to tap on the driver's partition and urge the coachman on when a sudden shifting of the shadows outside the window caught his attention. Whipping his head about, he was just in time to see a small figure come darting out from the mews that ran behind the row of town houses. Though the person wore a concealing cloak, he was aware of the same inner sense of recognition that he had felt the night before, despite the distance that separated them.

It was Lady Maura.

The figure moved with the same sort of furtive-
ness with which it had navigated the Viscount
Lanscombe's garden, and as he continued to watch,
it detached itself from the corner of the Daventry
house and hurried along the pavement toward a
nondescript hackney that he hadn't noticed before.
It sat far back along the curb, away from the light
of the streetlamps.

What the bloody hell was she up to now?

"Hawksley?"

Stonehurst's prompting had Gabriel starting in
his seat and tearing his gaze away from the cloaked
form as it climbed into the waiting hack. The man
had been so quiet that Gabriel had almost forgotten he was there.

"Christ, Hawksley, you look as if you've seen
a ghost," the viscount persisted, his tone edging
from irritation into outright aggravation. "Will
you kindly tell me what the devil is going on?"

Every bit of Gabriel's newfound resolve had
melted away, to be replaced by a thrill of anticipation. There could be no denying it now. She was up
to something. But what?

"I'm sorry, Stonehurst," he murmured, "but it
appears that we have somewhere to go this evening
after all."

The viscount stared at him as if he had lost his
mind as he reached up and rapped his knuckles
smartly on the partition.

"Driver, follow that coach!"

\* \* \*

Her mind awhirl with the events of the past several days, Maura peered out the carriage window at the night sky as they passed from the quiet neighborhoods of Mayfair into the bustling and more brightly lit environs of Pall Mall.

Here, close to the elegantly sprawling grounds of St. James Palace, tall and stately gentlemen's clubs and gambling halls lined the streets, their doors closed to all but the privileged few who could claim membership. Behind one of those doors, Lord Bedford was enjoying a hand of cards with his usual circle of acquaintances, little suspecting how the sanctity of his home was about to be invaded.

At the thought, Maura couldn't stifle a guilty wince. It had to be done to eliminate the baron as a suspect. She knew that. But that didn't mean she felt right about it. All this skulking about was hard on her conscience.

As if reading her mind, the other occupant of the coach leaned forward and placed a hand on her arm, distracting her from her ruminations.

"We don't have to do this, my dear," Violet Lafleur said with gentle compassion, her lightly freckled face rife with concern under its layers of powder and rouge. "Not if you are certain that the baron isn't the one."

Maura looked over at her with a grateful smile, not for the first time giving thanks that she had made the decision to seek this woman out. After running across Violet's name in her mother's journal and recalling that the marchioness had mentioned their past friendship with great fondness over the years, she had paid a call on the former actress in the hopes that she might be able to shed some light on the Lady Albright's life and past loves before she had met the marquis.

And from that initial meeting, an unexpected friendship had developed.

A buxom redhead with a bold, forthright manner, Violet had never achieved the same notoriety on the stage as Elise Marchand. So after her friend had wed Lord Albright, the actress had left the world of the theater to become the mistress of the Duke of Pembury. Upon his death, she had received a sizable fortune and the means to be independent, and she had seized that independence with both hands. Now, at the age of five and forty, she owned her own costume shop and lived life on her own terms.

She was not at all the sort of person Maura would have been allowed to associate with, but in the past fortnight they had formed a close bond despite their differences. Violet had been delighted to meet her old friend's daughter and eager to be of service in the search for Lady Albright's killer. And Maura had come to admire and respect Violet a great deal.

"The baron seems the least likely culprit," she told the woman now. "Despite his past relationship with Mama, I cannot see him fixating on one woman to the exclusion of all else. This is Lord Bedford we are speaking of."

"True. Cunnington is a distinct possibility, however. The man is a pig, and from what I can recall he was always possessive." Violet narrowed her hazel eyes in contemplation. "You are certain Lord Lanscombe can be ruled out?"

"As certain as I can be. His handwriting didn't match the letters at all. And I was so sure he was the one. He pursued Mama so relentlessly those last few months before her death that he just seemed the obvious choice."

"Well, as people are fond of saying, sometimes the obvious choice isn't always the correct one." There was a long pause, then Violet went on in a solemn tone, her sympathetic gaze never wavering from Maura. "You do realize, my dear, that the man who wrote these missives isn't necessarily the same man who killed your mother?"

"But it's a reasonable conclusion, isn't it?" Maura suppressed a shiver as the chilling words she had read, the words that monster had written, hovered before her eyes. "You haven't seen the letters, Violet. This man was obsessed with my mother, but at the same time it was almost as if part of him hated her, blamed her for making him feel that way. He reviled Hawksley and claimed he wasn't good enough for her, then in the next breath accused her of using men as playthings. I think he must have been quite mad. And if he thought that Mama was rejecting him in favor of the earl, I have no trouble believing that he was more than capable of committing murder."

"And that is just one of the many reasons why I can't help but be frightened for you. If this devil should discover that you are searching for him . . ."

"He won't. I promise I shall be most careful."

Violet sent her a rather stern frown. "As you were last night?" she queried with a hint of re-proach.

Heat seeped into Maura's cheeks at the reminder, and she regretted the moment of weakness that had led her to confess to the older woman about her confrontation with Lord Lanscombe's son. All she had succeeded in doing was rousing Violet's pro-tective instincts. She supposed it was a good thing that she had kept her subsequent run-in with Lord Hawksley to herself, though she wasn't at all cer-tain why she had chosen to do so.

Perhaps because she couldn't think about the scoundrel without recalling every passionate sec-ond she had spent in his arms or the way he had looked at her earlier that afternoon, as if he knew exactly what she was feeling and took the greatest pleasure in her discomfort.

Unwilling to let her thoughts stray any further in his direction, she shook off her preoccupation and gave Violet's hand a soothing pat. "Last night

I was caught unaware," she said firmly. "It won't happen again."

The words didn't seem to offer the older woman any reassurance, however, for her expression remained troubled. "I should be whipped for ever taking you to such a place. I could have gone without you, you know. I am capable of comparing handwriting samples."

"Nonsense. This is my burden, Violet. Not yours."

"But must you be so blasted stubborn about doing everything on your own? I am aware your father is ill and you don't wish to distress him at this point in his recovery, but surely there is someone else you could turn to? Perhaps this Mr. Tolliver you've spoken of?"

At the mention of the Bow Street Runner, Maura shook her head. "Mr. Tolliver is out of town pursuing a lead in one of his cases. And things are especially busy at Bow Street right now. The last time he came to visit with Papa he looked exhausted. I wouldn't want to add to his burdens. Never mind the fact that he would more than likely never allow me to have any part in the investigation."

"And I don't suppose I could persuade you to wait until your sister and her husband return home?" Violet prompted hopefully. "I'm certain they must have received your summons by now and are on their way even as we speak."

"Once they arrive, I shall be glad to let Jilly and

Connor take charge. But I can't sit around and do nothing until then."

"But I don't understand—"

"Please, Violet." Maura had told no one about the nightmares that drove her. About the vision she carried with her of her mother's eyes, begging her, pleading with her to find out the truth. And she didn't plan on doing so. That was her cross to bear. Alone. "As I said, I will use the utmost caution from now on, but I must do this. I must."

Violet heaved an exasperated sigh. "Well, you are certainly your mother's daughter. There's no mistake about that. Elise had that very same core of stubbornness."

The two of them became lost in their thoughts and did not speak again for quite some time as the hackney trundled along the cobbled streets toward their destination. Thus Maura was startled when Violet finally broke the extended silence with her announcement of their arrival.

"Ah. Here we are."

They turned off Regent Street and rolled into an alleyway behind a row of elegant and well-kept buildings, one of them a well-known boarding-house for gentlemen bachelors where the Baron Bedford maintained a suite of rooms.

The horses clomped to a halt, and as the driver jumped down from his box to open the door, Violet turned to Maura, her hand held out expectantly. "Do you have the letter?"

Maura hesitated, biting her lip. Earlier, as she had been making her preparations for this evening, she had realized that the letter she had taken with her to Lord Lanscombe's the night before had mysteriously disappeared, and she had turned her room upside down to no avail. She couldn't help but wonder and worry over where she might have dropped it, but she had been in too much of a hurry to do more than filch another letter from the packet and resolve to do a more thorough search later. She didn't want to take a chance on losing another one, however. "Perhaps I should be the one—" she ventured.

But the woman didn't even let her finish her sentence. "After last night? I think not, young lady. I'm afraid this is something that I must do."

"But how will you get into his room?"

"Oh, I have my ways." Violet's lips curved into a sly smile, and she reached up to pat her red curls into place before flinging back the edges of her satin-lined cloak, thrusting her ample breasts into prominent display over the low-cut neckline of her emerald gown. "I shall simply tell the landlord that I am a . . . friend of Lord Bedford's and wish to await his return in his room. Knowing the baron, such a request shouldn't arouse too much suspicion."

A laugh escaped Maura in spite of herself. "I suppose not," she admitted, reaching into the inside pocket of her cloak to extract the letter. "But do be careful. And hurry. We have no way of knowing how soon Lord Bedford will return."

Violet took the folded sheet of stationery from her and tucked it into her own pocket. "I shan't be long."

And with that, she stepped down from the hackney and the door closed behind her.

Minutes that seemed like hours passed, and with every agonizing one of them, Maura's impatience grew. She hated not knowing what was going on or how Violet's search was progressing, and the air inside the hack was so stifling that a fine sheen of perspiration coated her forehead. She couldn't help but be tempted to follow her friend inside the boardinghouse, but she managed to contain herself. Barely.

Just when she didn't think she could take the waiting for another second, she heard the mumble of voices from outside. The rough Cockney drawl of the driver, followed by an unintelligible murmur. Then the door of the hackney opened once again and a figure climbed aboard, settling into the opposite seat.

"There you are—" Maura began, but at that moment the light from the carriage lamp fell over the person's face, illuminating his features, and she stumbled to a disbelieving halt.

# Chapter 8

*"Today we eloped to Gretna Green. Though I know a large ceremony was out of the question in the circumstances, I do wish my friends from the theater could have been in attendance, especially Violet. But all of my little disappointments seemed to fade away when I looked into the eyes of the man I loved and promised to be his forever."*

From the diary of Elise Marchand,
August 15, 1794

For the second time in one day, Maura found herself gaping at the Earl of Hawksley in stunned amazement. There could be little doubt that his presence here was more than mere happenstance. Not even she could be so unlucky. The man was obviously following her, and the thought made her absolutely furious.

Clenching her hands into fists on her lap, she drew herself up in bristling indignation. "Get out," she hissed from between gritted teeth. "Get out at once!"

Instead of complying, however, he crossed his arms over his broad chest and leaned back against the squabs as if he had no intention of going anywhere.

"I think not," he drawled silkily, his mouth curving into a sardonic smile. "I've come for answers and I won't be leaving until I get them."

That did it. Enraged, Maura lunged forward, ready to fling herself from the hackney and enlist the driver's aid in ridding herself of this miscreant once and for all. But before she could even open her mouth to call out for assistance, one of his gloved hands shot out and captured hers as she reached for the door handle, lean fingers wrapping around her wrist in a gentle yet unyielding grip. The unexpectedness of it was enough to freeze her cry in her throat.

"You really don't want to do that," he said, almost conversationally. "After all, it wouldn't be a good idea to call too much attention to yourself, would it?"

Drat him, he was right!

She yanked free from his hold. "H-how dare you slink about, spying on me," she accused, the slight trembling of her voice rousing her ire even more. A pox on the odious man for being able to affect her like this! "I've been trying to convince myself that I was imagining things, that our encounter at Hyde Park today was only a coincidence. But it wasn't, was it? You're playing some sort of cruel game with me."

He lifted one shoulder in an indolent shrug, but his green eyes glittered with a curious sort of intentness as he surveyed her from under lowered lids. "Would I do that?"

"Of course you would." Aware of a vague tingling in her wrist left in the wake of his touch, Maura restrained the urge to rub it away and gave him a chilling glare, determined not to let him see how he had rattled her. "And I want it to stop. Now."

"And I want to know why you're here and who you're with. Now."

"I don't believe that is any of your business."

Hawksley's features hardened into a grim mask at her haughty statement, and even in the dim light, Maura noticed the abrupt tightening of his sculpted mouth, the ticking of a muscle in the taut line of his jaw.

"Unfortunately for both of us," he informed her in low, measured tones, "you made it my business last night, when you dropped this at my feet."

With a flare of alarm, Maura recognized the crumpled sheet of stationery he withdrew from the breast pocket of his coat, even before he unfolded it and began to read aloud.

The missing letter!

*My dearest Jezebel,*

*Why do you continue to torment me? To cast me inviting glances and coy smiles as you laugh and flirt and throw yourself at other men? I know who and what you are, yet I cannot seem to put you from my mind. I should make you pay for tempting me so. Do you do it deliberately, I wonder? Does it give you pleasure to know you can make me hate you and burn with want of you at the same time? I dream of you at night, of having you beneath me, at my mercy as I bury myself within you and take what you have been promising for so very long. I will not wait forever and I will not share. If I can't have you, no one can.*

Hearing the written words of her mother's possible murderer given voice in such a stark, matter-of-fact fashion was enough to send a ripple of gooseflesh racing over the surface of Maura's skin, despite the warmth of the summer night. Her heart pounding, she watched as Hawksley refolded the letter and returned it to his pocket, then settled back in his seat to regard her with upraised brows.

"An admirer?" he prompted, the mockery lacing the query unmistakable.

Maura bit her lip, at a loss for a reply. How

could she have been so careless? she wondered desperately. Thank goodness no actual names had been mentioned. Apparently the earl believed the missive had been meant for her.

*Stay calm. You have to stay calm.*

The admonition echoing in her head, she took a deep breath to steady her nerves, then lifted her chin at a mutinous angle before addressing him with icy asperity. "That letter is my property, my lord, and I expect you to return it at once."

He shook his head. "I think not. Not until you tell me what I want to know."

"And that is?"

"Just what sort of man have you managed to get yourself entangled with?"

Maura felt hysterical laughter bubbling up beneath the surface of her hard-won control, threatening to erupt at any moment. But she tamped it down with a supreme effort of will and quickly clasped her hands together in the folds of her cloak to disguise their sudden trembling.

"I'm sure I don't know what you mean," she said stiffly.

"And I'm sure you do." Something flashed in the depths of the earl's eyes. Something that—if Maura hadn't known better—she would have sworn was concern. "From the tone of this letter, my lady, he's no gentleman."

He had no idea how right he was. But that a man with the sobriquet of the Devil's Own would be the one to point out such a thing was beyond ironic.

Clinging to the frayed threads of her composure with ever increasing difficulty, Maura cast him a look of contempt. "Really, my lord, you are the last person who should be standing in judgment of anyone else. With your reputation, I would imagine there are more than one or two young ladies out there who have heard the same about you. In fact, after last night I believe I am more than qualified to state that you are definitely no gentleman." She waved imperiously toward the door of the carriage. "Now please leave."

There was a long, drawn-out silence. Then, to her shock, the earl actually threw open the door in one abrupt motion and climbed down from the hackney. But before she could congratulate herself on routing him so easily, he pivoted and held out his hand to her with an air of authority, palm upward.

"Come along," he instructed, for all the world as if he had every right to speak to her as if she were a recalcitrant child. "My patience is at an end, so if you were planning on meeting your paramour this evening, I'm afraid it will have to wait. We have much to discuss, and I refuse to do it here."

Maura gasped, her temper sparking to life once again. How dare he speak to her as if she were some nuisance to be dealt with? She wouldn't stand for it!

"I'm not going anywhere with you," she spat, pressing back into the far corner of the carriage and meeting his gaze with open defiance.

"Oh yes, you are." He paused, then angled his head so that the pale light of the moon spilled over his chiseled visage, giving him a vaguely saturnine appearance that sent a shiver running up her spine. "That is, unless you want me to take this letter to your father and let him know how and where I happened to come by it. I'm sure he would be interested to know that his daughter is in the habit of wandering about London on her own after dark, frequenting the sort of gatherings that well-bred young ladies should know nothing about."

Panic flooded through Maura, setting her pulse to pounding in her ears. As a threat, it was most effective. The last thing she wanted was for her father to become embroiled in all this, especially in his current condition. But if she failed to cooperate, she had little doubt that Hawksley would do exactly what he said he would.

It appeared she would have to give in to his demands. At least for now.

With a frigid glare, she gingerly placed one gloved hand in his, lifted her skirts with the other, and allowed him to help her alight.

The fog-shrouded darkness of the alleyway closed in around them, and their bodies brushed against each other, a fleeting, inadvertent contact. Catching her breath at the heat radiating off his lithe, muscular frame, Maura found herself swaying toward him, but managed to pull back at the last possible minute.

Had he felt it too? That tingling jolt of awareness? If so, he showed no sign of it. When she darted a glance up at him, his face was blank and impenetrable, reflecting none of his inner thoughts or emotions.

Flummoxed by her own unsettling response to his proximity, she waited and watched in sullen silence as he moved to the front of the hackney, where he exchanged a few quick, hushed words with the curious driver and pressed several pound notes into the man's hand before returning to her side.

"My lady, my carriage awaits just around the corner," he informed her without inflection, indicating with a slight bow and an inclination of his head that she was to precede him. "If you would?"

She whirled and started toward the street, fuming every step of the way as he followed close behind her. They hadn't gone very far, however, when a brisk voice rang out in the stillness, halting them both in their tracks.

"Here now! What do you think you're doing? Where are you taking her?"

Maura looked back over her shoulder to see Violet barreling toward them from the direction of the boardinghouse, her expression one of utter ferocity. With the hood of her cloak thrown back so that her red hair shone like a burst of pale flame in the moonlight, she resembled a vengeful Valkyrie advancing on the invading horde.

A lesser man might have quailed at the sight, for the former actress could be a formidable woman at the best of times. But Hawksley seemed unconcerned. Completely undaunted, he waited until she had pulled up short in front of them before greeting her in a coolly polite tone.

"Ah, Miss Lafleur. So you are the one serving as Lady Maura's companion this evening. I wasn't aware that the two of you were acquainted." He arched a questioning brow at Maura. "The nurse to your Juliet, I assume?"

Maura thinned her lips into a tight line, refusing to answer. She had no idea why it had never occurred to her that he and Violet would know each other. After all, they had more than likely moved in some of the same circles over the years, so she supposed it was only to be expected. But now that he had recognized her companion, it gave him just one more thing to hold over her.

Hands propped on her ample hips, Violet was busy eyeing him suspiciously. "Lord Hawksley, I don't know what you are doing here or where you think you are going with my charge, but I insist that you explain yourself at once."

"I apologize, dear lady, but your charge and I have something of the utmost importance that we need to discuss. Alone."

"You'll forgive me for saying so, my lord, but you have a rather strange way of going about requesting an audience. And I would have to be mad to allow such a thing. Why, if the two of you were discovered in each other's company without a proper chaperone, it would thoroughly compromise Lady Maura's reputation."

Even though they weren't touching in any way, Maura felt Hawksley stiffen next to her, his nonchalant manner melting away, to be replaced by a seething tension.

"And bringing her here to such a place at this time of night wouldn't compromise her?" Despite the softness of his voice, it held an underlying thread of steel that resonated just beneath the surface of his words. "Let us be honest, Miss Lafleur. As delightful as you are, I think we would both agree that no one would consider you a proper chaperone. I highly doubt that Lord Albright is even aware that she is in your company. And obviously her reputation means very little to either of you, judging by the situation I discovered her in last night."

Clearly shaken that Hawksley was aware of Maura's clandestine activities of the evening before, Violet's eyes widened in dismay. "Now see here—" she sputtered.

But Maura halted her with a subtle shake of the head. It would do little good to argue with the scoundrel at this point. Nothing had changed. If she refused to accompany him, he would do exactly as he had threatened and go to her father. For that reason alone, it would be best if she humored him for the time being. And it certainly wasn't as if she would be able to accomplish anything further as far as her own agenda was concerned. She couldn't tell from Violet's expression what—if anything—the woman had uncovered in her search of Lord Bedford's room. But that revelation would have to wait until later, when the two of them could speak privately.

"It's all right, Violet," she said aloud, meeting her friend's gaze and doing her best to inject a note of reassurance into her tone. "Truly. Lord Hawksley is correct. We do need to talk."

The older woman looked far from convinced. "Are you certain, dear?"

No, Maura thought with a wry quirk of her lips. No, she wasn't certain at all. But what else could she do? "Of course."

"Excellent." Lord Hawksley gave them both an enigmatic look before glancing back over his shoulder toward the entrance to the alleyway. "Stonehurst?"

At the earl's summons, a large figure suddenly materialized from out of the darkness close to the street and came toward them, and Maura barely stifled a gasp as the light from a lone streetlamp fell over a countenance of stark contrasts. While the bluntly carved planes and angles of the man's face held a harsh sort of masculine beauty, the overall effect was marred by the jagged, silvery line that slashed along his right cheekbone, running from his temple to the corner of his mouth.

"I was beginning to wonder if you even remembered I was here, Hawksley." He spoke in a gravelly rumble, and something about the familiar way he tilted his head struck a spark of recognition within Maura.

It was the same man she had seen the earl speaking to in Lord Lanscombe's garden the evening before.

Hawksley beckoned him closer, then turned back to Maura and Violet. "Lord Stonehurst, allow me to introduce Lady Maura Daventry and Miss Violet Lafleur. Ladies, my good friend, the Viscount Stonehurst."

The viscount swept off his hat and sketched them a stiff bow, revealing a head of shaggy, shoulder-length dark brown hair badly in need of a trim. He was slightly taller and built along bulkier lines than the earl, but Maura guessed he was at least a few years younger than Hawksley. And in spite of his frosty gray eyes, his intimidating mien, and the livid mark that gave one corner of his firm lips an unnatural twist, there was a boyish sort of appeal to his crooked smile. "It's a pleasure, Lady Maura. Miss Lafleur."

"As I've already paid the driver and it appears you are in need of a hackney, perhaps you wouldn't mind seeing Miss Lafleur home," Hawksley suggested to his friend, gesturing to the coach that still sat in the shadows behind the boardinghouse.

Stonehurst seemed momentarily nonplussed at the suggestion, but quickly recovered. "I would be delighted," he said gruffly.

Caught off guard, Violet gave a flustered little huff. But before she could offer up another protest, Maura interrupted her once again.

"Please, Violet. You go with Lord Stonehurst. I shall be fine. Once Lord Hawksley and I have concluded our conversation, he will return me safely home." Some saucy little imp prodded her into tucking her arm through his and fluttering her lashes up at him in deliberate provocation. "You needn't worry. I'm certain that the earl will be a perfect gentleman. Isn't that right, my lord?"

To her surprise, instead of stiffening up again at her coquettishness, a flicker of humor lit his eyes and a wickedly seductive grin stole across his fallen angel face, leaving her feeling decidedly nervous.

"Would I ever be anything else?" he murmured.

And with that, he led her away into the night.

# Chapter 9

*"Needless to say, Philip's father was less than pleased by our elopement. Though we paid a call on him upon our return to town, our visit accomplished little in the way of mending fences. The marquis ranted and raved, and Philip's elder sister, Lady Olivia, did nothing to help the situation with her disapproving silence."*

From the diary of Elise Marchand,
August 27, 1794

Now that he had the Lady Maura exactly where he wanted her—ensconced within the confines of his own coach and on the way back to Belgrave Square—Gabriel allowed himself a brief moment to regroup and to mull over how best to proceed with the mulish female seated across from him.

From under lowered brows, he studied her as

she stared out the window, the hood of her cloak thrown back from her face to reveal a flawless profile outlined by the soft glow of the carriage lamp. She hadn't spoken a word since they had parted from Stonehurst and Miss Lafleur, and it was obvious by the tense set of her shoulders and the obstinate tilt of her chin that she was angry with him.

He supposed he couldn't blame her. He had treated her more than a trifle high-handedly, but what else could he have done? He had been desperate to make her listen to him. Couldn't the bloody-minded female see that he was only concerned for her welfare? If she continued to behave in this reckless fashion, she ran the risk of jeopardizing all that her family had worked so hard to regain. And as he was the poor sapskull who seemed destined to keep rescuing her from the consequences of her misadventures, he thought the least he deserved was a few answers.

But judging from the way she deliberately avoided his eyes, getting her to cooperate in giving him those answers would be far easier said than done.

Shifting in his seat, he racked his brain for a way to begin the conversation diplomatically, finally deciding that it would be best to just plunge right in. Maura already had her back up, and it was highly doubtful that she would welcome anything he had to say, no matter how he phrased it.

"If memory serves," he drew out in a deceptively

casual tone, "Violet Lafleur was once an acquaintance of your mother's. A fellow stage actress, wasn't she?"

He left the question hanging in the air, but it soon became apparent that Maura had no intention of either confirming or denying his observation. In fact, she showed no sign at all of having even heard him. Her unblinking gaze was focused on the landscape rolling by outside the window, and her features remained locked in a taut, emotionless mask.

At her lack of response, Gabriel stifled an oath. *You will not lose your temper with her*, he told himself sternly. *Remember, she has no reason to trust you.*

Struggling to hold on to his patience, he leaned in toward her, determined to draw her out no matter what it took. "Is that what this is all about? Have you struck up a friendship with Miss Lafleur that your father wouldn't approve of?"

Still no reply. But as he examined her, taking in every nuance of her expression, he could have sworn he saw her flinch at the mention of the marquis.

"She is the one who has been leading you astray, isn't she?" he pressed, mentally willing her to look at him. Perhaps if he could see into her eyes, he would be able to tell if he was coming close to the truth. "And I would wager that she was the one behind your presence at Lord Lanscombe's masquerade as well."

He paused, one hand going to the pocket of his coat, where the letter he had found was tucked away. Even now, the missive's explicit, lust-filled ramblings floated before his eyes, taunting him. For reasons he didn't want to analyze too closely, the thought of some nameless, faceless man fantasizing about this woman, believing he had the right to declare his ownership in such ominous and unequivocal terms, filled him with the overwhelming and violent urge to seek out the scoundrel and bash his face in.

"Is she the one who introduced you to your current admirer?" he prodded her, his increasing aggression causing him to speak more sharply than he intended. "If so, I must say that her idea of an appropriate suitor leaves much to be desired."

It was his last derisive comment that finally got Maura's attention. Her head whipped in his direction and her eyes flashed with annoyance, glittering like twin sapphires in her delicate face.

"You haven't the slightest notion what you are talking about," she told him coldly.

"Then please do explain it to me."

"I owe you no explanations. But I will say that Violet has nothing to do with any of this. She's helping me. That's all."

"Helping you to do what?" Crossing his arms over his chest, Gabriel met her frosty glare with one of his own. "Court disaster?"

Maura gave a nonchalant shrug. "As I said

last night, I can't imagine why you would care."

That was a very good question. If he had any sense at all, he'd dump her in her father's lap and wash his hands of all of it. He certainly didn't need the added complications she brought into his life. But somehow she had worked her way past his defenses, and dismissing her had become an impossibility.

Bloody hell, but he was every bit as obsessed with her as the bounder who had written the letter!

And as his father had been with her mother.

Forgetting his resolve to hold on to his temper, he tore off his hat and tossed it on the seat next to him, then raked one hand back through his hair in frustration before leveling Maura with a fierce scowl. "Perhaps I simply can't stand to see you behaving just like *her*," he bit out from between clenched teeth.

There was no need for him to elaborate. He could tell by the way she drew herself up in righteous indignation that she knew exactly whom he meant.

"You think you have the right to pass judgment on my behavior?" she hissed. "You, of all people?"

"How can I not? Just look at you. Slipping out of your house in the middle of the night in the company of a woman we both know your father would forbid you to associate with, in order to meet a

man who obviously thinks you little better than a
harlot." He regarded her contemptuously. "This
from someone who insisted that she wanted to be
nothing like her mother. I suppose that makes me a
fool, because I actually believed you."

She shook her head. "You're wrong. It's not
what you think."

But Gabriel was beyond hearing, for he was being driven by a dark and roiling emotion that he
couldn't even begin to put a name to.

"I wonder what your father and sisters would
think of you if they read this letter," he mused
aloud, his voice dangerously soft. "Or your dear
friend, the dowager duchess. Or for that matter,
what about the Marquis of Waldron?"

Freezing like a startled doe at his mention of the
marquis, Maura eyed him with suspicion. "What
do you know about Lord Waldron?"

The laugh that escaped him in response to her
query was harsh and humorless. What did he
know about it? He would have to be deaf, dumb,
and blind not to know that Waldron had shown an
interest in Maura this Season. And as much as the
thought of her being courted by a man old enough
to be her father had disturbed him, the thought of
her in the arms of her admirer filled him with a
towering rage that left him far more shaken than
he cared to admit.

"You'd be surprised by what I know," he said
bitterly. "Snaring him would be quite the coup for

you, wouldn't it? He would give you precisely the sort of marriage you once told me you wanted. Safe and passionless. But then perhaps you plan to keep seeing your lover behind your husband's back. Arrange illicit assignations, revel in the thrill of an adulterous affair."

Maura's face leached of color at his obvious disdain, but she straightened her shoulders nonetheless and stuck her nose in the air with icy hauteur. "Of course. But why stop at just one lover? I'm certain if I only apply myself, I could entice at least half the men in London to my bed."

Her taunt pierced him like a razor-edged sword, ripping and tearing at something raw and primitively possessive deep inside him that he hadn't even known was there. A red mist of jealous fury clouding his vision, he lashed out without forethought. "Indeed. And perhaps one of those men will have a wife and child you can torment by flaunting your infidelity in public. That would truly make you your mother's daughter, wouldn't it?"

He had gone too far. He knew it the moment the words escaped him, but it was too late to do anything except curse himself for his callousness. Looking utterly devastated, Maura emitted a strangled cry and recoiled from him as if she had been struck.

A wave of remorse washed over Gabriel, and he reached out to her, his immediate instinct to find some way to alleviate the pain he had caused. But before he could even touch her, she threw herself forward, pummeling away with both fists.

"You loathsome cur!" she choked, striking out almost blindly, her blows bouncing ineffectually off his chest. "How dare you say such things? You know nothing about me or my mother! She wasn't . . . You don't know . . . There's so much none of us knew. . . ."

It all sounded like incoherent babbling to him, so he didn't even attempt to try to make sense of any of it. Instead he captured her by the wrists and tugged her onto his lap, into the snug circle of his arms, bringing a halt to her frenzied attack. Though he was well aware that he was the last one she would want to accept solace from, and that he deserved whatever abuse she might care to dole out, in her nearly hysterical condition he was far more afraid that she was going to do an injury to herself.

And that was when the tears started, spilling over and trickling down her cheeks as sobs shook her small frame. Each heaving breath was like a hammer blow to Gabriel's heart.

"Shhh," he soothed in a low-voiced murmur, holding her close, his nose buried in the fragrant strands of her hair. "I'm sorry, sweetheart. I didn't mean it. I've been a complete bastard, and I don't blame you if you hate me. Hush."

For what seemed like a small eternity, he continued to whisper comfortingly in her ear. And as the minutes ticked by and she slowly began to relax, her sobs tapering off to an occasional hiccup, he became more and more cognizant of the lushly curved body nestled against him, even through the layers of material that separated them.

Christ, now was not the time to be letting his thoughts stray in that direction. He was a cad for even noticing. But she felt so good, so very right in his arms, and his body began to react in a typical male fashion to the stimuli. With each sway of the carriage, her firm, rounded bottom shifted in his lap, brushing up against his manhood and bringing it to rigid, aching life in a way he couldn't ignore, no matter how hard he tried.

Maura's swiftly indrawn breath told him the exact instant when she became aware of the signs of his growing arousal. Lifting her head from his chest, she peered up at him, her gaze rife with wariness. Even with her face flushed and tearstained and her midnight hair coming loose from its topknot to tumble about her shoulders, she was beautiful.

God, he had to touch her . . .

Unable to fight the urge, he gave an impatient growl and tugged off one of his gloves with his teeth, then lifted his hand to cup her cheek. Her skin was like satin under the rough pads of his fingertips.

"I am so sorry," he said huskily. "Can you forgive me?"

She contemplated him uncertainly for a long, silent moment. Then her lashes fluttered closed and she gave a shaky nod.

"Thank you, sweetheart. It's more than I deserve, I know."

He used his thumb to brush away a tendril of hair that clung to the line of her jaw, and she unexpectedly turned into his caress, smoothing her cheek against his palm in a way that had his mouth going dry with longing. Tenderly he tilted her chin and lowered his head until his lips were mere inches away from hers. "You are so very lovely."

Her eyes snapped open at his hoarse rasp, their blue depths swimming with a heartbreaking vulnerability that he could see even in the dimness. "Please don't."

"Please don't what? Don't want you? It's too late for that. I can't seem to help myself."

Gradually, making sure he gave her plenty of time to rebuff him should she choose to do so, Gabriel closed the distance between them and brushed her lips with his. Once, twice. He had no wish to frighten her, so he kept the initial contact light, tentative, before drawing back to gauge her reaction.

For what seemed like forever, they stared at each other. Then Maura blinked and spoke in a voice barely above a whisper. "My lord?"

"Yes, sweetheart?"

"Please . . . Could you do that again?"

*God yes!* With a ragged groan, Gabriel obliged. It was a long, slow tasting, a gentle melding that sent his blood racing in a scalding rush through his veins. Over and over, he took her lips with his own, thoroughly exploring their silken surfaces and savoring their sweetness before plunging his tongue into the warm cavern of her mouth. She hesitantly met his tongue with hers, and her honeyed flavor was so intoxicating that it took every bit of willpower he possessed to finally pull back long enough to draw a shuddering breath.

This shouldn't be happening, he realized dimly, taking in her dazed and slumberous expression. If he kept this up, things would soon be spiraling out of control. He knew that. But when she wound her arms around his neck in a sinuous motion and pulled him back down to her for another kiss, his head spun and his wits went begging. The powerful tide of his desire swept all before it, and he was caught in the undertow.

The woman was about to drive him mad.

Suddenly he forgot all the reasons he had for keeping her at a distance. If the Lady Maura was so determined to give herself to a man, why shouldn't it—why couldn't it—be he?

Raining kisses along the pale column of her throat, he reached up, loosened the ties on her cloak, and let it fall carelessly to the carriage floor before starting on the fastenings at the back of her modest day dress of dark blue sarcenet. Even with fingers that were less than dexterous, he made short work of the task, tugging the bodice of the gown over her shoulders and down her arms until it bunched at her elbows, revealing her sheer chemise. The slopes of her breasts mounded above the beribboned, scooped neckline in lush temptation.

He cupped one ripe globe, skimming his thumb over the distended tip of her nipple when it stiffened against the fabric, and he couldn't help but feel a fierce sense of satisfaction at the way she pressed herself eagerly into his hand, mutely importuning him to continue. Only too delighted to do so, he leaned forward and nuzzled the upper swell of one creamy curve, then nudged the strap of her chemise aside to expose the rosy crest of her breast to the loving attentions of his mouth.

A throaty moan escaped her at the first suckling tug of his lips, and her fingers twined in the strands of hair at the back of his head, her grip almost painful. But Gabriel was oblivious. Lost in the exquisite taste and scent of her, he savored the weight of her breast in his palm, plumping and molding it for his delectation as he drew almost voraciously at the taut, pebbled tip. Lashing it over and over with his tongue, nibbling delicately with his teeth, he reveled in her quavering sighs.

Taking the arch of her back, the involuntary thrust of her hips, as an invitation, his hand left her breast and traveled to her waist, then on to the hem of her skirts, sliding the material upward along her well-shaped calf until he could delve underneath. His fingers teased the soft skin of her inner thigh, and from there it took only a bit of subtle maneuvering to find the slit in her underdrawers that led to the fleecy nest of curls at the apex of her thighs.

Hot, moist velvet. It was the first thought that came into his mind as his index finger parted her gently and entered the liquid core of her. At the intimate touch, she gave a start and clutched at his wrist, but he shushed her with another languid, soul-stirring kiss.

"It's all right," he coaxed, leaving his finger nestled just inside the slick entrance to her feminine channel. He would never force her, but he had caused her so much pain, and all he wanted to do was make it better. He wanted to give her nothing but pleasure. "You're so beautiful here, sweetheart. So warm and wet and welcoming. I just want to touch you. Will you let me?"

Maura sank her teeth into her lower lip, and for a fleeting instant he was positive she was going to call a halt, regardless of his reassurances. But after a brief hesitation, she released him and placed her dainty hand against his chest in a gesture of such trust that his heart lurched.

He began to stroke her again, teasing, shallow strokes that ventured just a little farther into her clinging dampness each time. Before long, her breath was coming in quick pants, and her hips began to rock against his hand, the motion increasing with each penetration of his fingers, each brush of his thumb over the swollen, sensitive bud hidden within the folds of her cleft. Maintaining the rhythm, he delved even deeper—and came into contact with a telltale barrier that confirmed what he had only just begun to suspect.

The discovery filled him with a sense of elation that he couldn't explain. The Lady Maura was still a virgin. Whatever the identity of her admirer, he had yet to claim her physically.

Exultant, Gabriel studied her face with an intent gaze. He wanted to watch her as he took her over the edge for the first time. The look in her eyes was one of slowly dawning wonder. She was so very close . . .

*Come for me, sweetheart,* he urged mentally, and with a final expert flick of his thumb over her clitoris, he sent her up and over the crest. A low, keening cry escaped her, and her hands fisted in his coat as she quaked and shuddered in his arms in the throes of a powerful climax, her head thrown back and her expression one of supreme ecstasy.

When the convulsive aftershocks of her shattering orgasm had finally subsided and she lay draped across his lap, flushed and spent, Gabriel pressed one last kiss to her lips and rested his cheek against her temple, his mouth curving in an indulgent smile. Never mind the discomfort of his own painful erection throbbing against her bottom. Never had he found such joy in giving a woman pleasure without taking anything for himself.

"Well, that was a bit of a revelation," he murmured, unable to disguise his honest delight at her uninhibited response.

But his words didn't elicit the reaction he had hoped for. Maura quite abruptly stiffened against him, then began to struggle, her palms shoving at his chest in an attempt to make him loosen his hold.

"Let me go," she hissed. "Let me go right now!"

Caught off guard, he complied and watched in consternation as she scrambled away from him, righting her clothing as she went.

Apparently what had happened here hadn't made quite the same impression on her as it had on him.

Plopping down on the opposite seat, she hugged herself in a defensive gesture, holding the sagging bodice of her gown in place as she leveled him with a glare every bit as chilling as any she had given him in the past. It was so unexpected after her sweet surrender that Gabriel wasn't certain how to even begin to proceed.

"Sweetheart—" he began, but she cut him off with a sharp exclamation.

"Don't. Don't you dare call me that. Your other conquests might have been susceptible to your machinations, but it will not work with me. I know what this was all about and I think you are beneath contempt."

A muscle flexed in Gabriel's jaw, and he narrowed his eyes at her in renewed irritation. What the bloody hell was she babbling about now? "Well, since it appears that you have managed to uncover my nefarious plot, perhaps you would be kind enough to enlighten me as to the finer points. Just to refresh my memory, you understand, as I can't seem to recall devising such a scheme. Nefarious or otherwise."

"Please don't insult my intelligence by pretending you weren't taking advantage of the situation." In a jerky motion, she scooped her cloak up off the floor of the carriage and hastily wrapped it around her, as if needing the added protection of its concealing folds. "Is this how you usually get what you want from females, my lord? Affect concern for their welfare and then take the opportunity to seduce them into submission?"

Her accusation stung. "You think I was trying to manipulate you?"

"Weren't you? Given who you are, it seems a natural assumption. I'm not precisely the sort of woman you usually show an interest in, am I?"

He couldn't deny that. When it came to sexual relations, his preferences had always run to mature and experienced females. Widows, courtesans, and unhappily married women who were content to part ways without clinging once he grew bored. But in the past year, those preferences seemed to have undergone a marked transformation, and it was all due to the infuriating chit seated across from him.

Goaded beyond all endurance, he waved an impatient hand, indicating the clearly visible bulge that tented the material of his breeches. "Do you really believe that my body would react in such a fashion if what just happened between us had merely been an attempt to pry answers from you?"

A bright tide of pink flooded her cheeks, and she hastily averted her eyes. "I'm sure I wouldn't know."

"Damn it, Maura, listen to me—"

"No! I'm through listening to you. And I'm through allowing you to bully and interrogate me. What I do is none of your concern, and I can't believe that I let myself forget even for an instant just what sort of man you are. That I let you . . . let you . . ."

She made a strangled sound, and before he could stop her, she rose from her seat. It wasn't until she flung open the carriage door and practically threw herself from the conveyance that he realized they had finally arrived on Belgrave Square and were pulled up to the curb a short distance from the Albright town house.

Enfolded within the dark material of her cloak, she was little more than a silhouette, her face a ghostly oval in the shadows as she glared up at him. "Stay away from me from now on, my lord," she warned him, her voice trembling with ire. "Don't ever come near me again."

She gave him no chance to speak, simply pivoted

on her heel and stormed off in the direction of the mews that ran behind the row of houses.

Leaving him staring after her, aching with unfulfilled desire, and no closer to discovering what secrets she hid than he had been before.

Yanking the carriage door closed with a vicious curse, he retrieved his glove from the seat and tugged it on, then curled his fingers into an impotent fist. He had never felt more helpless in his life. Maura seemed set on placing herself in harm's way, and it was obvious that her father was incapable of reining her in.

But perhaps there was someone who *was* capable of it . . .

Straightening his shoulders with grim purpose, Gabriel called up to his driver. "To Park Lane, please. Maitland House."

# Chapter 10

*"We have taken up residence at Philip's cottage in Dorset, part of his inheritance left to him by his mother. After what transpired with the marquis, we could no longer bear to remain in London. It is so quiet here, so peaceful. Philip can pursue his scholarly ambitions to his heart's content, and I am happy to merely love and be loved."*

From the diary of Elise Marchand,
September 19, 1794

**"M**aura? Maura, are you paying attention?" The incisive voice rang out in the confines of the Albright carriage, possessing the impact of a whip crack and startling Maura out of her brown study with a jolt. Tearing her unseeing gaze away from the pastoral panorama rolling by outside the window, she glanced over to find her aunt observing her with eyes narrowed in clear disapproval.

Folding her hands in her lap, she did her best to affect an air of contrition. "I'm sorry, Aunt Olivia. I'm afraid I was woolgathering."

Olivia elevated her nose with a haughty sniff. "Yes, that was rather obvious. But I suggest, young lady, that you attend to what I have to say. I'm sure I needn't tell you how important this weekend is. You'll not only have a chance to socialize with some of the more influential members of society, but it will offer you the opportunity to make an impression on the Marquis of Waldron. If you are wise, that is an opportunity you will not squander."

"Yes, Aunt Olivia."

"Very good." Appearing pleased with Maura's seeming meekness, her aunt gave a satisfied nod. "Now, as I was saying, do make sure you thank the duchess personally for including us on the guest list for this weekend, but don't be overly effusive. You want to present a picture of genteel refinement. And as for dinner this evening . . ."

Olivia continued to drone on, but Maura once again found her attention drifting away, her aunt's list of instructions fading until it became little more than an annoying buzz in the background. She had been listening to the same maddening blather ever since they had departed London early that morning, and she was convinced that if she was forced to endure it for much longer, she was going to scream.

She sent an envious glance in the direction of her lady's maid, Phoebe, who had nodded off in the corner of the carriage, her head slumped forward, her mobcap perched precariously on her carroty curls. With each exhalation, the girl's breath whistled through her nostrils in a snuffling snore.

What Maura wouldn't give to be able to escape into such oblivion.

It was the weekend of the Duchess of Maitland's house party, and they were on the road to Hampshire and the country estate of the duke and duchess, Rosemont Hall. Aside from a brief stop at a posting inn earlier in the afternoon, where they had partaken of a light repast, they had been trapped within the close environs of the coach for well over ten hours.

And Maura's tolerance had just about reached its breaking point.

Taking a calming breath, she bowed her head and peered down at the dusty toes of her boots, just peeping out from underneath the hem of her high-necked, French gray traveling dress. Though she knew just what her presence at this gathering could mean to her family's future, a part of her dreaded their arrival. The thought of talking and laughing and pretending all was well with her world when so much was wrong made her feel physically ill.

Not to mention the fact that she hadn't wanted to leave her father. Though the marquis had shown remarkable improvement in the last several days, he was still frail and weak and needed the assistance of his nurse to rise from his bed or to perform any of his daily ablutions. But when Maura had expressed her reluctance to leave his side the evening before, her aunt had nearly had the apoplexy.

"Tell her, Philip," Lady Olivia had railed, her eyes flashing with diamond-hard brilliance as she had paced back and forth at the foot of her brother's bed. "Tell your daughter how foolish she would be to refuse the duchess's invitation when she is already expecting us. It simply isn't done." Coming to a halt with hands on her hips, she had glared resentfully at her niece. "We have worked so hard to be accepted again, to be welcomed and respected by society. Now that we are so close, I won't stand by and watch you ruin it!"

She had slammed from the room, and Maura had turned to find her father watching her with gentle understanding.

"It's all right, darling," he had assured her, taking her hand in his. Despite the alarming gauntness of his once athletic frame, his hand was as strong as it had ever been, and his fingers had enfolded hers with a warmth that had given her comfort. "You should go. The Duchess of Maitland doesn't plan such affairs often, and procuring an invitation to one is well nigh impossible. I shall be fine. I have my nurse and Aimee to do for me. And according to the letter we received from Jillian this morning, she and Connor are on their way home and should be arriving any day."

"But, Papa—"

"No, Maura, your aunt is right. Whether you believe it or not, she only wants what is best for this family. And in any case, I'm sure Theodosia went to some trouble to convince her stepdaughter-in-law to add you both to the guest list."

He had paused, his eyes sorrowful, as if he were reflecting on something that brought him a great deal of regret. And when he spoke again, his voice had been noticeably softer. "I know that Olivia can be difficult to get along with and that it has been hard for you girls to accept her in our lives. But she does have a reason for being the way she is. There was a man once. Your mother and I were living in Dorset then, and Olivia has never been forthcoming with me about it, so I don't know many of the details. However, I do know that she loved him very much and it ended badly. In part, I think, because of the scandal generated by my relationship with your mother. Livvy was heartbroken."

Looking back on the conversation, Maura remembered the wave of sadness that had washed over her at her father's tale. Discovering that Olivia's anger and bitterness had stemmed from a lost love had struck a chord of sympathy within her, and she had resolved to try to be more patient with her aunt's abrasive manner. But that resolve had lasted barely beyond the first quarter hour of the journey.

So here she was, on her way to a house party she had no desire to attend, in the company of a woman who was about to drive her mad with her incessant carping and criticism. In fact, the only good thing about the coming weekend was that the Marquis of Cunnington would be present at Rosemont Hall as well. She hoped she would be able to use her time at the estate to her advantage and find a way to either ascertain his guilt in her mother's death or cross him off her list.

After all, the man was now Maura's last hope. Her lone suspect. It had been a week since the trip to Lord Bedford's boardinghouse, and her brief meeting with Violet at her costume shop the following day had revealed that the woman had found several pieces of correspondence in the baron's flat. The subsequent handwriting comparison had effectively eliminated him as the culprit.

To Maura's dismay, Violet had also taken the opportunity to question her about what had transpired with Lord Hawksley. But thankfully her friend hadn't pressed her for more than a few vague details. Maura had no intention of ever telling anyone what had taken place in the privacy of the earl's carriage. It was bad enough that the memory had been emblazoned upon her own mind.

Every time she recalled the way the man had kissed her, the way he had touched her in places she had never even thought to touch herself, she felt herself grow warm all over with shame. Draped over his lap like some carnal offering, she had practically begged him to take her. How could she have behaved like such a wanton? He had stirred sensations in her she had never before experienced, stroked her into a state of mindless submission. She had been weak, and now she was forced to face the fact that the very emotion she had once feared was something he was capable of arousing within her all too easily.

Passion.

But it was something that wouldn't happen again. If nothing else, last night had proved to Maura how right she was not to confide in him. She needed to stay as far away from him as possible, and she was going to do just that.

So she and Violet had parted ways, each set on her own course of action. The former actress had promised to continue her own search for answers by visiting some of her old contacts in the theater world in the hopes that someone might recall Elise Marchand and the men who had been close to her during her time on the stage. There was only a very small chance that she would be able to find out anything, but it was all they had at this point, other than the letters and Cunnington. All Maura could do was hold out hope.

And be thankful that for the next three days at least, she would be far away from the Earl of Hawksley.

"Ah, here we are."

Her aunt's announcement brought her back to the present once again, and she glanced up just in time to see a sprawling, majestic-looking home come into view around a bend in the road.

Rosemont Hall.

The coach turned onto a long, winding, tree-lined drive that ended in a circular carriageway, and Lady Olivia poked Phoebe into wakefulness just as they rolled to a halt in front of the marble steps that led up to the massive front doors of the house. Several footmen, resplendent in their elegant and brightly colored livery, came hurrying to help them alight and to aid the driver in unloading their belongings.

As Maura stepped down onto the cobblestones, she couldn't help but stare in awe at the gray stone structure that loomed over her. She had seen large and impressive homes before, but none to equal the size and grandeur of this one, with its jutting wings and soaring towers. The late afternoon sun glinted off the mullioned windows, casting a hazy glow over the surrounding gardens and vast, sloping lawns.

Her aunt brought an end to her gawking by prodding her toward the foot of the steps, where Felicia Rosemont, Duchess of Maitland, awaited them.

As they approached her, the woman offered a tight-lipped smile of greeting that didn't quite reach her icy blue eyes. "Lady Olivia, Lady Maura. Welcome to Rosemont Hall."

Thin and pinch-featured, with graying hair and a rather dour disposition, the duchess had always struck Maura as a very harsh and unyielding sort of person. As a leading pillar of society, she used her lofty position to pass judgment on those who failed to live up to her exacting standards, and she had made it clear on more than one occasion in the past that the Daventry family fell far short of the mark when it came to those standards.

Another nudge from her aunt prompted Maura to sink into a low curtsy. "Thank you for inviting us, Your Grace."

The duchess inclined her head in acknowledgment. "Of course. I'm so happy you could attend."

Despite the veneer of politeness, an underlying note of patronizing insincerity belied her words, and the hostile aura that vibrated in the air was so tangible that Maura bit her lip to keep from wincing. It was clear that she and her aunt weren't wanted here. Obviously the threats and ultimatums that Theodosia must have been forced to resort to in order to secure their invitations had caused more than a fair amount of resentment.

It seemed this weekend was going to turn out to be every bit as strained and difficult to get through as she had feared.

Her stomach a tangle of nerves, Maura left Phoebe directing the footmen and followed the duchess and her aunt up the steps and into the spacious, high-ceilinged foyer of the house. The entry hall was decorated with dark, heavily ornamented furnishings and well lit by a massive crystal chandelier. A set of carved double doors on the far side of the room had been thrown back to reveal a central gallery, where Oriental rugs covered the flagstone floor and the walls were lined with family portraits and expertly woven tapestries. Off to the right, through another archway, a set of wide, carpeted stairs spiraled upward, ascending to the upper reaches of the house.

Completely oblivious to the still lurking tension, Lady Olivia was chatting away, more animated than Maura could ever remember seeing her.

"We have been looking forward to this weekend, Your Grace," she was saying as she removed her bonnet and gloves and handed them to the butler who hovered nearby. "But I couldn't help noticing that no one is about. Are we the first to arrive?"

"Not at all." The duchess glanced back at them over her shoulder. "Several of the guests have been here since this morning and are resting in their rooms or preparing for dinner. And the others should be arriving any moment." Something indiscernible flashed in the depths of those hard eyes as her assessing gaze settled on Maura, and her smile turned razor-sharp. "We've had a few last-minute additions to the guest list that should make things most . . . interesting."

"How intriguing!" Lady Olivia exclaimed.

A break came in the conversation as some footmen scurried by on their way to the stairs, bearing the few trunks and valises they had unloaded from the Albright carriage. Then the duchess gestured to a stout woman who had been waiting unobtrusively in the corner. "This is the housekeeper, Mrs. Nash. She will show you to your room and make sure your lady's maid is settled in the servants' quarters. Should you need anything at all, do not hesitate to let her know."

Feeling more than a trifle nervous, Maura swallowed and placed a hand against her unsettled stomach. How she would have loved to see a friendly face right about now. She had hoped that Theodosia would be here to greet her upon her arrival, but the elderly lady was nowhere in sight.

She cleared her throat and stepped forward. "Pardon me, Your Grace, but has the dowager duchess arrived yet?"

The duchess surveyed her with a coolness that almost made her regret asking the question. "As a matter of fact, she has. But I'm afraid the journey from London was very tiring for her, and she is taking a nap in her chamber. She will be down shortly, I expect." With a careless wave of her hand, she dismissed the subject and moved toward the doors on the far side of the room. "Now I'm afraid you will have to excuse me, as I need to see to the preparations for dinner. Please feel free to do a bit of exploring until the rest of the guests arrive. But do be careful. The property is quite extensive, and we wouldn't want you to get . . . lost."

With one last curl of her lips, she turned and vanished through the doors into the gallery, her skirts rustling.

Maura shook her head, staring after the woman with a grimace. There could be little doubt that this weekend was going to be a nightmare, she thought with chagrin, whirling about to follow her aunt and Mrs. Nash up the winding stairs.

The housekeeper led them along several lengthy and narrow corridors to an elegantly appointed suite of rooms in the west wing, then left them with the announcement that dinner would be served promptly at seven. Their trunks awaited them, and they immediately started to work on getting settled in. After a while, however, Maura grew tired of Olivia's barked orders and Phoebe's fluttering and decided that she could do with a breath of fresh air as well as some distance from her aunt. So after changing from her traveling clothes, she quit the room.

It took a bit of navigating and directions from a few passing servants, but she eventually found her way back to the first-floor gallery and wandered out through a set of French doors to a stone terrace that overlooked the walled-in garden. There she sank down on a nearby bench, closing her eyes and letting the sun beat down on her uptilted face as she contemplated the weekend ahead of her.

Somehow, over the course of the next three days, she would not only have to figure out a way to get hold of a sample of Lord Cunnington's handwriting, but she would also have to find time to make an impression on the Marquis of Waldron, as well as associate with people who had once treated her and the other members of her family little better than the dirt beneath their feet.

She couldn't think of a way that things could possibly be any worse.

But for now, she would try to forget all that. It was so restful, so peaceful out here with the soft chirping of birds and the drone of insects drifting to her from the garden. She would have been content to stay in this spot forever and simply avoid the unpleasantness that was sure to come.

It was not to be, however. A sudden shift in the way the warm breeze caressed her cheek, a blotting out of the light behind her eyelids, told her that someone had joined her on the terrace and was about to interrupt her blessed solitude.

Reluctantly she lifted her lashes to find the tall figure of a man standing before her. At first, with the glare of the sun behind him, casting him in silhouette, she couldn't make out his features. But as he tilted his head and leaned toward her, his identity was revealed in stark relief.

No! It wasn't possible!

"Hello, sweetheart," he softly drawled, and the tingle that ran up her spine in response to that familiar baritone told her with undeniable certainty that it *was* possible.

It was the Earl of Hawksley.

# Chapter 11

*"Philip and I welcomed our first child yesterday. A daughter named Jillian. Though I had a bit of a difficult time of it, it was worth every moment of pain, and we both already adore her. Of course, we have heard nothing from Philip's father or sister, not even an acknowledgment of the birth . . ."*

From the diary of Elise Marchand,
April 7, 1795

Watching as Maura's blue eyes widened in horrified recognition, Gabriel braced himself for the inevitable explosion.

He didn't have long to wait.

"You!" The word escaped her on a shrill note, and she flung herself from the bench she'd been sitting on, pressing herself back against the stone balustrade that ran the length of the terrace as if attempting to get as far away from him as possible. "This can't be happening."

"Oh, I assure you, it can." He curved his lips into a sardonic smile, and some imp of Satan prodded him into closing the distance she had put between them with a few slow, measured steps. Standing in front of her once again, he bent his head until his lips were mere inches away from hers. "Shall I kiss you and prove it?"

Her nostrils flared, like a doe scenting danger, and one of her hands flew to his chest to hold him at bay.

"Don't you dare," she lashed out at him in an enraged whisper, her gaze darting over his shoulder as if checking to see if anyone had followed him from the house. "Don't you dare touch me!"

"Now, Maura, I'm desolate. After the other night, I thought we had become so close. And now you tell me you don't want my kiss?"

At the obvious mockery that laced his voice, she sucked in an audible breath and drew herself up, meeting his stare with righteous defiance.

"I am not a plaything for your amusement, my lord, and this situation is far from humorous. What happened between us the other night never should have happened, and I cannot believe that even you would be dastardly enough to remind me of something I am so very ashamed of."

Despite the effort she made to present a bold,

stalwart façade, her chin quivered and her words ended in a trembling rush, making it obvious that she was fighting desperately to hold on to her composure.

And quite suddenly he felt like a cad. He didn't know what compelled him to antagonize her in such a fashion. How could he ever expect to win her confidence if they were constantly at daggers drawn?

She appeared so young and fragile in her white muslin frock. The fabric was dotted with tiny lilac flowers, and a matching sash fastened in a bow just beneath her full breasts, emphasizing her tiny waist. With her blue-black hair braided and wound in a coronet about her head, only a few wisps left free to curl becomingly at her temples, she looked lovely.

Almost as lovely as she had looked climaxing in his arms. The mere memory of her face in that instant had been enough to keep him awake, tossing and turning in his lonely bed every night for the past week.

Though he would never admit it aloud, it had been difficult staying away from her. But the dowager duchess had insisted it was for the best. The elderly lady had warned him in no uncertain terms that if Maura had any inkling at all that he planned on attending the house party this weekend, she would never show up.

So he had bided his time and kept an eye on her from afar. It had been a definite test of his willpower, but now that the waiting was over, he couldn't allow himself to weaken where she was concerned. He was finally going to have all his questions answered, no matter what he had to do.

"I don't understand." Maura was still talking as she stared up at him with an apprehensive expression, apparently unaware that his mind had wandered. "What are you doing here?"

Trying his best to appear nonchalant, he gave a careless shrug and propped a lean hip against the low balustrade next to her in an indolent pose. "I was invited."

She shook her head vehemently. "No. You're lying. The Duchess of Maitland would never invite you to a gathering such as this. Not when she knew my aunt and I would be present. She is too conscious of stirring up gossip, and that is exactly what you and I in attendance at the same social function would accomplish."

"Perhaps." He hesitated, debating the best way to give her the news, then decided he might as well just come right out and say it. Phrasing things delicately wouldn't soften the blow in the end. "However, it wasn't the Duchess of Maitland who invited me. It was the dowager duchess."

Maura went deathly white, and there was a long, drawn-out silence.

When she spoke again, there could be no ignoring the pain that vibrated in her reed-thin voice. "I don't believe you."

Once again, Gabriel felt a sharp pang of compassion. No doubt she felt hurt and betrayed. But he was the last person Maura would believe if he tried to tell her that the dowager only had her best interests at heart. "It's true. Once I told her about your recent nocturnal activities, she was most anxious for me to attend."

"But why? Why would she do that to me?"

Even with his defenses in place, her wounded cry crept under his guard and made him want to wrap her in his arms and hold her. But he settled for reaching out and tenderly brushing a stray curl back from her cheek. "Maybe she thought it was about time you were honest with me about a few things. And maybe she's worried about you. Just like I am."

"Don't say that!" Jerking her head back to avoid his touch, she pushed away from the railing and began to pace before him, her hands clenched into angry fists at her sides. "Don't pretend that you care about me. Why you are so determined to get involved in my life, I have no idea. But I never dreamed that you would be devious enough to approach Theodosia and turn her against me as well."

"I haven't turned her against you. If you would just listen—"

She came to an abrupt halt, cutting him off with a sharp gesture as she leveled him with a fierce glare. "I have no desire to listen to a word you have to say, so you might as well save yourself the trouble. If you hadn't proved to me the other night just how loathsome you are, this would have certainly confirmed my low opinion of you. And whatever you think you have won by getting yourself invited here this weekend, I promise you that I will make you sorry you ever thought to interfere."

She whirled and started for the terrace doors, but Gabriel strode after her, catching her by the arm before she could reach them.

"Maura, please—"

Their bodies inadvertently brushed together, and the same sparks that always seemed to leap to life whenever they touched flamed up, higher than ever. But after a second, she stiffened and looked up at him with eyes rife with such a confusing mixture of anger, pain, and sadness that he bled for her.

"Let me go, Hawksley," she hissed. "Now."

"But all I want—"

"Let. Me. Go."

The words emerged from between gritted teeth, and it was apparent that she was at the end of her rope. In spite of everything, a large part of Gabriel wanted nothing more than to comfort her. But it was hardly likely that she would accept sympathy from him, and he didn't want to push her too far.

Slowly, reluctantly, he released her, staring after her as she stormed away and disappeared into the house.

Well, that had gone well.

With an unsteady exhalation of air, he bowed his head and lifted a hand to rub wearily at his temple. He had known that she wouldn't be happy to see him, but never had he dreamed that she would react so violently. If Theodosia Rosemont had known just how badly this was going to go, she might have never made the choice to champion his cause.

The dowager duchess hadn't been at all pleased when he had awakened her from a sound sleep by pounding on the door of Maitland House and demanding an audience after his confrontation with Maura last Saturday evening. But once he had explained the circumstances, he had gained her rapt attention. Of course, he had left a few things out of the tale he had told her. Somehow he had a feeling that she wouldn't appreciate hearing about what had transpired between him and Maura in his darkened carriage.

When he had finally finished talking, the elderly lady had grown strangely quiet and introspective, and after pacing the confines of her parlor for quite some time with the aid of her cane, she had lowered her plump figure into a chair with a sigh.

"There are many things you deserve to know, my boy," she had admitted, something unreadable shimmering in the depths of her anxious eyes. "Things that I am not in a position to reveal to you. However, if you truly are concerned for Maura, if you truly do care what happens to her, then I believe I have an idea . . ."

That was when she had proceeded to tell him all about the house party at Rosemont Hall and had offered to exert her influence to get him included on the guest list. Because he was caught off guard, his first instinct had been to refuse. By handing the problem over to the dowager duchess, he had hoped that he would finally be able to put Maura from his mind and get on with his own life. He'd had no intention of becoming further embroiled in her troubles. But when the elderly lady had pointed out that it was quite possible that Maura's admirer might be present this weekend, he hadn't been able to stay away.

After all, someone had to look after the stubborn chit, and it seemed the job fell to him. Apparently Maura's father was recovering from a rather serious illness, and with her brother-in-law out of town on an extended trip, there were no other close male family members to watch out for her. Not to mention the fact that the dowager had intrigued Gabriel with her puzzling statement. What had she been referring to? What "things" did he deserve to know? And what did they have to do with Maura?

He hoped to find out the answers to those questions over the next few days. And in the meantime, a reluctant Viscount Stonehurst had agreed to remain in town for a short while in order to keep an eye on Violet Lafleur. Surely between the two of them they would be able to get to the bottom of the matter before too long.

"Well, that was an extremely interesting little scene."

The coolly amused feminine voice cut into Gabriel's thoughts, jarring him, and he jerked his head up with a frown at the intrusion.

Lydia Stratton, Viscountess Lanscombe, was climbing the terrace steps from the garden, her glittering eyes focused on him with a piercing and unsettling intent.

Damnation! he thought, stifling a savage imprecation. She was the last person he needed to deal with in addition to everything else he had to worry about. As Lord Lanscombe was a good friend of the Duke of Maitland, he supposed he should have expected their presence here this weekend, but it hadn't even crossed his mind.

And if the viscount and viscountess were here, that meant that the viscount's son, Lord Stratton, was more than likely in attendance as well. Given the hostility that had always existed between him and that arrogant son of a bitch, he couldn't think of a way that things could get any worse.

Her icy blond beauty emphasized by a close-fitting gown of aquamarine silk, Lady Lanscombe crossed the flagstones toward him. "Really, Hawksley," she purred, her full red lips curving into a brittle smile as she drew near. "I do believe that's the first time I've ever seen a woman walk away from you. Usually it's the other way around."

A muscle jumped in his jaw, but he managed to keep a tight rein on his impatience and address her with nothing more than a raised brow and a stilted inclination of his head. "Lady Lanscombe, I would imagine there is a first time for everything."

"Indeed." Coming to a stop next to him, she stared at the terrace doors for a long, silent moment before tucking her arm through his in an almost proprietary gesture. "That was one of Albright's daughters, wasn't it?"

It would do little good to deny it. "Yes, it was."

"I see. I don't suppose I realized that the two of you were so well acquainted."

"We aren't. Not really."

"Yet you know each other well enough to argue, and rather vehemently." The viscountess's grip on his arm tightened and she tilted her head, scrutinizing him with probing intentness. "I do hope for your sake that you haven't been foolish enough to make the same mistake your father did, darling. I would hate to see you throw your life away on some cheap little tart."

That was it. He simply didn't have the time or the inclination to curry to this vicious cat right now. He had to find Maura and try to get her to listen to reason. To placate her in some way. If he couldn't gain her trust and convince her to confide in him, he would never find out what she was up to.

With controlled, deliberate motions, he loosened Lady Lanscombe's grasping fingers and slid his arm from her hold before offering her a stiffly polite smile. "I thank you for your concern. But if I have made a mistake, my lady, it is mine to make. Now, if you'll excuse me."

Ignoring her stormy countenance, he sketched her a brief bow and stalked from the terrace.

# Chapter 12

~~~ ⌒ ◯◯ ⌒ ~~~

*"For the first time in years, Philip has received word from his father. The marquis is gravely ill and requests his son's presence in London. Of course, being the man he is, my husband could not ignore the summons, though I cannot help but wonder whether this is a sign that our lives are about to change."*

From the diary of Elise Marchand,
February 4, 1808

**M**aura found the dowager duchess in one of the second-floor sitting rooms, leaning on her cane and staring out the wide dormer windows at the verdant landscape. Beyond the glass, the lush green expanse of lawn stretched downhill to meet the dense foliage that marked the edge of the surrounding woodlands.

At the sound of footsteps, the dowager glanced back over her shoulder, a welcoming smile curving her lips at the sight of Maura. "There you are, child. I wondered where you had wandered to. I'm sorry I wasn't downstairs to greet you, but Maitland's harpy of a wife failed to inform me of your arrival." Turning, she moved toward a grouping of overstuffed chairs close to the windows. "I trust you and your aunt are all settled in?"

Maura had come to a halt just inside the doorway, feeling as if she were afloat on a sea of confusion and unable to focus on anything the elderly lady was saying. The sense of betrayal that gripped her was almost crippling.

Theodosia knew what sort of man Lord Hawksley was. So why would she align herself with him? Why would she bring him here to serve as another reminder for all those present of just why the members of the Daventry family had never been accepted?

Licking her lips, Maura finally managed to force one word from her paralyzed throat. "Why?"

The dowager duchess looked up at her questioningly as she lowered her stout form into a chair and set aside her cane. "Why what, dear?"

Maura shook her head and wrapped her arms about herself in a defensive pose, praying that there was a logical explanation for all this. "I'm trying to understand, Your Grace. But it doesn't make sense. Why would you invite Hawksley?"

The color slowly leached from the dowager's face, leaving it as pale as old parchment. When she spoke again, her voice was a hoarse and brittle rasp. "You've already seen him?"

"Yes. He approached me out on the terrace. And you can imagine my shock when he told me that you were the one who added his name to the guest list. I didn't want to believe it."

"No, and I don't suppose I blame you. I'm sorry you had to learn about it in such a way. I had hoped . . ." There was a long pause, then the older woman sighed and lifted a hand to beckon Maura closer. "Child, please come and sit down. We'll make ourselves comfortable and talk about all of this."

"I'd rather stand, Your Grace. I—"

"Please? All I ask is that you hear what I have to say."

The appeal was so imploring, so full of genuine entreaty, that Maura would have felt churlish to deny it, so she crossed the room to perch rather stiffly on the edge of the settee directly across from the elderly woman.

Her eyes rife with sincerity, Theodosia leaned forward in her seat.

"I promise you it was not my intention to hurt you by inviting Hawksley," she explained earnestly. "But he came to me with a story that caused me a great deal of concern. He said that he had discovered that you have been slipping out of your house in the dead of night, and that you've been turning up in some rather . . . questionable places. He mentioned a masquerade at Lord Lanscombe's home as well as a boardinghouse off Regent Street that serves as a residence for gentlemen bachelors." Her brow furrowed in obvious anxiety. "Is this true?"

Maura bit her lip, at a loss. She could not bring herself to lie to the one person who had done so much for her family, but she was well aware that telling the truth would only lead to more questions and recriminations. It seemed the only viable solution was to say nothing.

Her silence, however, was answer enough for Theodosia. "I see. I was afraid of that. Especially since he also showed me a piece of correspondence that I found quite distressing."

Taking a deep breath, Maura lifted her chin and managed to speak despite the lump in her throat. "I suppose he told you that he believes I am involved in some sort of illicit affair? That I have taken up where my mother left off?"

"He did express some concerns along those lines, yes. But I don't believe a word of it."

The dowager's firm and unequivocal statement caught Maura off guard, and she found herself gaping at the woman in utter stupefaction before she managed to pull herself together enough to stammer out a response. "Y-you d-don't?"

"No, I don't. I may not have spent as much time in your company as I have with Jillian, but I do know you. And I know that after all of the pain your mother's behavior caused you, you would never put your family in the same position by following in her footsteps."

"Of course I wouldn't. Which only proves that Lord Hawksley hasn't the slightest idea what he's talking about and should mind his own business."

"What it proves, young lady, is that Lord Hawksley isn't aware of all the facts." Theodosia gave her a narrow-eyed look. "You're up to something. And I want you to tell me what it is."

Maura had to fight to smother a hysterical burst of laughter. How? How could she possibly admit that she had actively taken up the search for her mother's killer?

When Maura once again failed to reply, the dowager's countenance softened, and she reached out to give Maura's arm a reassuring pat. "It's all right. I believe I can figure out most of it for myself. Jillian has confided in me, and I know that she suspects that whoever killed your mother was someone from among her circle of close admirers. You were at Lord Lanscombe's masquerade, and I happen to know that the boardinghouse Lord Hawksley found you lurking outside of is also the address of the Baron Bedford." Her unwavering stare was knowing and far too perceptive for Maura's comfort. "This is about your mother, isn't it?"

Sudden tears blurring her vision, Maura lunged to her feet and went to stand before the window, her back to the room as she valiantly blinked the moisture away and struggled to get her teetering emotions back under control.

But Theodosia wasn't about to let things go. The swish of the dowager's skirts as she rose from her chair could be heard in the stillness of the room, as well as the thump of her cane on the floor as she came to stand at Maura's side.

"Child, I can see how much this is tormenting you. No matter how my invitation to Lord Hawksley has made it seem, you must know I am on your side. You can always trust me."

Maura turned her head to meet Theodosia's sympathetic gaze, and the compassion written on the dowager's wrinkled face was more than she could bear. Everything that had been building up within her over the last three weeks overflowed and the dam finally broke, the whole story pouring out in a rush. Her discovery of her mother's diary and the packet of letters. The nightmares that had led to her determination to get to the bottom of who had written them. All of it.

And when she was done, she subsided into an apprehensive silence as she awaited the dowager's reaction to her revelations.

Appearing shaken, Theodosia closed her eyes and leaned heavily on her cane, her grip on the handle visibly tightening. "Elise was being threatened? But she never mentioned any letters to me."

"From the few references she made to them in her journal, I received the impression that she didn't consider them a serious threat. She brushed them off, told herself they were harmless. But this person, whoever he is, is far from harmless."

Those piercing brown eyes shot open again and pinned Maura in place with unnerving intensity. "And yet you continue to put yourself in danger."

Maura straightened her shoulders, steadfast in her resolve. She would not be dissuaded. Not even by Theodosia. "I don't know how to explain it or how to make you understand, but I have to do this. After the way I—" She stumbled to a halt, the guilt that stabbed at her rendering her mute.

"I do understand, my dear," Theodosia told her gently, tucking her arm through the crook of Maura's elbow and guiding her back toward the grouping of chairs. "But that doesn't mean I think this is a good idea. At least when Jillian involved herself in your father's cases, she had Mr. Tolliver there to rely upon. You have been virtually on your own in this, aside from the occasional assistance of Miss Lafleur."

"But I can't stop now!" Maura clutched the elderly lady's hands as they both sank back down on the settee together. "I have already eliminated Lords Lanscombe and Bedford. That only leaves Lord Cunnington. I'm so close, I just can't give up."

Theodosia cast her gaze toward the ceiling, as if importuning the heavens. "And here I thought our lives would settle down once Jillian married her

Mr. Monroe. How could I have been so foolish?"

"Please, Your Grace. You must see how important this is to me. Please say that you won't make me stop."

Minutes ticked by like a small eternity, but the dowager finally expelled a soft breath and acquiesced with a grudging inclination of the head. "Very well. I don't like it. But no, I won't stop you. I doubt it would do any good for me to try. In your own way, you're every bit as stubborn as your sister."

A glad cry flew from Maura's lips, and she started to fling her arms around the woman's neck, but Theodosia halted her with a stern look. "Just a moment. Before you become too effusive in your gratitude, this leads me to my reasons for inviting Lord Hawksley here." A hesitation. Then, "I believe the time has come for you to think about telling him the truth."

The suggestion washed over Maura like a thorough dousing with icy water, freezing her in her seat in stunned disbelief. Surely she couldn't have heard correctly? Or perhaps it was some sort of joke.

But the dowager's visage was utterly serious. "Only consider, my dear. Now that you have enough evidence to lend support to the theory that his father was innocent, it seems rather unjust to leave him in the dark. In his own way, he has suffered just as much as you and your sisters. And

I think that he could help you if you would let him."

"I beg leave to doubt that, Your Grace. And you must see that his presence here this weekend will only make things that much more difficult for me. Aunt Olivia will be furious, and it will give rise to all sorts of gossip."

"Perhaps. Or perhaps if the other guests see that the two of you can attend the same party, even be in the same room, without attacking each other, they will be forced to realize that there is nothing for them to gossip about." Theodosia squeezed Maura's hand. "In any case, should you wind up in any sort of danger, I will feel better knowing he is here to look after you."

"Look after me? Why on earth would he do that? He cares for nothing and no one but himself."

"I'm afraid I must disagree with that assessment, my dear. You didn't witness his behavior the night he came to see me about you. He was like a caged animal, pacing the room and railing about the sort of man you were becoming entangled with and the danger you were placing yourself in by wandering about London after dark. I must say, his vehemence surprised me. He acted like some overprotective father. Or jealous suitor."

At Theodosia's assertion, Maura's mouth went dry and her heart took off at a gallop, hammering wildly in her chest. "That is utterly absurd!"

"Is it?" The dowager tilted her head and peered

at Maura with an intentness that wouldn't allow her to look away. "You know, I sensed something between the two of you that afternoon in Hyde Park. There is more going on than I know, isn't there?"

Maura's mind flashed back to her very first meeting with Hawksley in Lord and Lady Grafton's study. To the numerous times over the last year that he had come to her rescue. But she wasn't about to go into all that.

She cleared her throat, but before she could voice the denial that hovered on her lips, the dowager cut her off with a wave of her hand. "No, no. Don't bother to try and pull the wool over my eyes, dear. I may be well into my dotage, but I still know attraction when I see it."

"Attraction? I am *not* attracted to him."

"I will not belabor the issue, child. But I will say that it is not at all usual for a man who cares about no one to concern himself with the welfare of a young lady who means nothing to him."

"He's not concerned for my welfare!" Unable to be still for another minute, Maura shot to her feet and began to march back and forth in front of the settee, her cheeks flushed with the heat of indignation and her hands on her hips. "He merely enjoys tormenting me. This is all a game to him. I am the daughter of the woman he thinks tempted his father away from his mother, and he sees me as some sort of challenge."

"I don't think so."

"And why not? Do you really believe I am any different than any of the other females he has seduced over the years?" Maura shook her head. "No. I mean nothing to him and he means nothing to me. He's not the sort of man I could ever care for. He makes me feel—"

When she came to an abrupt halt, Theodosia eyed her curiously. "Feel what, child?"

*All sorts of emotions that I don't want to feel. That are so strong they frighten me.*

But Maura refused to repeat aloud the words that echoed in her head. "It doesn't matter. He has more than earned his nickname, Your Grace, and I can't imagine why you would want me to have anything to do with him."

"Because after speaking to him the other night, I believe the Devil's Own is a far better man than he lets on. And surely if anyone can understand what he has suffered, it would be you. It is all about society's expectations, isn't it? You fight against them while he attempts to live up to them. But you are both driven by the same grief and despair."

"Perhaps. But that doesn't mean we are the same."

"No. But it does mean that you aren't quite as different as you might think," Theodosia said solemnly. "Please, at least consider telling him the truth. He deserves to know his father was innocent."

Maura's head was spinning. She knew that the dowager had a point, but part of her feared what would happen if she did confess to Hawksley. He already hated her mother. Would he blame her family for the false accusations that had condemned his father? And what if he forced her to turn over the letters to the law and refused to allow her to have anything more to do with the investigation? What if he couldn't understand that doing this herself was the only way she felt she could atone for her mistakes?

So many questions and not enough answers. And she had no idea what she was going to do.

Bending over, she pressed a kiss to Theodosia's forehead, trying her best to smile reassuringly despite her worries. "I'll think about it. I promise."

"I suppose that's all I can ask," the elderly lady sighed. "Now, you'd best hurry along and make ready for dinner or you'll be late."

The rosy glow of the setting sun outside the window gave credence to the dowager's words, so Maura hugged the woman one last time before she excused herself and departed the room.

Only to collide with Lord Hawksley in the hallway.

Knocked off balance, she let out a gasp, clutching at him involuntarily as his hands shot out to catch her by the elbows in a steadying grip.

And held on.

Looking up into his eyes, she felt her lungs

seize and her heart stutter at the heat that blazed in those green depths. They were so close to each other, she could smell his clean male scent, a blend of evergreen and musk. And even through the material of his gloves, she could feel the familiar tingling spreading up her arms, his touch igniting fires within her that threatened to burn her alive.

*This* was why she feared him. *This* was why she had to continue to avoid him at all costs. Every time she was in his vicinity, she seemed to lose control of her thoughts and actions. Even now, knowing she should be running in the opposite direction, she couldn't bring herself to break away from his hold, and everything she and Theodosia had discussed raced through her mind.

Had he really behaved like a jealous suitor? . . .

His deep, questioning voice broke the spell. "Maura?"

Oh God, she wasn't ready to deal with this. Not yet.

With a muffled cry, she finally found the strength to pull free from his grasp and hurried off down the corridor, intent on putting as much distance between them as possible.

# Chapter 13

❧

*"We attended our first ball this evening as the Marquis and Marchioness of Albright, and things were every bit as dreadful as I had feared they would be. The stares and pointing fingers. The cruel whispers and snubs. I do not mind so much for myself. But seeing Philip reviled because of my presence at his side is my worst nightmare come to life."*

From the diary of Elise Marchand,
April 3, 1809

"**I** am utterly appalled!"

Even though her voice was little more than a furious hiss, Lady Olivia easily made herself heard over the laughing chatter that surrounded them as she turned to face Maura, her expression one of outraged affront.

The two of them stood in an out-of-the-way corner of the large front parlor, on the very fringes of the handful of party guests who had adjourned here after dinner. And though they had been doing their best to pretend that nothing was amiss, it was growing more and more difficult with every second that passed to ignore the smirks and knowing glances being cast in their direction.

Apparently Olivia had finally reached the limits of her tolerance.

"This is a disastrous turn of events," she went on, her thin frame practically bristling with the force of her indignation. "That . . . that man is ruining everything!"

There was little need for her to elaborate. Maura knew precisely which man she was referring to. In fact, she could feel his eyes right now, burning into her from the far side of the room. Devastatingly handsome in his dark evening clothes, Lord Hawksley leaned indolently against the wall, seeming completely unaffected by the furor his presence had wrought.

Plying her lace-edged fan with particular vigor, Olivia turned an icy glare on their hostess, who was deep in conversation with a group of matrons across the way. "I simply cannot credit that the Duchess of Maitland, of all people, could make such an oversight. She is usually so very meticulous when it comes to her guest lists. What have we ever done to cause her to deliberately set out to humiliate us like this?"

Maura quickly busied herself by smoothing an imaginary wrinkle from the satin overskirt of her evening gown. She had no intention of informing her aunt that it had been Theodosia who had added Hawksley at the last minute. Olivia didn't need another reason to dislike the dowager. "I'm certain it wasn't meant as an intentional slight to us."

"Well, of course it was! How could it be anything else? And I am utterly appalled by it."

"You've said that, Aunt Olivia. Several times."

"Yes, well, it certainly bears repeating. After all of the work I have done to restore this family to its former standing among society, this weekend was to be the start of better things for us. And now look. It is no different than it ever was. People pointing and laughing behind our backs. And all because of that devil."

It was true. Before Hawksley had appeared in the dining room earlier that evening, most of the guests had greeted Maura and her aunt with a certain amount of civility and had seemed prepared to extend at least a tentative acceptance. But once the earl had made his entrance, all that had changed. From that point on, dinner had become a miserable and strained affair, with speculative whispers traveling the length of the table and all eyes trained upon the Daventry women with avid interest, as if waiting to see which of them would be the first fly up into the boughs and cause a scene.

The only person who hadn't abandoned them

had been Theodosia, and once she had retired for the night, they had been left to their own devices.

*Hold your head up*, the dowager had counseled Maura before she had departed the room. *Don't let them see that they're getting to you. If you show them his presence doesn't bother you one way or another, they will soon forget all about it.*

But that had proved to be easier said than done.

"We should be upstairs, packing to go home," Olivia said now, drawing Maura out of her musings. "I fail to see any way of salvaging this debacle."

Maura felt a flare of panic. They couldn't leave! Not when the Marquis of Cunnington had yet to even put in an appearance. She still had to come up with a way to ascertain whether he was the one who had written those terrible letters to her mother.

Struggling to keep her dismay from showing on her face, she addressed her aunt in what she hoped was a fairly calm and reasonable tone. "Nonsense. If we flee as if we have done something wrong, it will only supply the rumormongers with even more to gossip about." She straightened her shoulders, her lips tightening as she felt a familiar prickling at the nape of her neck. She didn't need to look to know that the rogue was still watching her, and she had to resist an overpowering urge to whirl about and stick her tongue out at him in a childish display of temper. "Besides, I refuse to give Lord Hawksley the satisfaction of believing he made me run away."

"There is that," her aunt conceded thoughtfully. "And of course it would be a shame for you to miss such a wonderful opportunity to further your acquaintance with Lord Waldron." A sudden shadow passed over her features, and her eyes narrowed to hard, glittering slits. "But I plan on making sure that Maitland hears of my displeasure."

Before Maura could comment, the Duke of Maitland himself appeared at their side, as if the mere mention of his name had summoned him.

"Ladies." His manner humbly contrite, he swept them a formal bow and spoke in an earnest, low-pitched murmur so as not to be overheard by anyone who hovered nearby. "On behalf of myself and my wife, I must offer you my most abject apologies. Until I saw him at dinner, I had no idea that Lord Hawksley was even in attendance. How such a grievous error has occurred, I can't even begin to fathom, but I assure you that no insult was intended. Indeed, had I but known sooner, I would have taken steps to ensure that his invitation was rescinded."

Lady Olivia acknowledged his words with pursed lips and a stilted nod, but the poor man looked so anxious that Maura felt sorry for him. His heart was in the right place, even if he gave the impression that he was more than a trifle ineffectual when it came to dealing with his wife. It was quite evident from her avoidance of Maura and her aunt that whatever embarrassment they might be suffering was of little concern to the duchess. In fact, based upon the rather pointed comment she had made to them regarding last-minute additions to the guest list, Maura suspected that the woman was taking a sadistic delight in their predicament.

Maura gave the duke an understanding smile. "No insult was taken, Your Grace," she told him gently. "It is a bit awkward, to be sure, but these things do happen."

"Thank you, my dear." He pressed her hand in gratitude. "You are most gracious to be so forgiving."

With one final bow, he made his excuses and hurried away.

Lady Olivia frowned at his retreating back in clear displeasure. "The least he could have done was offer to toss that blackguard out on his ear," she sniffed.

Maura shook her head. That was a highly un-likely scenario, but before she could voice that thought aloud, they were once again interrupted. This time by the approach of Lords Waldron and Bedford.

Both gentlemen bowed gallantly, earning favor in Maura's estimation by making no reference what-soever to the stir Hawksley had created. And once the customary pleasantries had been exchanged, Lord Waldron turned to Maura and offered his arm with an air of expectancy. "My lady, I was wondering if you would do me the honor of taking a turn about the room with me?"

Her first impulse was to politely decline. She had received enough unwanted attention this evening, and parading about on the marquis's arm would only serve to draw more. But Lady Olivia gave her a less than delicate nudge, and she decided that she would much rather subject herself to the bold stares of the ton than risk her aunt's wrath should she refuse.

So instead, she inclined her head courteously. "I should be delighted, my lord."

As Lord Waldron tucked her hand through the crook of his elbow and began to stroll with her around the perimeter of the parlor, she felt another frisson of awareness shiver its way up her spine. It was even more pronounced than the tingles she had experienced before, and the strength of her reaction made it impossible for her to resist seeking out the source of her discomfort.

Hawksley hadn't moved from his spot against the wall. In fact, it didn't look as if he had even shifted position. But something about the way he held himself, the leashed tension she could sense lurking just beneath the surface of that aloof façade, told her even across the short distance that separated them that he was not nearly as indifferent as he appeared.

In fact, as she and Waldron passed by him, she

noticed a slight stiffening of his tautly muscled frame, and a scowl marred his forehead as his heated stare focused on her fingers where they curled around the marquis's arm.

Was it possible . . . ? Did it actually bother him to see her with Lord Waldron?

But she shook off the possibility almost as soon as it occurred to her. Of course not. She was being utterly ridiculous. Hadn't she already decided that he was simply playing games with her? What could it possibly matter to him if she was being courted by the marquis?

She returned her attention to Waldron, and he met her gaze with a charming smile. "Please pardon my presumption, Lady Maura, but I cannot help but notice how very lovely you look tonight."

"Why, thank you, my lord. You look quite dashing yourself."

And that was no less than the truth. A handsome, distinguished gentleman with silvery hair that gleamed in the lamplight, the marquis possessed a tall, athletic frame and a lean, unlined face that belied his years.

But when she looked at him, there was no leap of her pulse, no pounding of her heart, no flutter in her stomach. She felt none of the dizzying, disconcerting emotions she felt when she peered over her shoulder once again to see the brooding figure of Lord Hawksley still leaning against the wall. Still staring at her.

Only now someone else had joined him.

The Lady Lanscombe.

In an off-the-shoulder evening gown of emerald silk with a décolletage so low that her plump breasts threatened to spill over the top, the beautiful, blond viscountess was pressed up against his side, her hand resting possessively on his arm as she leaned in close to whisper in his ear.

For a fleeting instant, Maura could have sworn someone had plunged something sharp into her chest. Her breath seized in her lungs and an angry red mist abruptly clouded her vision. Good heavens, he was letting that . . . that woman practically drape herself over top of him. And a married woman, at that!

But of course. Since when had that ever stopped the Devil's Own?

Finally managing to suck in a calming gust of air, she told herself firmly that what he did and who he did it with shouldn't matter to her at all. But shutting out the little voice in the corner of her mind that insisted it did matter was next to impossible.

With a supreme effort of will, she forced herself to focus on the marquis, who was speaking to her as if oblivious to her momentary distraction.

"As much as I hate to bring up an unpleasant subject, my dear, there is something I feel that I must tell you, and then we won't speak of it further." He skirted around a potted plant before drawing her to a halt next to a set of French doors.

The moonlight shining through the glass illuminated his serious expression. "I know this has been a most trying evening for you, but I wanted you to know how much I admire the grace and dignity you have shown in the face of the shameful treatment you have received here tonight. I cannot think of many other young ladies of your age who would have been able to handle this situation with such strength of character."

Though genuinely touched by his words, Maura couldn't help but wonder where his support and encouragement had been earlier. "I don't know what to say. You are too kind."

"Not at all. Your father would be very proud of you, I'm sure." His brown eyes were warm with sympathy as he studied her. "In any case, I am glad that we shall have a chance to get to know each other better this weekend."

"As am I, my lord."

"Good." He patted her gloved fingers. "Now, I'm afraid I will have to cut our stroll short, my lady, as I see Lord Leland beckoning to me. I have a few things of importance that I need to discuss with him. And as your aunt and Lord Bedford seem to be headed in this direction, I shall leave you to their care. If you will excuse me?"

"Of course." Maura curtsied to him as he bowed low over her hand. "Good evening, Lord Waldron."

"Good evening, my dear."

She watched as he walked away and disappeared with Lord Leland through the archway into the next room. Then, anxious to finally return to her bedchamber and put this nightmare of an evening behind her, she turned to await Lady Olivia and Lord Bedford's approach.

Only to realize that there was someone else coming toward her.

With long, predatory strides, Hawksley covered the distance between them, magically clearing a path through the small clusters of people that milled about the center of the parlor. Lady Lanscombe was no longer with him, and his burning gaze was fixed unerringly on Maura.

Her mouth went dry, and the chamber spun sickeningly around her. No! She couldn't believe that even he would dare!

But of course, he would.

He reached her side just a few seconds before her aunt and the baron, and Maura couldn't help but notice that the look of smug satisfaction Olivia wore was swiftly replaced by one of horror when she recognized the man who loomed over her niece.

"Lady Maura." His voice was deep, throaty, stroking the syllables of her name like a velvety caress.

Instantly the buzz of conversation ceased, and all eyes focused on them. The silence was deafening, the very air charged with a sense of expectation as those around them waited with bated breath to see what would happen.

Theodosia's advice from a few hours before echoed in Maura's ears, as clearly as if the dowager herself were standing right next to her. *Hold your head up. Don't let them see that they're getting to you.*

It gave her the courage to take a deep breath and reply in an even tone that betrayed not a sign of her nervousness. "Lord Hawksley."

His mouth curving upward in a devilish grin, he sketched her a bow, the white slash of his teeth gleaming against the swarthiness of his skin. "I could not help but notice that your escort was forced to leave your side without completing your turn about the room. I should like to offer my services in his stead, if I may."

In the stillness, someone gasped. And for some reason, that tiny sound acted like a prod to Maura's pride. All of a sudden, all the anger and resentment that she had kept buried for so long came bubbling to the surface and spilled over, filling her with an overwhelming rush of righteous fury.

After a year of playing the part of the dutiful daughter, of the genteel and circumspect young lady who behaved in all the ways that society dictated she should, she had finally had enough. None of it had done her any good and she was tired of trying to prove herself. It was time to start living life on her own terms, and she would not be intimidated any longer. Not by Hawksley. Not by her aunt. And not by the small-minded members of the ton.

"I accept, my lord."

"Maura, you can't—"

She halted Lady Olivia's protest with an upraised hand. "It is all right, Aunt Olivia. Perhaps if Lord Hawksley and I show everyone here that we can put our families' past differences behind us and behave as civilized adults, they will see that it is finally time for them to do so as well!"

Leaving her aunt clinging weakly to a visibly disgruntled Lord Bedford, she sent a pointed glare around the parlor at the blur of pale, gawking faces, tucked her arm through Hawksley's, and let him lead her away.

Behind them, a sudden babble of voices rose up. But Maura ignored them. Chin lifted at a lofty angle, she sailed along, barely restraining the compulsion to throw back her head and laugh wildly at the exhilaration that filled her.

She had finally cut the strings, and it was quite a heady sensation. It felt so freeing to be able to cast off the strictures of society and simply do as she pleased. Was this the way her mother had felt on the day that she had finally decided to be true to herself and had stopped trying in vain to play the role of a proper marchioness?

"Now you've done it."

At Hawksley's enigmatic statement, she glanced

up at him to find him examining her with inscrutable eyes.

"Done what?"

"Given them something to talk about."

She lifted one shoulder in a shrug, using her free hand to tuck a stray dark curl back into her elegant chignon. "They were going to talk anyway. If they were going to do so, I would rather it be about something that is true rather than something that is not. Besides, Theodosia seems to think that if we pretend we don't loathe each other, sooner or later they will lose interest and the tongues will quit wagging."

He raised a brow. "I thought you were angry with me."

"Oh, I am. Make no mistake about that. I just happen to be angrier with them at the moment."

"Then I suppose I should be thankful for that."

"Yes, you should."

They lapsed into silence as they took the turn at the corner of the room, passing a trio of elderly dowagers who eyed them askance over their fluttering fans before turning away to converse among themselves in hushed murmurs.

Once they had left the women behind, however, Hawksley spoke again, his voice now laced with a perceptible tension. "Is Lord Waldron your mysterious admirer?"

Instead of answering, Maura sighed and looked away. "As I've said before, that really isn't any of your business."

"So he's not. I didn't think so, but I had to be sure." Out of her peripheral vision, she saw his head swing in her direction, felt his gaze skim over her face as if he were attempting to read her very thoughts. "Will you accept his suit? Waldron's, I mean?"

"My aunt believes it would be an excellent match."

"And what do you believe?"

What did she believe? The question plucked at the threads of her composure, filling her with a mad urge to laugh and cry at the same time. Did what she believed even matter anymore?

"Of course it matters!"

Maura didn't even realize that she had uttered her thoughts aloud until the exclamation exploded from Hawksley with a vehemence that sent several young debutantes who had been assembled nearby scurrying from their path with fearful expressions.

The earl didn't even notice. Coming to an abrupt halt, he frowned down at her, a muscle ticking in his jaw. "I understand that you are angry. And believe it or not, I am sorry for all of this. As I tried to explain to you out on the terrace this afternoon, it was not my intention to hurt or embarrass you by coming here this weekend."

Fighting to keep her countenance serene and a false smile in place for the benefit of any onlookers, Maura spoke through gritted teeth. "Then what *was* your intention, my lord? Just what did you think would happen? That I would thank you for giving the ton a reason to gossip about me again?"

His features drawing into a mask of taut rigidity, he drew her subtly closer to him. "Damn it, Maura," he bit out. "Do you think I am enjoying this? Do you think that I like the fact that I can't seem to stay away from you, no matter how hard I try? That I can't get you out of my head? Watching over you has become a compulsion for me that I am incapable of ignoring. The more I fight it, the more it pulls me in. Like bloody quicksand."

The words were harsh, grating, sounding as if they had been torn from his throat against his will, and they washed over Maura with a seductive power that made her heart stutter. But she was determined not to let him sway her. Heaven knew the man was well practiced in the art of getting what he wanted from women. It was all an act, and she doubted he meant a word of it. "Do not say such things when you don't mean them."

"I do mean them. And if your secret admirer is in attendance this weekend, someone must be here to keep you from making any rash mistakes. At the very least, this man has designs on your virtue. And more than that, I truly believe he means you harm. If you can't see that, I must make you see it."

Incensed, Maura tugged at her arm in an attempt to free herself from his grip, but he reached up to cover her hand with his, holding it pressed against his forearm. Even through his sleeve and the material of her glove, she could feel the warmth of his flesh, the flex of muscle, and it angered her that even now, when she was enraged with him, she could be so aware of him on a completely primal level.

"How dare you pretend that my reputation, my welfare, means a thing to you after your attempted seduction of me only last week," she hissed. "I don't understand why you insist on continuing to play this game with me! Is there so little of interest in your own life right now that you must attempt to orchestrate mine in order to relieve the tedium?"

"It's not like that." His green eyes glowing with a fierce light, he held her gaze as he brushed his thumb over the pulse point in her wrist once, twice. It was almost as if he were daring her to deny her reaction to him. "What happened in that carriage happened because I could not keep my hands off you any longer. Something has been growing between us for the past year, ever since we met at Lord and Lady Grafton's ball. You can deny it all you like, but—"

"Stop!" She didn't want to hear it, couldn't bear to listen to him any longer. With every word, he enticed her closer, tempted her to forget who and what he was and to trust in him. She couldn't let that happen. There was far too much at stake. "I know what you are doing, my lord, and it will not work. I will not be manipulated. So do your worst. But I will show you that two can play this game."

With that, she finally managed to free herself from his grip and stormed away, leaving him standing alone among the crowd of party guests, staring after her.

# Chapter 14

~~~⌒⌒~~~

*"It seems that no matter what I do, I shall never be accepted by society as the wife of the Marquis of Albright, and I am weary of being made to feel inadequate in every way. It has placed a terrible strain upon my marriage, for not even Philip understands my feelings of frustration and loneliness. The only person who has shown me any kindness is Theodosia Rosemont, the Dowager Duchess of Maitland. I grow more grateful every day for her unswerving friendship and support."*

From the diary of Elise Marchand,
July 30, 1809

**P**erched in an overstuffed armchair in Rosemont Hall's well-appointed library, Maura stared out the window at the gray, dismal-looking landscape. Raindrops still misted the glass from the thunderstorm that had awakened her from a restless sleep early that morning, and a heavy fog hovered over the estate. All the outside activities scheduled for the first half of the day had been either postponed or canceled.

With a soft sigh, she reached up to rub at an aching temple. She had long ago lost track of the amount of time she had spent just sitting here. Initially she had sought out the library with the sole intention of finding a book with which she could while away the spare hours. But once she had stepped into the quiet chamber and the atmosphere of hushed tranquillity had washed over her, she hadn't been able to make herself leave.

In truth, after spending most of the morning listening to a lengthy lecture on her deplorable behavior of the evening before, all she had wanted to do was get away from everything. While the other guests had filled their plates from the sumptuous repast spread out on the buffet table in the breakfast nook, Lady Olivia had filled the air with a diatribe so scathing and vitriolic that Maura's ears were still ringing.

"What on earth were you thinking?" her aunt had hissed, shooting a furtive look over her shoulder as if to make sure no one was close enough to overhear. "To accept an invitation to stroll with Lord Hawksley, of all people! You should have given the bounder the cut direct instead of promenading with him about the parlor as if it were something to be proud of. Any more of that sort of nonsense, young lady, and we will be lucky if we are ever received in polite circles again."

By the time Olivia had finally wound down, Maura felt nauseated and more than a trifle numb. And when those of the younger guests who were close to her in age had separated from the rest of the party for a round of parlor games, she hadn't even felt slighted that they had failed to include her. Her only thought had been to escape.

She heaved another weary breath and smoothed down the muslin skirt of her modest day gown. She was well aware that she couldn't hide here forever, but surely she could afford to linger for a while longer? Her aunt had assumed that she would follow the other young people to the parlor, so no one would be looking for her right away.

At that moment, a faint clinking sound broke the stillness, drawing her attention to the archway on the far side of the room. Curious, she got to her feet and wandered past the rows of bookshelves to peer into the adjoining chamber. It appeared to be the billiard room, and Lord Hawksley was leaning over the green baize table, sighting one of the colored balls that littered its surface down the length of a cue stick.

Maura stifled a gasp of dismay and whirled with every intention of fleeing before he saw her, but his voice cut across the distance separating them, halting her in her tracks. "Don't rush off on my account, Lady Maura."

Too late.

She glanced back to find him standing with one hip propped against the table, observing her with hooded eyes.

"I promise I don't bite," he went on, the corner of his mouth quirking slightly. "Although after last night, I'm forced to wonder about you. Your teeth are much sharper than I expected."

"If I were of a mind to bite you, my lord, it would certainly be no more than you deserve."

Maura's furious statement had his blond brows arching skyward, and the heated look in those green eyes as they traveled over her sent a shiver running up her spine. "Please feel free to nibble on me wherever and whenever you like, my lady."

After all she had been through in the last several hours because of him, she had little patience for his provocative innuendos. "I am glad you find this situation so humorous, Lord Hawksley," she said, icy resentment lacing her tone. "But I can assure you that I see nothing amusing about any of it."

He abruptly sobered. "I know, and I apologize." Rounding the billiard table, he laid aside his cue stick and folded his arms, regarding her with a grave expression. "Whether you believe me or not, I meant what I said last night. I did not accept the dowager duchess's invitation to come here with the purpose of hurting you. I honestly assumed that

I would bear the brunt of the gossip, and I never dreamed they would focus most of their attention on you."

Something about the way he said it made her want to believe that he was telling the truth, but she couldn't quite bring herself to do so. Who knew better than she how persuasive he could be?

Her chin held high, she brushed by his tall form and advanced farther into the room, coming to a stop next to the billiard table. There she stood with her back to him as she pretended a particular interest in the cue stick he had left lying on its cloth-covered surface. "It really doesn't matter what you meant. The best of intentions could not fix the damage that has been wrought. So if my mood is a bit less than amiable this morning, you have only yourself to blame."

She flinched when she heard his footsteps approaching her, but didn't turn to him, even when he halted at her side.

"I agree," he said softly. "I'm only sorry that you have suffered in any way because of my presence here."

He was too close. Far too close for her comfort. She could practically feel the heat of his body radiating off him, feel him willing her to look at him. But that was something she refused to do. She could not meet his eyes. Not when he might be able to read in her own just how much he was affecting her.

Taking a step away from him in an attempt to remove herself from his unsettling proximity, she reached out to run her finger absently along the length of the discarded cue stick. "If you truly wished to make amends, you would pack up and leave now."

"I came here for a reason, my lady, and I'm not going anywhere."

His response was firm and unequivocal, and it had Maura finally spinning about to face him, her nostrils flaring in indignation. "Then your apologies obviously mean nothing."

"That isn't true. But though I realize you have a right to your anger, I can't——I won't—leave. I have tried to explain my reasons. All we can do now is make the best of the situation. And I promise that I will do nothing further to draw any undue notice to our association."

Maura bit her lip. He sounded so earnest, so sincere . . . "But I still don't understand why—"

"Do you play, my lady?"

Coming as it did in the middle of their conversation, the question caught Maura off guard. Her anger drained away, and she blinked at Hawksley in bewilderment for a second before following his gaze to where her hand rested on the cue stick.

"Changing the subject, my lord?" she inquired with false sweetness, narrowing her eyes at him.

He shrugged. "I only wondered. You seemed rather absorbed by that cue stick."

With a sniff, she picked it up. "Not at all. Though I must admit to a certain amount of bafflement as to why men seem to enjoy the game so much. Knocking a few balls about on a table is a rather inane way to pass the time." She turned the stick over in her hands so that she held it lengthwise and aimed experimentally at one of the balls closest to her with the tip. "Though it doesn't look all that difficult."

A low chuckle from Hawksley had her whipping her head in his direction once again. "And just what are you laughing at, sir?"

"If you hit it like that, you will either end up flipping the ball off the table or miss your shot entirely." He moved forward. "Here, let me show you."

Before she knew what he was about, he had fitted himself up against her and reached around from behind, effectively trapping her within the circle of his arms.

At his touch, she froze in place.

"If this is another attempt to manipulate me . . ." she whispered.

There was a moment of silence, then she felt him press in closer, his muscled chest grazing the length of her spine. "I am merely trying to help you, Lady Maura," he said next to her ear, his breath caressing the lobe in a way that sent a wave of gooseflesh rippling across the surface of her skin. "But I can stop, if you want me to."

Yes. Yes, he should stop right now, she thought dimly. But it felt so good to be next to him like this . . .

"No. Don't stop."

"Then let me show you. You hold it like this." Suiting his actions to his words, Hawksley slid his hands over hers, adjusting her grip on the cue stick. His palms were warm, the pads of his fingers slightly rough. "There, you see. And lean forward enough to line up the shot . . ." A single nudge of his hips brought the cradle of his strong thighs into contact with her bottom, making her instantly aware of the rigid, throbbing proof of his arousal. Her nipples tightened to tingling points beneath the material of her bodice, and she could have sworn she heard him release a shaky hiss before continuing his instruction in a husky murmur. "Let the tip slide out from between your fingers just . . . so, and when you strike the ball, make sure you tap it very, verrrrrrry . . . gently."

The damp flick of his tongue just behind her ear served as a punctuation, making her jump, and the cue stick jumped along with her. But it still managed to strike its target. The ball spun across the table, banking off the edge and sinking into the corner pocket.

"Bravo, Lady Maura!"

At the sardonic drawl, Maura muffled a startled cry and sprang away from the table, her cheeks heating in distress as she looked up just in time to see the Viscount and Viscountess Lanscombe, Quincy Stratton, and the Marquis of Cunnington enter the room.

What had they seen?

Hawksley handled the interruption much more calmly than she had. With smooth efficiency, he returned the cue stick to the rack on the wall, then rounded the billiard table in a few loose-limbed strides to take up a casual stance on the far side. But while he appeared undisturbed, Maura suspected he had deliberately placed the table between himself and their unexpected companions to hide the effects of their lesson.

"What ho?" Lord Lanscombe, a tall, spare gentleman with thinning gray hair and a beaked nose, ogled Maura through the lens of his quizzing glass. "Who knew you were an expert billiard player, my dear?"

She swallowed and lifted a hand to make sure her dark hair was still pinned in its tidy coronet, doing her best to seem as unruffled as Hawksley. "I'm not, my lord. The earl was just showing me—"

"Yes, we saw what he was showing you." It was Stratton who interrupted her. Flinging himself into a chair next to the door, he slung a leg over the arm and swung a booted foot lazily as he surveyed her from under the limp strands of brown hair that fell across his forehead. "You make a most apt pupil."

"Indeed." This came from Lord Cunnington, who moved to take up a position at the corner of the table, less than an arm's length away from her. He was a squat, florid-faced man with thick lips and beady eyes, and just looking at him was enough to make Maura shudder.

This was the last suspect on her list. The person who might have been responsible for her mother's death.

"I must say, however, that you look as if you have a natural talent for it," he went on slyly, his gaze trained on her modest décolletage as if trying to see through the thin fabric. "As I'm certain you are naturally talented at many, many things."

Maura frowned. Was this cur actually insinuating what she thought he was insinuating?

He didn't give her a chance to respond, but moved to take a cue stick down off the wall, tossing her a wink over his shoulder. "I don't suppose you'd like to indulge in a game? I could show you a few . . . techniques of my own."

Lady Lanscombe, who clung to her husband's arm, gave a melodious laugh. "Really, Lord Cunnington, how improper of you to suggest such a thing." Despite the amusement in her voice, there was no trace of humor in the frosty blue eyes that scrutinized Maura. "I'm certain that Lady Maura's chaperone wouldn't approve at all."

"A pox on what's proper! Lady Maura doesn't seem like the sort of young lady who would let a bit of impropriety keep her from having fun. Wouldn't you agree, Lanscombe?"

The viscount waved a hand airily. "Quite right. After all, the chit must have inherited a bit of brass from her mother or she wouldn't be keeping company with Hawksley."

Cunnington leaned in toward her, so close she could smell the eggs and kippers he must have eaten for breakfast. It made her stomach roll. "I knew your mother, my dear. Quite well, as a matter of fact." A strange light entered those ratlike eyes as they trailed over the slender curves of her body, and he licked his lips lasciviously. "A tasty little morsel, Elise was, if a bit too spirited. She needed a firm hand, that one. And I would imagine a luscious little filly like yourself would know just how to make a man—"

"Lady Maura was just leaving."

It was a grating rasp, and all eyes went to Hawksley, who still stood on the other side of the table. He didn't look nearly as calm as he had earlier. His mouth was set in a grim line and a muscle flexed in that taut jaw.

"I'm certain her aunt must be searching for her by now," he said, leveling Maura with a look that she couldn't quite interpret.

Cunnington raised a brow, then twirled the cue stick with a pudgy hand as he considered the earl. "And what about you, Hawksley? Are you up for a game? If you'd like, we could make it more interesting. Lay a small wager on the outcome, perhaps?"

"Gambling in mixed company, Lord Cunnington?" Lady Lanscombe released her husband and strolled forward to join the group around the table. "How very naughty of you!"

A harsh bark of laughter escaped Stratton, who had been observing the proceedings with a sullen countenance. "A wager? Are you mad, Cunnington? You've got nothing to wager with! Your pockets are to let, remember?"

His father nodded. "My boy's right, Cunnington. You still owe me a rather large sum from our round of faro over a fortnight ago."

"I am a bit lacking in funds at present," the marquis admitted. "But I did recently purchase a pair of high-steppers from Tattersall's. Excellent breeding." He examined Hawksley. "Of course, should you win I could simply write you an IOU."

An IOU.

Maura felt her pulse spike. After the hours she had spent racking her brain to come up with a way to catch a glimpse of the marquis's handwriting, could it really be this easy?

"Not now, Cunnington," the earl said impatiently, starting around the table toward Maura. "I need to escort Lady Maura back to her aunt."

A slow smile crept over Maura's face. *Oh, I don't think so, my lord . . .*

"Lord Hawksley." Folding her hands together in front of her, she drew her full lips into a pout. "I believe I should like to stay and watch you and Lord Cunnington play."

He pulled up short, as if he had slammed into a brick wall, and his hands fisted at his sides, the knuckles showing white with tension. "That is not a good idea, my lady."

The words were gritted out from between clenched teeth, as much a warning as the fierce look in his eyes. But she strengthened her resolve. She had made up her mind that she would not be intimidated by this man, and she had no intention of letting him bully her.

"On the contrary. I think it is a very good idea, my lord. After all, you seem to be such an expert." She tossed her head, her manner deliberately provoking. "Surely you aren't worried that the marquis could beat you?"

"That has nothing to do with—"

"Really, Hawksley, what could it hurt?" Lady Lanscombe cut across his objection by resting a hand on his muscled biceps. "If the child wants to watch, then let her watch. I admit, I have a rather keen desire to see you trounce Cunnington myself."

The sight of those pale, delicate fingers against Hawksley's sleeve set off something sharp and painful deep inside Maura, but she shoved it away and turned to Lord Cunnington, fluttering her lashes flirtatiously. "Perhaps you could demonstrate a few of those techniques you mentioned, my lord?"

The marquis preened. "I should like that, my dear."

Maura had to struggle to keep her features from hardening. *And I should like to prove that you murdered my mother, you monster.*

And three quarters of an hour later, as she watched Lord Hawksley slip the Marquis of Cunnington's IOU into the breast pocket of his coat, she knew she would very soon have her wish.

# Chapter 15

*"For the past few months, Philip has been very withdrawn, almost brooding. He closes himself in the library for hours at a time and buries himself in his articles on criminology. I know that the duties of his new position weigh heavily upon him, but when I try to speak to him of it, he brushes me off as if it is nothing. I can feel him drifting away, and it frightens me."*

From the diary of Elise Marchand,
January 13, 1810

From the concealing shadows of a curtained alcove, Maura waited and watched with bated breath as a rather harried-looking footman came hurrying along the second-floor corridor on his way toward the stairs, muttering to himself. With his head bent, he didn't seem to notice her peering out at him as he passed by, and she heaved a grateful sigh once he had disappeared from sight.

Making a conscious effort to calm her rattled nerves, she stepped out from her hiding place and took a second to get her bearings in the dimness. Though the rain had finally stopped a few hours earlier, the day was still overcast, and what light shone in through the windows at the other end of the hallway was gray and muted.

Hawksley's room should be just a little farther ahead. Three doors down and on the right.

It hadn't taken much sleuthing to discover where the earl's guest chamber was located in the Hall. It seemed that even the staff was abuzz with his presence, and Phoebe had been a veritable wealth of information after spending her free hours last evening chatting with a pair of gossipy housemaids. With Aunt Olivia resting in her room in preparation for tonight's ball, Maura had decided that now seemed as good a time as any for her to accomplish her self-appointed task.

Filled with a sense of anticipation, she started down the corridor with stealthy footsteps, counting doors as she went until she had reached the designated one. Then, hesitating, she listened intently for any sounds that would indicate that someone might be within. When she heard nothing, she slowly reached out to grip the handle and pushed the wooden panel open.

Inside, all was dark and still. The draperies of

burgundy damask that hung at the windows had been drawn back by their tasseled gold cords, but as in the hallway, little light spilled in, and only a single lamp burned on the nightstand. It cast its pale glow over the heavy mahogany furnishings and the large canopied bed with its burgundy and gold hangings.

Closing the door behind her, Maura moved forward into the room, her gaze darting here and there as she debated where to begin looking. Though the surface of the nearby chest of drawers and the table near the window were bare of any accoutrements, the writing desk in the far corner held a few scattered pieces of paper along with some other odds and ends.

She wasted no time in crossing to it and sifting through the items. But to her disappointment, the sheets of paper turned out to be blank stationery, and there was nothing else of interest. Her subsequent rifling of the armoire was equally as unsuccessful.

No IOU.

What could the infuriating man have done with it?

Growing more and more frantic with each second that ticked by, Maura continued her search, digging through drawers and even rummaging in the linen chest at the foot of the bed, all to no avail. She was just getting ready to turn away from a fruitless ransacking of the drawers in the bedside table when someone spoke up from behind her.

"Well, this is an unexpected pleasure."

The wry voice caught Maura off guard, sending her heart into her throat, and she whirled about with a gasp.

Hawksley lounged in the doorway, arms crossed and one broad shoulder propped against the frame as he regarded her with an unreadable expression.

Blast! Now what was she going to do?

Taking a stumbling step backward, she swiftly weighed what few options she had, and for one wild instant she actually contemplated making a bid for escape by attempting to flee past him into the hallway. But she discarded that notion almost as soon as it occurred. With his large frame blocking her path, it wasn't likely that she would make it by him before he could stop her.

As if he had read her mind, the earl levered himself away from the door and advanced into the room, kicking the panel closed behind him with a booted foot.

"You know," he drawled smoothly, "you seem surprised to see me. Which is puzzling, considering that this is my room." One of his eyebrows arched upward. "And that leads to a very interesting question. Just what are you doing here?"

Maura bit her lip and eyed the door behind him in wistful longing. It was quite obvious she wasn't going to get out of this until she had answered Hawksley's questions to his satisfaction. And she supposed she couldn't blame him for that. He had found her looting his room, after all. But she was far from prepared to tell him the truth, so what on earth could she possibly say to explain it?

The smile she forced was small, uncertain, and far from steady. "I don't suppose you would believe that I merely got turned around and wandered into the wrong room?" she offered rather lamely.

"Tsk, tsk, my lady." Hawksley clucked his tongue and gave an almost sorrowful shake of his head, even as he stalked ever closer to her. "Surely you can do better than that? That excuse might have held a bit more water if I hadn't overheard you use the exact same one with that sot Stratton the night of the Lanscombe masquerade."

Oops. She had forgotten that.

Why oh why hadn't she planned for this eventuality? Maura wondered frantically. She had been so anxious to get her hands on Lord Cunnington's IOU that it hadn't even occurred to her that Hawksley might return before she'd had a chance to finish searching his room.

Now she had placed herself in a potentially hazardous situation. Though Hawksley didn't sound angry, the unwavering intensity in those green eyes made her more than a trifle uneasy. And it had all been for naught. She hadn't even found what she'd been looking for and she . . . she . . .

A sudden image flashed through her mind. A picture of Hawksley in the billiard room earlier, tucking Cunnington's IOU into the inside breast pocket of his coat.

The coat that he still wore.

Of course! If he hadn't had the opportunity to visit his chambers since early that morning, then the IOU must still be in his pocket. All Maura had to do was figure out how to get her hands on it.

The earl now stood less than an arm's length from her, and she let her gaze stray from that finely sculpted face, down over those sloping shoulders, to the solid wall of his chest. The superfine material of his coat stretched across that broad expanse, fitting him to perfection and subtly hinting at the muscled strength that lay beneath.

Her mouth went dry and she swallowed convulsively. There was one avenue she could try. A way she could possibly make him lower his defenses and get him out of that coat. But could she do it?

The answer was all too obvious. She *had* to do it. There simply wasn't any other alternative. If finding her mother's killer meant using whatever limited seduction skills she might possess, then so be it. Hadn't she made up her mind just last night that she was going to start living life on her own terms? She wasn't the Marchioness of Albright's daughter for nothing, and Hawksley had already proven that he was more than willing to use the same sort of tactics on her to get what he wanted. If she turned the tables, it only served him right.

She had warned him that two could play this game, and play it she would.

So, taking a deep breath, she placed one hand on her hip, leaned in toward him, and reached up to trail one finger along the lapel of his coat.

"Why, my lord," she purred, lowering her lashes and doing her best to affect a sultry mien, "I've come to give you what you've been claiming to want."

He froze at her change in demeanor, his eyes flaring with something stark and primitive. She was so close to him, she could feel the thrumming tension coiled in his taut, powerful frame, and even as it alarmed her, it also filled her with an unexplainable thrill of excitement.

"And just what is that, sweetheart?" he murmured, his voice dangerously soft.

"Me."

He didn't trust the scheming little minx for a minute.

As much as Gabriel wanted to believe every word that had just spilled from that exquisite mouth, he couldn't. Despite the provocative pout, the coy flutter of her lashes, he had seen the panic that had passed over Maura's face when she had looked up to see him standing in the doorway. And the transformation to enticing seductress had simply been too abrupt.

No, this was just another ruse meant to divert him from his suspicions.

But the fact that he was well aware this was all an act didn't lessen its impact on him. With such a small amount of space separating them, he could smell her familiar flowery fragrance, feel the waft of her breath against his cheek, and his body stirred to aching life, just as it always seemed to do in her presence.

The tantalizing stroke of her finger back and forth over the lapel of his coat wasn't helping matters either. He could feel it burning right through the layers of fabric, heating his skin. Every touch, every look reminded him all too powerfully that aside from their brief, unsatisfying interlude in his carriage over a week ago, it had been longer than he cared to remember since he had last indulged himself with a willing woman. And though he could have easily sought out one of his past conquests or visited Madame Desiree's to ease his needs, he knew it would have been little more than an empty release.

It was maddening, frustrating, and impossible for him to comprehend, but it seemed that an emotionless mating was no longer enough for him. He had no desire for any woman other than the one standing before him.

Which made this situation highly volatile, he thought now. At this point, it was far too tempting to convince himself that she meant what she was saying, to swoop her up in his arms and carry her to the bed so that he could proceed to take her up on her invitation. But he couldn't allow himself to be distracted. And he had no intention of letting the luscious Lady Maura know just how much she was affecting him.

Struggling to maintain a stoic countenance, he reached up and captured her wrist, effectively halting the teasing motion of her finger. "Would you care to repeat that?"

At his coolly remote tone, she tilted her head back to meet his gaze, one elegant dark eyebrow flicking upward in question. "Forgive me, my lord. Did I misread the situation? Last night I could have sworn you told me that you wanted me. And this morning you gave every indication that you still did."

Her reminder of that morning had him stiffening in more ways than one. The memory of their lesson, of the feel of her rounded bottom squirming against the most sensitive part of him, sent a shaft of heat spiraling straight to his very core. And recalling the way she had flirted with Lord Cunnington added a hefty dose of possessive jealousy. For the briefest instant, he had actually entertained the notion that the marquis might be her secret suitor, but it hadn't taken him long to dismiss the idea. He refused to believe that Maura would let herself get entangled with one of her mother's former lovers.

Which meant that something else was afoot. Something that involved Cunnington. But what?

"I do want you," he finally admitted, releasing

his hold on her wrist and taking a step back to remove himself from the sensual spell she was weaving about him. "But surely you can understand why I might appear to be a bit skeptical? I was left with the impression that you would rather be boiled in oil than allow a man like me to touch you."

"I know, and I'm sorry for that." Clasping her hands together in front of her, she gave him a repentant look that he couldn't quite bring himself to trust. "It was a defense, as you said. I didn't want to admit what I feel for you. You saw the way everyone behaved at just the sight of the two of us strolling together. Can you imagine the talk it would give rise to should any of them ever discover that we had an . . . interest in each other?"

Oh yes. He could imagine. In fact, he had spent half the long night berating himself for exposing her to further speculation by approaching her. But after seeing her on the arm of the Marquis of Waldron, he hadn't been able to resist.

He shook his head. "Then what changed your mind?"

She gave a shrug and closed the distance he had placed between them, apparently far from dissuaded by his standoffishness. "Perhaps I am tired of constantly trying and failing to please everyone else. Perhaps I want to escape from my tidy little cage and experience all the delights that life has to offer. To forget what society thinks of me and be more like my mother and sister." Her eyes held his, alight with an irresistibly alluring glow. "Perhaps I have decided that you were right and my admirer is not the man to show me the way."

Going up on tiptoe, she pressed against him, the lush curves of her breasts brushing his chest in a titillating fashion as she murmured in his ear. "I want that man to be you, my Lord Hawksley."

Gabriel suppressed a groan. God, how he wanted that to be the truth! The thought of being the first to show her the passion she was capable of, the first to have her in his bed, to be inside her, was a heady prospect. But there was more going on here than met the eye. He could not forget that he had just caught the little baggage searching his room and that this was nothing more than a ploy on her part.

Just how far was she prepared to take this? he wondered grimly.

Crossing his arms, he fought back the over-whelming urge to seize what she was offering with both hands and surveyed her with an expression that he prayed revealed nothing of what was going on in his head. "Convince me."

Maura blinked, the look of tempting challenge on her face fading away to be replaced by one of bemusement. "I beg your pardon?"

"You heard me. Show me how much you want me." He eyed her dispassionately, even as he longed to reach out and touch her. To bring back that wanton look. "I refuse to make love to you, only to have you turn around and accuse me of attempting to seduce you into revealing all of your secrets again. So this time you'll have to make love to me, sweetheart."

He watched as Maura's face paled. It was obvious that he had shocked her, that she hadn't expected him to make such a suggestion. Any second now, she would be backing off, stammering her way through a list of excuses for her reluctance.

But she surprised him.

Her teeth sinking into her lower lip, she faltered for a fraction of an instant, then slowly lifted a trembling hand and laid it on his cheek.

"Show me how," she whispered.

He shuddered as the warmth of her palm seeped into his flesh. Sweet Christ, this woman would be the death of him! "It's easy, sweetheart," he rasped, barely able to hear himself over his pulse pounding in his ears. "Just use your instincts."

"What do I do?"

"Kiss me."

Following his instructions, she once again went up on her toes, pressing a soft, tentative kiss to his lips. It was a mere caress, a feather-light contact, and was over before it had truly begun.

"Is . . . is that all right?" she asked with such diffidence that he couldn't hold back an indulgent smile.

"It will do to start. Try again."

She did, and this time the kiss was longer. But

there was still a timidity that had Gabriel clenching his fists to keep from yanking her into his arms and taking over. She changed the angle several times, nudging his lips fleetingly with her tongue, but didn't seem to know how to go about showing him what she wanted.

When she pulled away from him, she was flushed and panting and clearly frustrated. "I can't do this if you won't cooperate!" she hissed.

Her disgruntled exclamation startled a low chuckle from him. "Remember, sweetheart. You're the one in charge. You have to tell me what you want."

"I want you to kiss me like you did in the carriage."

Thank God! "As you wish."

Cupping her cheek, Gabriel lowered his head to claim her mouth in a voracious kiss. This time it was a thorough and lengthy exchange. They teased, tasted, and devoured each other over and over, their tongues entwining with scorching need. And when they drew back from each other, their lips clung damply.

Maura took an audibly shaky breath before she attempted to speak. "Could . . . could we move to the bed?"

Feeling more than a trifle weak in the knees himself, he nodded. "Of course."

He was never sure how the two of them managed to make it across the room to the bed, where they sank down on the edge of the high mattress. They were both so wrapped up in each other that everything else had become a blur.

Maura's hands rested on his shoulders, and after stringing several more nibbling kisses along the line of his jaw, she let her palms trail down the front of his chest to push at the edges of his coat. "Perhaps if you could take this off . . ." She let her voice trail off suggestively.

He lifted a brow, regarding her through slumberous, half-closed eyes. "Take it off for me."

With fingers that were obviously far from steady, she unfastened the buttons on his coat and pushed the sleeves down his arms before drawing it off with his help. Then she paused for a moment with the material bunched in her hands, staring down at it as if not quite certain what to do with it.

Gabriel felt his heart catch. *Please don't let her be having second thoughts.*

"Maura," he prompted gently.

But when she glanced up at him, her features held no hint of doubt. In fact, she smiled as she laid aside the coat and reached up to loosen his cravat.

"Now let's get you out of that shirt." She drew the words out like a verbal caress, each syllable coinciding with the gradual inching up of the lawn fabric until she was able to pull it off over his head. By the time she finally put her hands on his bare chest, he was ready to jump out of his skin. Her fingers traced the hard muscles of his pectorals, the rippled contours of his abdomen, with loving attention to detail.

"I didn't know a man could be so beautiful."

He gave a choked laugh at her awed-sounding observation, then covered her hand with his, trapping it against the unsteady beat of his heart. "Oh, sweetheart, men aren't supposed to be beautiful." His free hand lifted to skim over the curve of her cheek, his touch rife with a reverence of its own. "But you . . . I've never seen anyone so lovely. You are utter perfection."

And she was. With her lips swollen and red from his kisses and her blue eyes sparkling with a fervent light, she was gloriously alive in a way that illuminated her beauty from the inside out.

But she didn't seem convinced. Something shadowy shifted in the depths of her eyes, and she shook her head. "I'm sure you've said that to every woman you've slept with."

He tilted her chin up with his knuckles, unwilling to let her dismiss him so casually. "But this is the first time I've said it and meant it."

The truth of that statement was enough to frighten even him.

Their lips met in another devastating give-and-take that seemed to last for a small eternity. Gabriel's tongue plunged deep into her mouth, stroking and exploring, and Maura came up on her knees on the mattress, wrapping her arms around his neck and tangling her fingers in his hair so that she could return the kiss with equal ardor. And when his lips left hers and blazed a path down the pale column of her throat, nuzzling the pulse point just above the lace of her ruffled collar, he felt her shiver against him.

"Please," she urged, her head falling back to give him better access. "Please, Hawksley."

"Please what, sweetheart? You have to tell me what you want, remember?"

"Touch me."

Gabriel was only too happy to oblige, and his palms slid down over her shoulders to tenderly cup her breasts through the fabric of her gown, his thumbs sweeping over her rapidly hardening nipples in small, tormenting circles. "Like this?"

"Mmmm. Oh yes . . ."

Driven onward by her sighs, he deftly undid her gown, tugging one sleeve down her arm along with the strap of her chemise so he could nip delicately at the bare upper curve of her breast.

She gave a quavering moan, and the next thing he knew, she had shoved him back on the bed and moved to straddle him, her skirts bunched up around her thighs, revealing pale, smooth, mouth-watering skin above the sheerness of her stockings. The move staggered him, as did the bold intent in her gaze. With her hair wild about her shoulders and the bodice of her gown sliding down so that the tops of her breasts mounded above the material, she was as far removed from the prim and demure society miss as a pagan goddess from a vestal virgin.

Every time he thought he knew what to expect from this maddening, mercurial female, she managed to knock him off balance.

"I thought I was supposed to make love to you," she said throatily, gliding her hands over his chest once more. But when her fingers reached the waistband of his breeches, she paused, peeking up at him from under her lashes with just the slightest hint of hesitancy. "You've been with so many women. Women who know how to please you. Tell me what to do so that I can please you too."

"Sweetheart, anything you do will please me."

The smile she gave him in response to that was a reward in itself. But when she leaned forward to cup the hard, swollen length of his shaft through the material of his breeches, he knew he'd died and gone to heaven. His hips bucked and he made an inarticulate sound, his hands fisting in the bedclothes as she stroked and molded him with questing fingers.

"Do you believe me now?"

At first Gabriel was so lost in arousal, so centered on that teasing touch, that he wasn't positive he had heard her correctly. But as soon as her words came together to make some sort of sense, he went numb. The knowing query rang like a death knell in his mind.

How could he have let himself forget for a moment that this was only her way of outmaneuvering him?

Immediately he snagged her wrist, stilling her inciting caresses, and his warning emerged through gritted teeth. "Maura, whatever game you are playing, whatever this is in aid of, it's about to go too far. You might want to think about that before you keep doing what you're doing. This is something you can't take back."

Their eyes locked for a long, drawn-out moment. Her face turning an alarming shade of white, she gave a strangled cry and jerked her hand from his grasp, scrambling from her position atop him as she held the sagging bodice of her gown in place.

"Please turn around."

"Maura—"

"Please!"

Her tearful command shook him, so he complied, listening to the soft rustle of cloth from behind him as she put her clothing back into some semblance of order. It was followed by a short beat of silence.

And then the slamming of the door.

Damnation!

Lunging to his feet, Gabriel crossed the room with a few long, furious strides and flung open the panel. But by the time he poked his head out into the hallway, she was gone.

With a growled imprecation, he raked both hands through his hair and swung back into the chamber. He should have known better than to turn his back on her. Now he would never know what she had been doing here. Not to mention that this was the second encounter with her when he had been left aching and unfulfilled. It was enough to make a man wish he were a eunuch.

It was as he stood there, brooding, that he noticed that his coat lay on the floor near the door, and he picked it up rather absently. He could have sworn that Maura had laid it on the bed after she had taken it off him, so what was it doing lying on the rug halfway across the room?

Wait a minute . . .

Struck by a sudden possibility, he slid his fingers into the pocket of his coat. It took him less than a second to ascertain that he had been correct. It was gone. There was no crinkle of paper. Nothing.

What the bloody hell did she want with Cunnington's IOU?

# Chapter 16

"*At the opera last night, Philip and I somehow became separated in the crush at intermission. I found him chatting with a group of gentlemen in the foyer, and I approached just in time to hear one of them say something extremely insulting about me. I waited for my husband to rush to my defense as he has so often in the past, to call the man out, but he said not a word. In that instant, I discovered what it meant to have a broken heart.*"

From the diary of Elise Marchand,
March 24, 1810

The handwriting didn't match.

Sick with dismay, Maura stared down at the IOU she held clutched in her hands, unable to bring herself to accept what her eyes were telling her. She had been so sure. But once again, she had been wrong. The differences were so glaringly apparent that she didn't even need to take out the letter for comparison.

Cunnington hadn't written the threatening missives to her mother.

The words blurred and wavered before Maura as tears misted her vision. Her last hope was gone.

Crumpling the paper in her fist, she sank down onto the bed in her chamber. She was at an utter loss. She had believed so strongly that Lady Albright's killer had to be one of the three men on her list that she hadn't even let herself consider any other possibilities. She supposed all she could do now was wait and see if Violet had been able to turn up any information or additional suspects after questioning her contacts at the theater. Otherwise she was at the end of the road.

A tear slipped free and trailed down her cheek, and she quickly brushed it away. After everything she had been through in the last few weeks, the crushing disappointment was almost more than she could bear. How she had longed to be the one to place her mother's diary in her father's hands, along with the answer to the mystery of who had been responsible for her death. But now it seemed that was not to be.

A sudden stirring from the dressing room that connected her guest chamber to Lady Olivia's alerted her to the fact that her aunt had risen from her nap and would more than likely soon be seeking her out. Not wanting to listen to any more lectures or make any explanations for her tearstained face, Maura decided it would be for the best if she beat a hasty retreat. If she could just get away from the house for a short while, perhaps go for a walk about the grounds and clear her head, she would feel better prepared to face everyone once it was time to return and ready herself for the ball this evening.

Hesitating, she glanced down at the IOU once more. Her convulsive grip had torn a hole in one corner of the paper. Sooner or later she would have to find a way to return it to Hawksley's room, but the thought of doing so now filled her with a panic that threatened to overwhelm her. No, she couldn't do it now and risk running into him again.

Not after what she'd done.

Her cheeks warmed as she recalled her behavior. Heavens, but she had played the part of seductress so well that she had been in danger of forgetting that it was only a role. There had been something wildly intoxicating in taking control of their lovemaking, and it had unleashed a wanton side of her nature that she hadn't even known she possessed. With the earl's glittering green eyes urging her on and his long, lean body bare to her gaze, spread out on the bed before her, she hadn't been able to resist the temptation to explore his masculine perfection. His skin had been so smooth and sleek under her palms, stretched over muscles like tempered steel.

And he had wanted her. There could be no denying that. She had seen the evidence of it. Felt the heat and hardness of it through his breeches. The savage need that had marked his handsome features had compelled her to keep stroking, to keep caressing that pulsating length until she had given him the same rush of mindless, scalding pleasure that he had given her that night in the carriage.

Thank goodness he had finally made a move to stop her, to call her on her actions. If he had remained silent, there was no telling what could have happened. She might have . . . might have . . .

But she wouldn't let herself think about that. She had to get out of here before her aunt came in and cornered her.

Smoothing out the crinkled IOU, she tucked it into her mother's diary along with the letters and packed it away in her traveling valise, then hastily quit the chamber.

Outside, the sun had finally peeked out from behind the clouds, and the younger set was playing a game of croquet on the south lawn, their laughter carrying on the breeze. A small group of ladies, the duchess among them, observed the proceedings from the stone terrace that overlooked the gardens, so Maura instantly discarded her idea of a stroll among the flowers. Instead she set off along the path that led down the slope on the north side of the house. Long and meandering, it wound its way past the carriage house and stables, through a short stretch of woodland, and ended near the lake that bordered the Maitland property.

It was quite a distance, but she didn't mind. Here, away from the condemning stares of the other party guests, she felt lighter, more carefree. There was no one to whisper or point an accusing finger, no one to judge her or find her lacking. With the house out of sight on the other side of the trees and the sparkling surface of the lake dappled with dancing prisms of sunlight, it was if she were in a magical world of her own. All was quiet except for the chirping of birds and an occasional quack from the family of ducks who waddled through the reeds at the water's edge.

It was perfect, and Maura couldn't help but think that this must have been the sort of contentment her mother had felt when they had all still lived in their little cottage in Dorset, back before their lives had been so cruelly torn apart.

All too soon, however, her peaceful idyll was shattered. Becoming aware of hoofbeats on the path behind her, she stopped walking and whirled about just in time to see a large chestnut gelding bearing down on her, Lord Stratton on its back.

Just before he reached her, he pulled up sharply, causing his horse to rear and paw the air several times before he managed to bring the animal back under control.

"Well, well." He drawled the words in an insolent tone as he scrutinized her from underneath lowered brows. "It seems that I have stumbled upon a wood sprite."

Maura tried her best to appear calm in the face of her apprehension. This vile man was the last person she wanted to see, for bad things happened whenever she had the misfortune to end up alone in his presence. But she had no intention of letting him know just how much he frightened her.

"Lord Stratton."

"Lady Maura. I trust you are enjoying your stroll?"

"I was, yes. But I fear it is much later than I had suspected, and I need to return to the house if I am to make ready for the ball. So, if you will excuse me."

She moved to walk by him, her heart pounding, but he halted her by swinging down from the saddle directly in her path.

"One moment, my lady." The cold smile that curved those thin lips didn't quite reach his eyes. "You know, if you keep insisting on rushing off whenever I come near you, I could be excused for thinking you were trying to avoid my company."

Backing away, she wrapped her arms protectively about herself and regarded him with trepidation. She didn't know what he was up to, but she absolutely refused to take part in one of his verbal games. He knew very well why she stayed away from him.

"And if I were? Could I be blamed for that, my

lord? You haven't precisely proved yourself to be the most pleasant companion in the past."

"And Lord Hawksley has?"

That succeeded in freezing her in her tracks. Her mouth went dry, and she had to force her reply past the lump in her throat. "I'm sure I don't know what you mean."

"Of course you do." Tethering his horse to the branch of a nearby tree, Stratton sauntered forward, tapping his riding crop carelessly against his boot as he closed the distance she had placed between them. His icy stare never wavered from her face. "You needn't play coy. No one missed the little scene between the two of you in the parlor last night. And this morning in the billiard room, you both appeared to be very cozy."

"It was nothing."

"And was your visit to his chamber earlier this afternoon nothing?"

Despite Maura's best efforts, her stunned reaction to his knowing query must have shown in her expression, for he gave a malicious smirk.

"That's right. I saw you come running from his room. And I must say, my dear, you looked a bit worse for wear. Hair falling down, cheeks flushed, lips swollen. I think I would be safe in assuming that you weren't discussing the weather."

He shook his head, sending her a look of mock reproach. "Really, Lady Maura. Stringing along Lord Waldron. Flirting with Lord Cunnington.

And now it seems you have crawled into bed with the son of a murderer. You've turned into quite the Jezebel. But then I suppose I shouldn't be surprised, given who your mother was. I've known all along that your prim and proper act wouldn't last, and I only had to bide my time."

Maura drew herself up, her temper igniting at his insinuations. "You don't know what you're talking about."

His features suddenly hardening into a mask of hostile resentment, he reached out and snared her arm with a speed that startled a gasp from her. "Don't I? Believe me, I expect I would know better than most. Your trollop of a mother used what was between her legs to lead my father around by the nose, leaving him to pant at her heels for whatever scraps of attention she was willing to fling in his direction. She flaunted herself like a bitch in heat, and she wasn't content until she had every male in her vicinity under her spell." He gave her a shake that was far from gentle and leaned in toward her, his voice a harsh rasp in her ear. "But I won't be led, and I won't wait any longer. If you're doling it out, I want my share, and I intend to take it now."

Outraged that he would once again dare to put his hands on her in such way, Maura fought against his hold. "Let me go!"

"Make me, my lady."

With one particularly vigorous yank, she succeeded in freeing herself from his grasp. But the impetus of it sent her flying backward, knocking her off balance. Her bottom landed in the dust with a teeth-jarring thud, and she sat with her legs stretched out before her, stunned and winded.

Stratton's laughter held a chilling note of menace as he cast aside his riding crop and stalked toward her, working at the laces on his breeches as he advanced. "Isn't that appropriate? A whore on her back in the dirt, where she belongs."

The evil intent glittering in those cruel eyes sent Maura's fear spiraling into pure, heart-stopping terror, and she started to scramble backward as fast as she could. But her skirts hampered her progress, and she didn't get very far before her tormentor caught up to her. Bending over to seize her by the ankle, he covered her with his wiry body in one swift motion, pinning her in place.

She screamed, thrashing out in an attempt to get away and pushing at his shoulders with all her might, but he held her with very little effort. The hand on her ankle tightened, biting painfully into her skin, then slid upward to toss up her skirts, even as his other hand continued to fumble to free himself from his breeches.

*Please!* Maura thought wildly. *Someone please help me!*

And then, like an answer to a prayer, her attacker was gone.

Struggling to regain her breath, she pushed her tumbled hair out of her eyes and managed to lever herself to a sitting position, only to be greeted by an altogether unexpected sight. Lord Stratton lay sprawled several feet away, half in and half out of the water at the lake's edge, one hand cradling his rapidly swelling jaw.

A tall, broad-shouldered figure loomed over him. Hawksley.

The earl stood over Stratton like an avenging angel, his muscular frame practically vibrating with the force of his anger and his green eyes blazing with fury.

"You son of a bitch," he spat, the words emerging from between gritted teeth. "I ought to kill you right now for putting your hands on her."

Wincing, Stratton propped himself up on an elbow and dabbed at a glob of mud that ran down his cheek with the sleeve of his coat. "Really, Hawksley, this is becoming a bit of a habit, isn't it? I must say, your insistence on playing the white knight of late is rather puzzling, considering your own reputation when it comes to the fair ladies of the ton." He jerked his head in Maura's direction. "And in this case, I'm afraid your heroics are sadly misplaced. You're not the only one to dip your cock in that honey pot. But then you've had occasion to find that out for yourself, haven't you?"

A soft, feral growl rumbled up from deep in Hawksley's chest, and he took a threatening step toward the other man. "Get up, Stratton, so I can knock you back down."

Maura noticed the brief flare of alarm that flashed in Stratton's eyes before he swiftly veiled them and lurched to his feet, confronting the earl with his hands balled into fists.

"You won't touch me, Hawksley," he said scornfully. "Do you know why? If you do, I will make sure to spread the tale of your little afternoon assignation with the Lady Maura all over Rosemont Hall. I'm sure the duke and duchess's guests would enjoy hearing about her visit to your room, from which she emerged looking flushed and well tumbled." Crossing his arms, he tilted his head to contemplate his opponent with a brow arched in taunting challenge. "But then maybe that doesn't matter to you. Maybe bedding the daughter of the infamous Lady Albright will only add to your reputation as a whoremonger. But we both know that Lady Maura's life will be destroyed."

His mouth tightening into a grim line, Hawksley visibly stiffened. "You bloody bastard."

"So it does matter!" The snarled response elicited a derisive sneer from Stratton. "You fool, you've gone and fallen for the little harlot, haven't you? I never would have believed it was possible. The Devil's Own in love with the spawn of London's most notorious Jezebel." He paused, casting a scathing and venom-laced glare at Maura, and something shifted in his expression. Something dark and unreadable that wrung a shiver from her. "But then the women in that family do tend to have that effect. They lead a man into sin against his better judgment, tease and torment him, then open their legs for the next male in line like a common strumpet."

In a move so swift it was almost a blur, Hawksley caught the other man by the lapels of his sodden coat and drew him up onto his toes, his face a mask of rage, and Maura felt her blood run cold. Dear God, if she didn't do something, they were going to go for each other's throats like a pair of rabid dogs. And for some unfathomable reason she didn't care to contemplate, she couldn't stand the thought of the earl getting hurt because of her.

She called out pleadingly, unable to hide the anxious quiver in her voice, "Hawksley, don't. He isn't worth it."

Her admonition halted the earl in place, and he glanced back over his shoulder at her, a muscle flexing in his jaw. Several long seconds ticked by while he dangled Stratton like a limp puppet. Then, with a muttered imprecation, he lowered the man to the ground.

"Get on your horse and get out of here," he barked, propelling Stratton in the direction of his mount with a hard shove. "And if you're wise, you'll keep your mouth shut about the Lady Maura. For the sake of our fathers' past friendship, I would hate to have to call you out for maligning an innocent female's reputation, but I will if I hear so much as one whisper regarding anything you think you saw. I'm sure I needn't remind you that I'm a crack shot."

Stratton leveled him with a fierce glower, as if still debating his chances in a toe-to-toe match with the larger man. But he finally turned, stalked to his horse, and swung himself up into the saddle. Spurring the animal with the nudge of a boot heel, he cantered off back the way he had come.

As soon as he had disappeared down the trail, Hawksley whipped about and crossed to Maura's side with a few long, ground-eating strides, his features now drawn taut in concern.

He knelt next to her. "Are you all right? Did he hurt you?" he asked huskily.

She stifled the hysterical urge to laugh. Was she hurt? Not any worse than usual, she supposed. Perhaps she had simply grown used to being pawed, groped, and tossed about at will. Inured to it, so to speak.

Something told her Hawksley wouldn't appreciate that observation, however, so instead of voicing her thoughts aloud, she released a shuddering sigh and swiped a few more tangled curls from her forehead. "No. I'm fine. I'm just a bit shaken up, that's all." She smoothed down her skirts as best she could, peering up at him hesitantly through lowered lashes. For some reason, she couldn't bring herself to fully meet his gaze. Never could she remember feeling so humiliated or ineffectual. "If you wouldn't mind helping me up?"

He didn't hesitate, but placed a gentle hand under her elbow and guided her to a standing position. But as soon as he started to release her, she felt the blood rush from her head, and she swayed on her feet.

"A bloody pox on this!"

The exclamation exploded from the earl with vehemence, and the next thing Maura knew, he had swept her up into his arms and was carrying her.

"Hawksley—"

"Shhh."

"But Hawksley—"

"Gabriel."

The single, gruff word stilled her tongue for an instant, and she blinked up at him in consternation. "What?"

"My name is Gabriel."

Gabriel. Not Lucifer, as she had once speculated. Somehow it was fitting. After all, what else would the man who appeared set on becoming her guardian angel be called?

The tension slowly seeped out of her body, and she allowed herself to settle back for a fleeting moment, to enjoy the feeling of being held, safe and warm, in his arms. He was bearing her toward a small, octagonal gazebo she hadn't noticed before, nestled just off the path in a small clearing. Though it was still within view of the lake, it was partially concealed from prying eyes by a surrounding screen of trees and flowering bushes.

Despite her added weight, he handled the steps of the structure with ease and placed her carefully on one of the cushioned benches. Then he took up a stance against the railing next to her, his countenance inscrutable.

Squirming under that intense regard, Maura threaded her fingers together in her lap and cleared her throat. "It seems that I owe you my thanks once again," she ventured. "I suppose you followed me from the house?"

He didn't speak, only inclined his head in a stiff nod.

"I should probably thank you for that as well. Here I've been trying to make you stay away from me for weeks, and now it turns out that I should be grateful you didn't listen." Moisture blurred her vision and she looked down at the gazebo's wooden floor, refusing to let him see her weakness. A sudden trembling had seized her small frame, and no matter how hard she tried to stop it, it only became more pronounced with every second that passed. "Aren't you going to deliver me a lecture? Scold me for wandering off alone again? Tell me I deserved that wretched man's pawing?"

To her amazement, Hawksley sank down on the bench next to her and covered her shaking hands with his. "No, I'm not. Because no matter what that bastard said to you, Maura, you didn't deserve what he did. None of it."

Her wide eyes jerked up to meet his. Though his

gaze was still rife with anger and frustration, there was also a genuine caring and compassion that she couldn't mistake.

"I wanted to throttle him within an inch of his miserable life," he finished roughly.

His honesty tore something loose inside her, and a sob ripped up from the depths of her, twisting and tearing at her throat like jagged shards of glass.

"All I wanted was to get away from the whispers and assumptions," she choked, her fingers grasping his. "But it follows me. Wherever I go, it follows me." A tear spilled down her cheek and dripped onto the back of her hand, but she didn't even notice as she looked at him imploringly. "He called me a harlot. But I swear to you, I'm not . . . I haven't . . ."

"Shhh." Hawksley lifted a finger to her lips, halting the flow of words. "I know, sweetheart."

"But how can you possibly know? After what happened in your room earlier, you probably believe every word Stratton said."

A small smile curved that chiseled mouth. "Remember that night, in the carriage? There are ways a man can tell when a woman is still innocent, Maura." He paused, then lifted his hand from her lips to cup her cheek, holding her still as his expression hardened. "But whatever it is you're trying to accomplish, you're playing a dangerous game, and I can't let you put me off anymore. I have to know—I need to know—what it is. Now."

# Chapter 17

*"I have come to a decision. After a year of struggling to win the ton's approval, of trying to be the perfect marchioness for the sake of my husband, I am finished attempting to be something I am not. What have my efforts gained me? Philip and I have drifted apart, and he no longer seems to care what I do. So why not behave exactly as I like? Society be damned!"*

From the diary of Elise Marchand,
May 2, 1810

Maura stiffened under his caress, her first instinct to pull away and escape from the interrogation she knew was coming. But she managed to remain still, though her gaze skated away from his nervously. "I don't know what you mean."

"Don't." Despite the softness of his voice, the

one word held a sharpness, an urgency that brought her eyes back to his face in spite of herself. "Don't do that. Don't lie to me."

"I'm not."

"You are!" Dropping his hand, the earl rose from the bench and stared down at her in renewed irritation. "Maura, contrary to your opinion of me, I do not lack intelligence. I caught you searching my room, and now Lord Cunnington's IOU is missing. I would have to be thick indeed to believe that you are not involved in something you shouldn't be." He paused, the little muscle in his jaw that was such a good indicator of his current mood leaping before he continued in a low, grating tone. "Tell me Stratton isn't your secret admirer."

Maura didn't know whether to laugh or be insulted. As if she would ever have anything to do with the likes of Stratton! Even if he wasn't an odious toad, there was something about the man that terrified her, and there was an underlying viciousness in the way he treated her that had led her to wonder on more than one occasion why he seemed to hate her so much. "Of course not!"

The relief that marked Hawksley's features was profound. "Thank God," he breathed, relaxing somewhat and reaching up to rub wearily at the back of his neck. "But that still doesn't answer all of my questions. You must see that this can't continue. Whoever this admirer is, he is obviously driving you to do things that can only lead to trouble."

His patronizing manner rubbed her on the raw, and the revelation burst from her lips before she could call it back. "Drat it, Hawksley, there is no secret admirer!"

"What?"

Maura bit the inside of her cheek so hard, she was surprised she didn't draw blood. But it was too late to regret the slip now. "You heard me. I have no secret admirer. The letter you found wasn't written to me."

The earl went rigid, every muscle in his body visibly tensing. Then he pivoted and stalked over to the railing, his back to her as he peered out through the veil of surrounding trees toward the lake. Maura waited with bated breath as several seconds of ringing silence ticked by.

Just when she was beginning to think he wasn't going to say anything, he spoke over his shoulder, sounding oddly choked. "It was killing me, to think that you might be—that you might let someone else—" He stumbled to a halt and turned, his eyes blazing at her across the short distance he had put between them. "Then where did you get the letter? Who wrote it and to whom does it belong?"

She shook her head. She had no idea what to tell him. If she admitted it was her mother's, she would have to go into the whole story, and she wasn't certain she was ready for that yet.

When she didn't reply, he pounded a fist against the railing, the blow causing the entire structure to shake. "Damnation, Maura, whatever it is you are trying to do, you're risking your reputation for it. What is so important that you would jeopardize your future in such a way?"

Unable to stay still any longer, she lunged to her feet and began to pace before him, her agitated steps carrying her from one end of the gazebo to the other. "What does it matter what I do?" she cried. "I've tried so hard to prove to them all that I am not what they think. None of it has changed their opinion of me in the slightest. So if I'm going to be condemned for crimes I haven't even committed, why not live up to their expectations?"

She heard him move away from the railing, and as she swept by him, he reached out and caught her by the arm, gently but inexorably turning her to face him. "Because that's not who you are."

"You don't know that. You don't know me."

"I do know you. Better than you think. And it's not that easy, Maura. It won't take the pain away."

The tears that still lurked so close to the surface threatened her composure once again, and she lifted a hand to dash one away before it could overflow. "You don't understand. You don't know what it's like."

The earl's visage darkened and he gave her a little shake. "Wait just a moment. Do you honestly think you are the only one who has ever been judged unfairly?"

"No, but—"

He didn't let her finish, but set her from him and strode back to the railing to stand with his head bent. He appeared to be struggling to come to grips with something, and when he glanced up again, the combination of pain and torment that marked his features startled her.

"From the time I was a boy, people looked at me and saw my father," he told her, the obvious turmoil that seethed just beneath the surface of his words making his voice gruff. "Society wrote me off as a future drunkard and philanderer before I even reached manhood, and it didn't seem to matter when I protested that being like him was the last thing I wanted. I hated him with every breath in my body. For the nights he came home smelling like liquor and perfume and made my mother cry. For the times my mother begged and pleaded with him for just one small crumb of his affection, only to have him turn his back on her and walk away. I was determined that I was going to be nothing like him."

He swallowed hard and swept off his hat, tossing it onto the bench and raking one hand back through his hair as if he needed a minute to collect himself before returning to his tale. "But there were those damnable expectations. The members of the ton watched me like vultures. Every time I had a bit too much to drink or flirted with a pretty young lady at a social event, it was my father in me coming out. Whenever I threw in my lot with the rest of the lads at school and indulged in some sort of mischievous prank or reckless pursuit, it was my wild blood showing itself. They were calling me the Devil's Own before I even earned the name."

Maura winced. And she was one of the ones who had decided without even truly knowing him that the name suited. Her heart bled for him, for she was well aware that he was exposing to her a vulnerable part of himself that he had more than likely never exposed to anyone else. It was clear that the strife between his parents had affected him deeply, just as the battles between her own mother and father had affected her.

Perhaps she should at least tell him what she knew about his parents' relationship. Why the late earl had turned to her mother for comfort. Surely he deserved to know that much?

"After a while," he went on, oblivious to her momentary preoccupation, "I got tired of fighting it. It was too exhausting to try and disabuse them of their opinions. So I made up my mind that if they wanted a devil, that was exactly what I would give them." He looked over at her, a plethora of emotions swirling in the green depths of his eyes. "But for the most part, it's a façade, Maura, no matter how it looks. Oh, I played the role to the hilt, and I'm far from innocent. But I'm not the devil everyone thinks me."

He moved back to her side, lifting a hand to

brush a stray tendril of hair away from her cheek. "So, you see, I do understand. Better than anyone else ever could. That's why I know that striking out in such a way doesn't solve anything. In the end, it only makes you more unhappy, more dissatisfied, because you aren't being true to yourself. And it's a very lonely state in which to live."

A lump filled Maura's throat. How often had she lamented her own feelings of isolation and alienation? Even with Jilly and Aimee, she had always felt apart from them somehow. Oh, she didn't doubt that they loved her, but perhaps because she had placed importance on things that weren't nearly as important to them, the two of them shared a closeness that didn't include her.

As if reading her mind, Hawksley spoke again, echoing her thoughts aloud. "I'd become so cut off from everyone, Maura, so apart from it all. Nothing really mattered to me anymore. Until the night you wandered into Lord Grafton's study and changed everything." His thumb skimmed over her lower lip, then tilted her chin upward until their gazes met. "For the first time, I felt a connection with someone. I felt as if I had met someone who could truly understand me."

She had felt that connection as well, Maura recalled now. That instant of powerful bonding. It had left her troubled and shaken. Over the last several months, she had fought it, tried to deny it. But it was still there, all the same.

"You're not your mother, Maura, and I'm not my father. Whatever happened with them has nothing to do with us. I see that now. I only wish you could see it too."

She reached up to capture his hand, holding it against her cheek as she peered up at him beseechingly. "I do. I just . . . I don't understand. It doesn't make sense. I have given you no reason to keep pursuing me. I lash out at you and push you away, yet you keep rescuing me. You keep coming back. Why?"

"I wish I knew the answer to that." Leaning in toward her, he rested his forehead against hers and settled his hands on the rounded curve of her hips to pull her closer to him. The heat radiating from his tautly muscled frame seared her like a brand. "I only know that I want you. And I can't seem to stay away."

A tingle of awareness raced through her veins at his confession. "S-surely you've wanted women before? How does that make me special?"

"I don't know. I only know that you *are* special." He pressed his mouth to her temple in a brief caress, a fleeting benediction. "And yes, I've wanted women before, but never like this. This is something . . . more."

"More?"

It was a mere breath of sound, but he heard her and drew back, bestowing upon her an indulgent smile. "More," he confirmed huskily.

Maura's pulse picked up speed and her mouth went dry with unmistakable need. If she was honest with herself, she could no longer deny that she felt the same way. Why continue to fight something that she longed for with every beat of her heart?

In a slow, tentative motion, she raised her arms to wind them about his neck. "I want you too . . . Gabriel."

Her shy admission was followed by a sudden, shocked hush. Then, as she anxiously awaited his reaction, Hawksley's nostrils flared and a tide of hectic color washed into his high cheekbones.

"Do you mean it?" he murmured hoarsely. "Are you sure?"

She nodded. "I don't think I've ever been so sure of anything."

The next thing she knew, they were locked together in a passionate embrace, his mouth on hers, warm and soft and urgent. And she was kissing him back just as ardently. Over and over, they devoured each other, their tongues entwining, mating hungrily, until Maura's legs threatened to buckle beneath her and she was forced to cling to him for support.

And suddenly she was floating, swept off her feet for the second time in as many hours as he cradled her in his strong arms and bore her to the padded bench. There he lowered her onto the seat and followed her down, pressing her back into the cushions even as they continued to exchange kisses and caresses.

Maura's head was spinning as she reveled in the weight of him atop her. He felt so good. Their bodies melded, a perfect fit, yet she couldn't seem to get close enough, and she was desperate to touch his bare skin.

Her hands left his shoulders, and her trembling fingers yanked at his cravat, parting the snowy folds. Then, tearing her lips from his, she trailed them down the line of his jaw to the strong column of his throat. The flesh there was smooth and sunbrowned and tasted slightly salty, and she felt his Adam's apple move convulsively under the damp glide of her tongue before he pulled back with a groan.

"Maura." Cupping her face in his hands, he held her still so he could look down at her, his penetrating stare scrutinizing every inch of her features, as if he were trying to discern her very thoughts. "I don't want you to regret anything that happens between us. If this truly isn't something you want, if there's a chance you might be sorry afterward, maybe we should stop now before it's too late."

"No!" Afraid that he really meant to call a halt, she clutched at him, her fingers digging into his biceps. "Please don't stop. I want you to make love to me."

"Sweetheart, someone might stumble upon us at

any moment. And you deserve so much more than a hasty toss out in the open. It's your first time. You should have a comfortable bed and satin sheets, not a hard, padded bench and—"

"I don't care about all of that!" she burst out, attempting to convey the depth of her need. "I'm so tired of being alone. I need to be with you. I need to feel you inside me."

Apparently her words were enough to convince him, for he shuddered and threaded his fingers through her hair so he could seize her lips in another devastating, soul-stirring exchange. And from that point on, they were lost in a world of sensation where nothing else mattered except pleasing each other, and time itself ceased to exist.

Amid deep, tongue-thrusting kisses that merged one into another, Maura managed to undo the buttons on Hawksley's coat and push it from his wide shoulders, just as he went to work on the lacings of her gown. Loosening her bodice, he tugged it down to bare her breasts to the cool air and his avid gaze. The rosy nipples hardened instantly, and he grazed one with his knuckles before cupping the ripe, creamy globe in his palm, plumping it up so he could brush his lips reverently over the high, rounded upper curve. Then, with a harsh, guttural groan, he latched on to the swollen, aching tip, drawing it into the heated cavern of his mouth, suckling at her fiercely.

Maura arched under his ministrations. The feel

of his hot, wet mouth on her breast, of his tongue lashing and laving the distended peak, was almost more than she could bear. Letting out a wavering cry, she tangled her fingers in the hair at the nape of his neck and held him to her as her head fell back and her eyes drifted shut . . .

And for some reason, a mental image of Hawksley doing the same thing to the blond and beautiful Lady Lanscombe flickered behind her closed lids. The vision stabbed at her like a knife. All too easily, she could recall the way the viscountess had pressed herself so provocatively against him the night before, those tapered fingers resting on his arm in such a possessive manner, and it was enough to send a wave of pain and jealousy crashing over her.

"I wish I were more experienced," she murmured next to his ear, her voice barely above a whisper. "Like the other women you've been with. Like Lady Lanscombe."

The earl relinquished her nipple and gave a low, desire-roughened chuckle, passing his thumb over the engorged tip before meeting her eyes with earnest warmth. "Sweetheart, it may be hypocritical of me, but I'm ecstatic that you aren't experienced. And Lady Lanscombe couldn't hold a candle to you." He hesitated, his expression suddenly serious. "Just so you know, I've never been with her. I won't lie and tell you I've never lain with another woman, but she wasn't one of them."

Maura felt a surge of relief. "Good. I wanted to tear her hair out."

"Bloodthirsty minx." He smiled at her, then slid one hand up under her skirts, stroking his palm over her calf before traveling upward to the pale flesh of her thigh just above her stocking. "Are you really sure, sweetheart? After what you've been through this afternoon with Stratton—"

She hushed him with another kiss. "You aren't Stratton. And I'm sure."

Taking him by the wrist, she guided his hand to the slit in her drawers. And from there he took over, delving into the thatch of curls that guarded the entrance to her feminine channel. Gently his fingers explored her velvet heat, sliding just inside the entrance to test how ready she was, his thumb brushing over the quivering, sensitive bud of her clitoris.

She hissed, her hips bucking at the tantalizing contact.

"You're so tight, so wet, sweetheart," he rasped. "I can feel your juices coating my finger. Like thick, rich honey."

He reached down to unlace his breeches and fit himself to the cradle of her thighs, that rigid, throbbing part of him that she had explored earlier sliding between her slick folds. But she felt no fear at the foreignness of it, only a restless, aching need.

He reared up, his eyes glittering down at her with a molten glow. "Only a little pain, sweetheart," he murmured tenderly. "Then nothing but pleasure. I promise."

With that, he entered her, filling her inch by inch, stretching her narrow passage gradually with his steel-hard thickness. Then, with an inarticulate sound, he flexed his hips and plunged deep. She gasped and bit her lip as she absorbed the shock of his invasion, aware that he was holding himself still above her, allowing her time to get past the pain.

For several seconds he hovered there, his face taut with strain. But when she finally relaxed a bit underneath him, he began to glide in and out, setting up a steady rhythm. With each earth-shattering stroke, the burning sensation faded to be replaced by a marvelous feeling of fullness, and her eyes went wide with wonder. Splaying her palms over the broad expanse of his back, she could feel the powerful flex of his muscles under the lawn of his shirt, bunching with every thrust, and she wrapped her legs around his pistoning hips in an attempt to bring him closer, to capture the elusive feeling that was building inside her.

They climbed the precipice together, slowly, thrillingly, until a sensation as powerful as anything she had ever felt before cascaded over Maura, carrying her with it, sending her flying in an explosion of such intensity that she was sure she could touch the very stars.

"Gabriel!"

A second later, he followed her over the edge, and she felt the scalding hot splash of his release as his lean body shuddered and quaked against her.

Afterward, they lay cradled in each other's arms, their breathing slowly returning to normal. Hawksley's hands caressed her hair, smoothed over her back, soothing her.

And once all was quiet, he cleared his throat and spoke hoarsely.

"Maura, as wonderful as that was, I haven't forgotten that our conversation isn't over. It can't be. Especially not now. I have to know what's going on."

"I— . . ." She paused, biting her lip. After all they had shared, she wanted to tell him. But no matter what had happened between them, she wasn't quite prepared to reveal everything. Not yet. There was so much to consider, and she needed to think.

"I need time, Gabriel. Just give me a little more time."

# Chapter 18

❦

*"I have renewed my acquaintance with
several gentlemen from my former circle
of intimate admirers: Lords Lanscombe,
Bedford, and Cunnington. It is flattering
to be wanted and admired once again, but
though they have all made it clear that
they would gladly indulge in an affair
with me, I cannot bring myself to cross
that line. Despite the chasm that exists
between us, I still love my husband."*

From the diary of Elise Marchand,
June 11, 1810

**T**he pale light of the moon shone down from
the velvety night sky, bathing Rosemont
Hall's manicured gardens in a softly luminescent
glow. From his perch on the low stone balustrade,
Gabriel stared out over the almost unearthly pan-

orama, basking in the peacefulness of his surroundings. The lilting strains of orchestra music drifted through the French doors that stood open behind him, and he could hear the animated voices of the guests assembled in the ballroom, but as of yet no one had wandered out onto the terrace to disturb his solitude.

Somewhere inside, among the throngs of people milling about the dance floor, was the woman who had occupied his thoughts to the exclusion of all else.

The woman he had made love to earlier that afternoon.

Rolling his shoulders to relieve some of the tension that had settled over him, he let his eyes fall shut and savored the feel of the evening breeze as it caressed his face. This was certain to complicate things, and he had no trouble admitting it. Never mind all the promises he had made to himself so long ago to avoid ever placing himself at any woman's mercy. These damnable feelings for Maura kept growing despite every attempt he made to keep them at bay, and he had no idea how to deal with them or what to do about them.

All he *did* know was that he couldn't be sorry for any of it. He meant every word he had said to her in the gazebo. He was tired. So tired of pretending to be something he wasn't. And tired of trying to put up a wall against the emotions she inspired within him. He was beginning to think that she just

might be the one person who could truly understand what he had suffered, who might be capable
of seeing the real person he was underneath his façade. What had happened between their parents
was in the past, and it was more than time to let it
go and look to their future.

He had felt so alone for so many years, but
Maura had come along and had drawn him from
the dark path he had been following, into the light.
And now he couldn't go back. He didn't want to.

Of course, Maura had never told him in so many
words that she cared for him, but he hadn't exactly
voiced his own feelings aloud either. He refused to
believe, however, that she would have given him
her innocence, that she would have come apart so
violently in his arms, if she didn't feel *something*
for him.

In the ballroom, the orchestra struck up a waltz,
and he glanced in the direction of the French doors.
For a second, he was sorely tempted to make his
way inside and seek her out, to ask her to dance.
God, to be able to take her in his arms, to hold her
close, and let the tongues wag as they would . . .

But no. He had made up his mind that for this
evening it would be best to give her a bit of space.
Perhaps without his presence to stir the pot, the gossips would relent a bit in their unflagging attentions.

At that moment, a faint rustling from the hedges
lining the path that led into the garden captured his
attention, and he whipped his head about, straining

his ears for any further sound. Almost immediately he heard a throaty and seductive feminine laugh, followed by a masculine murmur. A second later, a woman emerged from the brambles, tugging her bodice into place as she went and plucking leaves from her elegantly styled blond hair. A man was at her heels, straightening his coat.

The moonlight fell over their faces, and he recognized them almost instantly.

Lady Lanscombe and Stratton.

Gabriel stiffened, and his hands bunched into fists. After the way the bastard had attacked Maura this afternoon, part of him wanted nothing more than to bound down the steps, seize the man by the neck, and pummel him bloody. But as Maura had said, that was likely to only make things worse. So far he hadn't heard a hint of a whisper about Maura's visit to his room earlier, so apparently his warning had been heeded. However, if he pushed things and made Stratton angry, there was no telling how he would retaliate.

As he continued to watch, Lady Lanscombe turned to wind her arms around her stepson's neck and went up on tiptoe to whisper something in his ear. Then, with one last lingering kiss, they parted ways. The viscountess climbed the steps to the terrace, unaware of Gabriel lurking in the shadows as she crossed the flagstones and entered the ballroom through the French doors. And after waiting several minutes, Stratton followed.

Once all was still again, Gabriel pushed away from the railing with a shake of his head. It shouldn't surprise him at all that the two of them were involved. It was more than obvious what sort of man Stratton was. And Lydia had shown on several occasions that she possessed few scruples when it came to indulging her baser appetites. He doubted she would think twice about bedding her husband's son. And yet society welcomed the two of them into their midst with open arms, while a sweet innocent like Maura was reviled, ridiculed, and made to feel as if she didn't belong because of the crimes of others.

The bloody hypocrisy of it all made him furious.

Moving to stand before the French doors, he peered into the well-lit ballroom, past the throng of dancers, searching for a head of dark curls. And it didn't take him long to find her. His gaze was drawn straight to her as if by some invisible force.

Standing with her aunt and the dowager duchess on the far side of the room, Maura was lovely in a lace-trimmed ball gown of cerulean blue silk. The square-necked bodice revealed just a hint of the shadowed valley between her lush breasts, and her black hair was swept up into a sophisticated topknot, leaving the graceful, creamy throat he had pressed kisses to that afternoon bare except for the pearl choker she wore. She was the very picture of the demure young miss, but he knew precisely how to peel back those layers of prim modesty to reveal the fiery, passionate woman she was underneath.

The gentle smile he saw her bestow upon the dowager duchess at that moment warmed all the empty places in Gabriel's soul. She had shared so much with him today. Far more than just her body. He was well aware, however, that she hadn't told him everything. So there was no admirer waiting in the wings to seduce her away from him. That was one less thing for him to worry about, but it didn't explain the letter or what she'd been up to. And after all she'd been through that afternoon, he hadn't been able to bring himself to question her about Cunnington's IOU. The more she let slip, the more he became convinced that all this had something to do with their parents somehow.

But he wouldn't push her. She had asked for time, and he intended to give it to her. Now he could only pray that she would realize sooner rather than later that he could be trusted.

And that this damnable attraction between them was worth exploring, come what may.

"You know, my child, I've been meaning to tell you how very proud I am of you."

At Theodosia's soft words, Maura looked up from her perusal of the colorful swirl of dancers as they circled the ballroom floor, and raised an eyebrow at the dowager duchess in question. "Proud, Your Grace?"

"For holding your head high despite the difficulties you have faced this weekend." Her obvious concern lacing her voice, the elderly lady tucked her arm through Maura's and examined her with troubled brown eyes. "I'm aware that you haven't had an easy time of it, and I'm also aware that a great deal of the blame for what you have suffered lies with me. I can only hope that you have forgiven a meddling old woman her interference. I truly believed that inviting Hawksley was the right thing to do. That it would give the two of you a chance to come to terms."

Not wanting her aunt to overhear their conversation, Maura glanced back over her shoulder to make sure that Olivia was still busy chatting with Lord Bedford before giving the dowager's hand a reassuring pat. "There is nothing to forgive, Your Grace. I know you meant well. And in many ways it has all turned out for the best."

Theodosia tilted her head inquiringly. "Oh? How so?"

"If nothing else, it has helped me to understand a bit better what Mama must have gone through in those last few years before her death. And the whispers and speculative looks have died down considerably since last night. In fact, the majority of those in attendance this evening have been most kind to Aunt Olivia and me."

It was true. From the moment she and her aunt had joined everyone in the ballroom earlier, Maura had noticed a distinct thawing in the manner of the other guests toward them. Several of the older matrons had approached Lady Olivia to engage her in polite conversation, and Maura had even been asked to dance more than once.

"So it seems that your theory holds merit after all," she told the dowager as she guided the elderly woman away from the edge of the crowd and toward a quiet corner. "Now that the gossips have seen for themselves that Lord Hawksley and I can be in the same room without bloodshed, perhaps they will turn their attention to more interesting diversions."

"I see." Theodosia pursed her lips. "It pleases me that you and the earl have been able to put your differences aside, though I must admit to a certain amount of surprise. The last time we spoke, you appeared to be so set against him."

Maura lifted her shoulders in a slight shrug, trying hard to keep herself from blushing under the dowager's intent regard. "I suppose that is something else I have decided you were right about. The earl is not at all the devil that everyone believes him to be."

"So you have given what we discussed yesterday afternoon some thought?"

Pretending to contemplate the laughing group of people who were gathered about the buffet table nearby, heaping plates full of food, Maura mentally debated how best to answer that question. She had most definitely given the matter a great deal of thought. Especially in light of what had occurred between her and Hawksley that afternoon in the gazebo . . .

She closed her eyes against the memory of his strong hands caressing her skin, of his lips feasting on hers. Dear God, never would she have believed that he was capable of being so gentle, so giving. He had aroused sensations within her that she had never thought to experience.

But what had passed between them hadn't just been physical. He had told her things that she suspected he had never confided to anyone, had shown her the kind and compassionate man that existed behind that inscrutable mask. A man who was just as lonely and misunderstood as she was.

She had misjudged him terribly. And while she knew she should regret the loss of her innocence, she found that she could not. Being in his arms had felt so right that their lovemaking had seemed like a natural progression. Instinctively, she had trusted him with her body, and she was very close now to trusting him with her heart.

Perhaps it was time to start trusting him with the truth as well.

Before she could say anything aloud, however, the music ended and the dancers came to a halt. Amid the exodus of people from the floor and the general shifting of partners, the Marquis of Waldron appeared before them.

He greeted them with a low bow and a polite smile. "Your Grace, with your permission, I should like to ask Lady Maura for the honor of this next dance."

The dowager faced Maura, deferring the question to her. "My dear?"

Though she had no desire to do so, Maura found that she couldn't bring herself to refuse him. Not when he had been so kind to her the evening before. So she returned his smile and accepted his invitation with a nod. "I should be delighted, Lord Waldron."

As he took her gloved hand in his and led her to the middle of the floor, Maura couldn't help but surreptitiously search the crowd gathered about them, hoping to catch a glimpse of a tall, broad-shouldered figure with a head of golden curls. But of Hawksley there was no sign. So far this evening he hadn't put in an appearance, and for some reason that bothered her.

Could he be avoiding her? she wondered anxiously. Was he sorry for what they had done?

A stabbing pain pierced her heart, and she immediately pushed the thought away. She couldn't let herself believe that was even a possibility or she would very likely drive herself mad.

At that moment the orchestra struck up the next set, and as the marquis began to guide her through the intricate steps of a minuet, Maura noticed that he was studying her with a furrowed brow.

"Is something wrong, my lord?" she ventured, speaking just loud enough to be heard over the music. "You seem . . . troubled."

He paused, then inclined his head in a rather abrupt affirmation. "As a matter of fact, I am a bit troubled, my lady. Normally I wouldn't think of broaching such unpleasantness, but in this case I feel it is my duty to inform you that there is a rather disturbing rumor floating about."

"Disturbing?"

"Yes." He lifted an arm, allowing her to pass underneath in the next move of the dance before continuing. "As I told you last night, I was most impressed with the manner in which you have comported yourself in light of these most unfortunate circumstances, and I have been praising you most highly to those among my usual circle of acquaintances."

Ah, Maura mused. So that was why there had been a change in the way the other guests were treating her. The marquis had been singing her praises. She supposed it had been foolish of her to believe that anything she had done might have had any effect on their attitude, but she couldn't help a small stir of disappointment.

Lord Waldron was still talking, frowning down at her with a stern expression that put her in mind of a disapproving parent. "Of course you can imagine my shock when one of the gentlemen I had been conversing with repeated this most unsavory tale to me."

She shook her head, her stomach fluttering. Surely if Stratton had ignored Hawksley's warning and bandied about to all and sundry the story of what had happened that afternoon, she would have heard something before now. "I don't understand."

"Apparently you were seen this morning in the company of several of the duke and duchess's more . . . shall we say, notorious guests. And it is also being said that these guests, most notably the Earl of Hawksley and the Marquis of Cunnington, were indulging in some rather questionable behavior."

Maura blinked. "The billiard game?"

His eyes narrowing, the marquis lifted his chin. "I had heard that there was much more to the proceedings than a mere game of billiards, my lady. I was told there was gambling involved, and that you actually encouraged it."

"It was simply a small, gentlemanly wager."

"There is little that is gentlemanly in such behavior," Lord Waldron rapped out, his face reddening with displeasure. "And it was unseemly for a young lady of your station to even be alone in their company, much less to take part in such scandalous doings. Obviously your aunt has been neglectful in her duties as your chaperone. A future marchioness would never conduct herself in such a way."

Feeling her temper spark, Maura took a deep breath and waited until she had made another pass beneath the marquis's arm before attempting to defend herself. "Please, my lord, I—"

But he interrupted her before she could get the words out, his tone censuring. "I had thought much better of you, my dear. That you were a young lady of breeding and morals, despite your mother's common origins. Perhaps there is more of her in you than I had realized."

That did it. Maura's anger boiled over. How dare he scold her as if she were a child? And how dare he malign her mother? No longer would she stand aside and let Lady Albright be reviled and criticized.

Not caring if she was causing a spectacle, she stopped dead in the middle of the dance floor, hands going to her hips as she glared up at him. My God, how could she have ever believed she would be content married to such a man? He was no different from the rest of the hypocritical members of the ton, and the mere thought of lying in the same bed with him, allowing him to touch her the way Gabriel had, was abhorrent to her now.

"Perhaps there is, my lord," she said with asperity, her gaze never wavering from his rapidly paling visage. "And I'm more proud of that than you will ever know. My mother was a good woman, no matter what you or anyone else thinks, and I loved her. I would ask you to consider that the next time you start to publicly disparage her."

She sent him a look of contempt. "And as for conducting myself as a marchioness, I find I no longer have any aspirations in that regard. So perhaps it would be better if you turned your attentions elsewhere in your search for the future Lady Waldron, my lord."

For several long seconds after she fell silent, the marquis said nothing, merely stared down at her, a muscle ticking in his jaw. And though the music continued, she could feel the eyes of everyone in the room, could almost hear their cruel whispers.

*See? She's just like her mother. Didn't I tell you?*

"I see," Lord Waldron finally said stiffly, releasing her hand and offering her a perfunctory bow. "I am sorry that we have both wasted our time. If you will excuse me?"

With that, he pivoted and stormed off the floor, leaving her standing there alone among the other dancers.

Around her the murmurs began, muffled and insidious as they rose in volume, but Maura couldn't bring herself to move. All the blood in her body seemed to have pooled in her feet, and her limbs had gone cold and numb.

So it had come to pass. She had finally proven them all right. With a single display of righteous indignation, everything she had worked so hard for had been lost. No, it hadn't been lost. She had thrown it away with both hands.

And she couldn't seem to care.

A hand on her shoulder startled her, bringing her out of her stupor, and she looked up to meet the green eyes of her self-appointed knight in shining armor.

Never before could she ever remember being so relieved to see someone as she was to see Hawksley.

Concern shone clearly on his handsome face, but he made no mention of what had just transpired. Instead he caught her hand in his and lifted it to his mouth, his lips brushing the skin of her wrist just above her glove. The warmth and tenderness in that simple caress filled her heart to bursting.

"My lady, may I have this dance?" he asked softly.

She didn't even hesitate. Ignoring the circle of astonished faces around her, she curtsied to him and placed her free hand on his upper arm in acquiescence. "Yes, you may, my lord."

His slow smile made her pulse jump, and he swept her into his embrace. Suddenly everything looked brighter and nothing else mattered. Not even the sight of her aunt, slumped in Lord Bedford's supportive arms while she fanned herself frantically with a napkin from the buffet table, could diffuse the blissful haze that hovered over her.

Who cared that her reputation, her very future had been thrown into chaos? She had made a choice this evening, and she could not be sorry for it. And now her very own guardian angel was dancing with her, holding her close, keeping her safe from all harm. He had known she needed him, and he had come to her.

Tracing those perfect masculine features with loving eyes, Maura realized that there should no longer be any question in her mind as to whether she could trust this man. He had come to her rescue time and again, had shown himself more than willing to stand with her against the naysayers. He truly cared for her. Perhaps he could even come to love her. And how incredibly naïve she had been to believe she could live without the sort of passion he had brought into her life.

It was indeed time she told him everything. He deserved to know the truth. And who knew? He might even be able to help her figure out what to do. What the next step in the search for her mother's killer should be.

Going up on tiptoe, she put her mouth close to his ear. "Gabriel?"

He looked down at her, his eyes glowing with a fierce light. "Yes, my lady?"

"Tonight, after the ball . . ." She hesitated for only a second, then plunged ahead, sealing her fate. "I want you to come to my room."

# Chapter 19

*"It seems the only time Philip demonstrates any interest in me is when I have managed to anger him. This evening, upon returning home from our social rounds, he launched into a diatribe regarding my relationships with other men. Apparently I have acted the part of flirt too well. My own husband now believes that I am a faithless jade. I know I should try to protest my innocence, though a small part of me is glad to finally have his attention, even if it is for all the wrong reasons. Does that make me wicked?"*

From the diary of Elise Marchand,
August 26, 1810

Maura was sitting before her dressing table mirror, absently staring at her reflection as she brushed out her hair, when the light tap she had been waiting for came at her bedchamber door.

The sound had her heart flying into her throat in nervous anticipation. From the moment she had returned to her room after the ball, she had been trying to decide the best way to go about telling Hawksley the truth about his father. She had yet to come up with any answers, but it seemed her time had just run out. There could be no more putting it off.

It had been wrong of her to withhold the information from him for so long. She realized that now. In fact, she'd had a perfect opportunity to confess all this afternoon in the gazebo, but she had let it pass her by. She had been so caught off guard by the confusing thoughts and emotions pouring through her, so overwhelmed by the intensity of their love-making, that she hadn't been able to think straight. But she no longer had that excuse, and she couldn't continue to keep him in the dark.

Theodosia was right. In his own way, Hawksley had suffered just as much pain and grief as Maura had. And after he had been so honest with her, the least she could do for him was to be honest in return.

Rising from the padded bench, she took a calming breath and smoothed out the skirts of her ball gown before crossing the chamber to open the door.

Hawksley loomed on the threshold, still dressed in the elegant dark evening clothes that he had worn earlier. His broad-shouldered, leanly muscled form was backlit by the pale glow of the few sconces that illuminated the hallway, but his green eyes glittered down at her with a passionate hunger that was unmistakable, even in the dimness.

The heat of his regard was enough to rob Maura of breath, but she managed to ignore the fluttering it produced in the pit of her stomach and offered him a welcoming, if not quite steady, smile.

"Lord Hawksley." She greeted him in a low-pitched tone so as not to disturb those who slept behind the other closed doors that lined the corridor. "Won't you come in?"

He didn't hesitate, but stepped inside and shut the door behind him.

For a small eternity they stood close together, their gazes locked. For Maura, everything else faded into the background as she was held captive by the almost tangible force that had always drawn the two of them to each other like helpless moths to a flame. And after what had passed between them this afternoon, it was stronger than ever, vibrating through her with a powerful resonance that had her tingling from head to toe.

Licking her dry lips, she blinked and looked down at the floor. "Thank you for coming, my lord."

"Don't thank me." His expression serious, he tilted his head, studying her from under lowered brows. "If I had any sense, I would have stayed away. My presence here this weekend has already caused you enough pain, and if anyone were to see me coming and going from your room, society would wash its hands of you for good."

"Perhaps. But as I am already well along the road to perdition after this evening, I can't see that it makes any difference."

"I imagine your aunt would disagree with you. Especially if she should happen to wander in here and catch the two of us alone together."

Maura glanced over at the door of the dressing room that connected her chamber to the one next to it. Lady Olivia had been so distraught over the humiliating events of the evening that she had spent at least an hour furiously pacing their rooms, berating her niece, and insisting that they pack up all their belongings at once so they could depart the Hall first thing in the morning. It had taken the combined efforts of Maura, Phoebe, and a dose of laudanum to finally get her settled and tucked into bed. Given all that, it was highly unlikely that the woman would be wandering anywhere tonight.

But Hawksley was so sober that Maura couldn't seem to help teasing him just a little bit.

"Would you marry me should my reputation be compromised, my lord?" she asked with a flutter of her lashes.

He answered her question with another question, his solemn mien never wavering despite her flirtatious attempt at lightening the mood. "Would you want me to?" He paused, then reached out to cup her cheek with one hand, his thumb tilting her chin upward so she couldn't avoid his penetrating stare. "Would you really wish to be tied forever to the son of the man responsible for slaying your mother?"

Once again he had given her an opening to broach the subject of his father, to reveal what she knew. But somehow the words wouldn't come. She just couldn't seem to squeeze them past the constriction in her throat. And the feel of his fingertips against her face only disconcerted her further.

So instead she freed her chin from his grip and moved a few paces away, putting some much-needed distance between them before she faced him once more. "I wanted to thank you," she managed to say after a second or two, her voice more than a trifle breathless despite her best efforts at composing herself. "For what you did this evening. For coming to my rescue once again."

His countenance darkened, the sudden anger that marked his handsome features giving him an almost feral appearance. "I should have called Waldron out for walking away and leaving you standing there like that. If I hadn't known it would only complicate things, I would have."

She lifted a shoulder in a slight shrug, startled by the strength of his fury on her behalf. Did he truly care so very much for her? she wondered, her heart leaping at the prospect. "I appreciate your concern, my lord. But you are right. It would have only made the situation that much worse in the end."

"It's more than mere concern, Maura, and you must know that. I wanted to rip the bloody fool's head off. He didn't deserve you."

"I'm certain he thinks that I didn't deserve him."

"He would be wrong." Hawksley moved toward her, bridging the gap she had placed between them. This time, when he cupped her face, he used both hands, gently tipping her head back for his thorough perusal.

"But then he didn't really know you, did he?" he continued, his warm breath caressing her lips in a most titillating fashion. "I'm beginning to think you've never let anyone really know you."

Maura couldn't help but see the humor in that statement. "This from the man who has pretended to be the devil incarnate for years," she reminded him with a raised brow. "Tell me, where is that devil now? I do believe I rather miss him."

He shook his head and gave her a look of tender amusement before swooping in to cover her mouth with his own.

The kiss was slow and sensual, a leisurely exploration that melted Maura's bones and left her head reeling. Each tantalizing caress of his lips, each moist sweep of his tongue, teased and tempted her, fanning the flames of her desire ever higher. And before too long, she was burning out of control.

Wrapping her arms around his neck, she speared her fingers into the hair at his nape, reveling in the warmth that surged through her as his palms smoothed down over her shoulders. She had been so caught up in the sensations he stirred within her that she hadn't even realized he had loosened the tapes of her gown until the silken fabric slid down her arms and fell in a pool at her feet. The cambric and lace of her chemise followed, leaving her naked before him.

His gaze trailed over the curves of her body with a reverence that robbed her of breath, and when he lifted her high against his chest to carry her to the bed, she shuddered at the fierce need that blazed down at her from those green eyes. But something niggled at the edges of her consciousness, even as he laid her carefully on the mattress and lowered his long, muscled length over top of her.

*This isn't what you asked him here for*, a little voice whispered insistently at the back of her mind.

She froze, every muscle in her body going lax. There was so much he didn't know. She should stop this right now. Tell him everything. But part of her dreaded doing so with every fiber of her being.

Once Hawksley discovered what she had been concealing from him for so long, he might never forgive her. He might even end up hating her, and that was something she didn't think she could face.

Despite everything she had done to push him away, to deny her feelings for him, she was very much afraid that she was dangerously close to falling in love with this man, and the mere possibility of earning his hatred was enough to chill her straight to her soul.

Some of her tension must have transferred itself to him, for he propped himself up on his elbows and peered down at her with a concerned expression.

"Are you all right?" he murmured, brushing a tendril of hair back behind her ear. "If I hurt you this afternoon—"

"No," she rushed to assure him, halting his words. "I'm fine. A bit sore, perhaps. But you didn't hurt me. You couldn't."

He leaned forward to skim his lips over the bare curve of her shoulder, then traced a finger along the indentation of her collarbone and down into the valley between her breasts, wringing a shiver from her.

"You are so beautiful, Maura," he said huskily. "And I want you very much. But we don't have to do this again if you aren't sure. I don't want you to think that I expect any more from you than you have already given me."

A soft sigh escaped Maura as he feathered another kiss across her lips. And instantly she lost her train of thought. With his eyes and hands and mouth exploring every inch of her with such worshipful intent, that little voice that was trying so hard to remind her of what she had to do subsided to a faint mutter, becoming so distant and indistinct that it was all too easy to ignore it.

"I do want you, Gabriel," she whispered, barely able to speak past the lump of emotion that swelled in her throat. "And I want this. Please make love to me."

He made a broken sound at her quiet confession and seized her mouth again for a devastating and erotically charged exchange. Then, pushing himself to his feet, he stood next to the bed and shed his clothes as she watched in awe. The lamplight shimmered on his bronzed skin, illuminating the taut, striated muscles, the lean, whipcord strength of his body. That hard male part of him that had given her so much pleasure when they had come together before jutted proudly from between his thighs, long and rigid and swollen with need.

Like some golden Adonis, he loomed over her, a vision of masculine perfection. And when he came back to her, Maura spread her legs to welcome him without hesitation, her trembling moan mixing with his full-throated groan as he fit himself to her sleek warmth and entered her moist, clinging passage. The pink petals of her femininity parted smoothly as he slid deep, and this time there was no pain, only a slight discomfort before she was completely swept away by the sensation of him moving inside her.

They began to rise and fall together, her hips lifting to meet his slow, steady strokes in harmonious synchronization. Her climax, when it came, poured over her like a benediction, intense and profoundly moving. And when he shuddered and collapsed atop her, his own cataclysmic release leaving him weak and panting for breath, she savored the utter contentment that washed over her and the way their hearts pounded against each other in perfect rhythm.

This was where she belonged, she couldn't help but think as she drifted off to sleep in his arms.

She was finally home.

Gabriel awoke with Maura draped over his chest, the silken sheets tangled about their bare, perspiration-soaked bodies and the air redolent with the musky scent of their lovemaking.

Drawing in a contented breath, he reveled in the feel of her nestled against him and stroked a hand through her tumbled dark curls. He had lost track of the number of times they had come together, but each experience had been more deeply satisfying, more earth-shattering than the last.

She had been a revelation, he mused with an indulgent smile. An intriguing combination of innocent miss and wanton temptress. Inexperienced she might have been, but she had proven more than eager to learn whatever he had been willing to teach her.

He gently tugged aside the sheets, gazing down at her sleeping form, his gaze tracing over every inch of her creamy skin in appreciation. She was so very lovely. Lushly curved despite her small stature, like a veritable pocket Venus. Part of him longed to lean over, kiss her awake, and indulge in another heated bout of shared passion. But he knew he couldn't afford to linger. Though he had made sure earlier that the connecting door into the next room was locked, and Maura had assured him that her aunt had taken a liberal dose of laudanum before going to bed and wasn't likely to disturb them, he wasn't taking any chances.

As much as he enjoyed being with her, sleeping in the same bed with her, the thought of her being forced into a marriage to him simply because they had been caught in a compromising position wasn't something he could countenance. He didn't want her to feel pressured or compelled in any way to make a commitment she wasn't yet ready to make.

Strangely enough, the prospect of wedding her, of becoming her husband, didn't fill him with the sense of panic that he would have expected. After watching his parents' marriage disintegrate around him, he had often thought that he could live out the rest of his life quite happily without ever marrying. He had never felt a strong desire to acquire a wife simply for the sake of siring an heir to carry on such a shameful family legacy. However, the thought of tying himself to Maura, of sharing his future with her, of seeing her grow big with his child, made his heart catch and sent a jolt of excitement and anticipation racing through him.

But as sweetly as she had given of herself, she had made no mention of her feelings for him. And his feelings for her were growing more complicated with every second he spent in her company. He loved talking to her, sparring with her, getting to know her. He loved making love to her. And he could no longer deny that she had a hold on his heart. However, he wasn't sure if he was ready to acknowledge just exactly what that hold was.

There was simply too much that still had to be resolved between them. Too much that was still uncertain.

With a weary exhalation, he brushed a feather-light kiss against her temple, then reluctantly rose from the bed to slip into his discarded shirt and trousers. Once he had finished dressing, he would leave her a brief note to explain his reasons for slipping away while she was still asleep and return to his own chamber for a few short hours of rest before the dawn broke.

Sooner or later, they had to talk. He knew that. Just not now. Not before he'd had the chance to mull things over, to consider what it was he wanted to say.

And what it was he felt for her.

Gabriel turned, intending to cross the chamber

to the writing desk in the far corner in search of a pen and some blank stationery, when his booted toe struck something that had been sticking out from between the bed and the nearby armoire, knocking it over. Stopping in his tracks, he looked down to find a small traveling valise lying on its side, its contents spilling out in all directions.

He bent over to pick it up, and the first thing his fingers closed around was a small leather-bound book. As he lifted it, however, several pieces of paper fluttered from its pages and wafted to the polished floor, one of them landing face up at his feet.

It was instantly recognizable as Lord Cunnington's IOU. The same IOU that Maura had stolen from his coat pocket earlier that day and that he had almost forgotten about in the events of the last several hours.

*There are many things you deserve to know, my boy. Things that I am not in a position to reveal to you.*

The dowager duchess's voice echoed in his head, prodding at his doubts, stirring up his insecurities, and almost without volition, he reached for one of the other pieces of paper that had fallen from the book. Even as he unfolded it, he knew it was another of those damnable letters. The yellowed stationery was unmistakable, and the words jumped out at him, stark and menacing.

*Dearest Jezebel,*

*I can remember a time when I used to think you were an angel in disguise. When you used to shine upon the stage like some bright beacon, shining only for me. But I realize now that it was all a lie. You are nothing more than a whore, tempting and taunting men to their ruin with that sweet honey pot between your legs. Holding out hope to each of us that we just might be the one who could finally tame you, own you, only to jerk that hope away at the last minute and dance back to your husband. And now you are bedding that bastard Hawksley! How I loathe him! You are a harlot and a sinner, and you must be punished. I have decided I am just the one to do it.*

The blood drained from Gabriel's face and he sank down in one of the overstuffed chairs close to the bed, his stunned gaze never wavering from the note in his hand. It seemed quite obvious that this letter had been meant for Maura's mother. And the tone of this one was even more hostile than the one he had confronted Maura with. Whoever had written it sounded as if he had every intention of carrying out his threats.

And he had mentioned Gabriel's father.

His stare traveled from the letter to the book he held in his other hand. It appeared to be a journal of some kind, and he contemplated it for several minutes, torn. As much as he disliked the idea of invading Maura's privacy, an urgency he couldn't ignore compelled him to look inside . . .

He opened the book and began to read.

# Chapter 20

*"At the Palmerton ball last night, the Viscount Lanscombe introduced me to an acquaintance of his, Geoffrey Sutcliffe, the Earl of Hawksley. We engaged in a most entertaining conversation, and I laughed more than I have in a very long time. For a while, I was able to forget my painful estrangement from Philip and simply enjoy myself. I do believe that the earl and I are going to be quite good friends."*

From the diary of Elise Marchand,
March 8, 1812

**M**aura's eyes drifted open to a room that was dark and silent. Not a hint of sunlight shone in through the part in the curtains, so she assumed that it must still be well before dawn, though Gabriel was no longer beside her in the bed.

She missed the warmth and strength of his arms around her. Where had he gone?

Stretching languidly, she stared up at the canopy overhead, thinking back on all that had passed between them in the last few hours. She ached in some very interesting places, and her face heated even now as she recalled the many times—and the many ways—they had made love. And it had been making love. If she had been dangerously close to falling for him before he had taken her to bed, there was little doubt that she had now completely and wholeheartedly tumbled.

There could be no more denying it. No going back. She was in love with her guardian angel. Her knight in shining armor.

The Devil's Own.

And how on earth was she going to explain that to her family?

She sighed and brushed her hair out of her eyes before pushing herself to a sitting position. But an unexpected voice from out of the shadows had her stifling a gasp, freezing in place with the sheets clutched to her bare breasts.

"Looking for me?"

Her eyes darted around the room until they came to rest on a figure seated in one of the chairs on the other side of the bed, next to the armoire. The faint light from a nearby lamp cast just enough of a glow that she could barely make out his features.

"Gabriel." She relaxed back against the propped-up pillows with a sense of relief. "You surprised me. I thought you had left."

The laugh that wafted to her across the space that separated them held no amusement. "No. I'm still here. But I almost left. I almost walked out without knowing the truth."

Something about the flat monotone of his voice, the hard, utterly emotionless look in his eyes, sent a chill racing up her spine. "What are you talking about?"

"I've been doing a bit of reading."

When Maura recognized the leather-bound book he held up, her stomach did a slow, tumbling roll, and she went numb all over in horrified disbelief.

No! It couldn't be!

But it was. She knew it, even as she tried to convince herself that her eyes were playing tricks on her.

"It's my mother's diary," she whispered, her fingers twisting in the bedclothes so tightly, so convulsively, that her knuckles turned bone-white.

"I know."

"How did you find it?"

"Does it matter? I did."

She shook her head, a painful knot of fear and trepidation forming in her chest. He knew. He held all her secrets right there in his hands. God, how she wished now that she had never let herself be so easily distracted. That she had told him everything the moment he had stepped into the room. But she hadn't, and now she was going to have to deal with the consequences.

"Have—" She stumbled to a halt, swallowing back the bile that rose in her throat before trying again. "Have you read it all?"

A humorless smile curved his mouth. "As a matter of fact, I have. Fascinating stuff, by the way." Opening the book, he glanced up at her over the top of its cracked binding, his eyes holding hers in the dimness. "Listen to this."

He didn't give her a chance to refuse, but began to read aloud.

*Hawksley has been such a dear friend to me. It is sometimes difficult to stand by and listen to those around me denigrate him. I know he has his faults. But as much as he drinks and carouses, it is only to hide his pain. There was someone he loved once. Very much. He refuses to tell me her name, but I know that he was forced to give her up because his family did not approve. Apparently his marriage was arranged against his will. His wife is a sweet, shy creature, and I cannot help but feel sorry for her and their son, Gabriel. They have both borne the brunt of Hawksley's terrible unhappiness, and though I have tried to tell him it is not right to make them suffer for what he has lost, it is the one subject on which he turns a deaf ear to me.*

*It is ironic. I have seen his wife out and about in public, and she stares at me with such hatred. Little does she know that I am not the enemy she thinks I am. Hawksley and I have never slept together and never will. Neither of us could ever bring ourselves to ruin our friendship by doing such a thing. And while my heart still belongs to Philip, Hawksley still pines for his long-ago love . . .*

There was a long, drawn-out silence when the diary passage finally came to an end. And when Gabriel spoke again, it was in a harsh and accusing rasp. "When were you going to tell me that my father never had an affair with your mother? That he never touched her? That—"

"That everything you thought you knew about their relationship was a lie?"

"Damn it, yes!"

Maura wrapped her arms defensively about herself, knowing what his answer would be before the words even left her mouth. "Would you believe me if I said tonight?"

When he laughed this time, the sound was so jagged that she winced.

"Please don't insult my intelligence any further," he said contemptuously. He paused, studying her face as if trying to read her mind before gesturing to the stack of yellowed paper that was piled on the table next to him. "I read the rest of the letters. They were written to your mother, weren't they?"

She bit her lip and nodded.

"And?" he prompted when she said nothing further.

Truth time, Maura thought grimly. There could be no more stalling. The best way to do it was to simply say it and get it over with. A quick, clean cut would heal that much faster. She only wished she'd come to that realization sooner. "And I think whoever wrote them is the one who really killed my mother."

The revelation hit him like a bullet. She could almost feel him jerk at the impact, see his face whiten even in the dimness. His mouth opened and closed several times, as if he were at a loss. Then, drawing himself up, he finally managed to find his voice, though it sounded thick and choked. "You believe my father was innocent?"

"My older sister, Jillian, has always believed that. There were things about that night that didn't make sense to her, that didn't fit. She's the one who has worked with Bow Street in the past, and while she was working on an unrelated case last year she found a witness who claimed he was there that night and that he saw someone else come out of our town house."

"Yet no one thought to tell me?" Gabriel leaned forward in his seat, gritting the furious words out through clenched teeth. "No one thought I might like to know that he wasn't a murderer after all? I might not have been overly fond of the man, but he was still my father, and I deserved to know."

"There was no real proof. Not even the law believed it. The lone witness wasn't considered reliable, as he was only your father's former coachman. And the man died before he could be brought before Bow Street."

"I'd say these letters should be proof enough."

"Perhaps. But I—I only just found them. Not even my father or Jillian has seen them. Just me."

"But it doesn't make sense. If my father was innocent, if he wasn't in love with your mother, why would he kill himself?"

Maura's heart sank. Here was something else she had to tell him that was bound to cause him further pain. "I don't think he did, Gabriel. I believe that he was murdered. That the killer framed him for the crime and then made it look as if he pulled the trigger on himself. You must have seen the references to him in the letters. This man hated your father. He wanted him gone."

Gabriel stiffened, then lunged to his feet and began to pace, raking his hands through his hair, disordering the already rumpled strands as he marched back and forth next to the bed. "He was murdered? And all these years I thought . . . I believed—" He came to an abrupt halt and faced her, his eyes narrowing. "Then that means the killer is still out there. That's what you've been up to, isn't it? You've been trying to track down the person who wrote these letters."

"I've been comparing handwriting," she admitted, knowing there was little use in pretending she didn't know what he was talking about. "Whoever wrote these is very knowledgeable about my mother's years with the theater. He makes numerous references to it. He also alludes to an intimacy that makes me think they were involved at one time." She flushed and avoided his gaze by glancing down at her hands fisted in the sheets. "The only men besides my father that my mother ever had relations with were Lords Lanscombe, Bedford, and Cunnington."

"Which is why you needed Cunnington's IOU?"

"Yes. But none of the handwriting matched, and I don't know what to do now."

"I'll tell you what we are going to do." Gabriel sat down on the mattress next to Maura, reaching out to cover one of her hands with his. His touch caught her off guard, for she'd been certain from his angry reaction to what he had learned that he would never wish to touch her again. But a swift peek up at his face showed that some of his fury seemed to have dissipated, though his jaw was still set at a rigid angle.

"You are going to give me these letters and I'm taking them to the law," he was saying, his firm tone brooking no refusal. "To someone who knows how to handle this. And from now on you are staying out of it. Do you hear me?"

Ah. And there it was. The edict she had known was coming sooner or later.

Swinging her legs over the side of the bed, Maura made sure the covers were wrapped firmly about her before she stood and whirled to glare down at him, one hand propped on her hip. "You see? This is part of the reason why I didn't tell you. I knew you wouldn't let me be involved. That you would shut me out."

His expression was incredulous. "Bloody hell, Maura, are you mad? You never should have been involved with any of it to begin with. You should have taken your discovery to your father or someone at Bow Street."

"You don't understand. Papa was so ill, and I couldn't just wash my hands of it and let someone else take charge." She licked her dry lips, took a deep breath, and let everything that had been tormenting her for the last several weeks come spilling out. "I believed the lies, Gabriel. I believed all the terrible, awful stories I heard about my mother, and I hated her for it. And then I read her diary and found that none of it was true. She never let any of those men touch her once she was wed to Papa. Not Lanscombe. Not Cunnington. None of them. But I condemned her for it anyway."

It was her turn to pace, the sheets that swathed her nakedness rustling with every agitated step. "I felt so much guilt. I've been haunted by nightmares for weeks, and I suppose I thought that I could make up for it all if I could only discover who her killer was." She glanced over at Gabriel with importuning eyes. "And you said it yourself. I've felt so isolated from the rest of my family. I wanted to be the one to bring us back together and finally fix things for us. To hand my father the diary and see the happiness on his face when I told him that Mama's killer had finally been caught."

He captured her by the wrist, stopping her midstride. "But do you have any idea what sort of danger you could have placed yourself in if Lanscombe or Bedford or Cunnington had been the killer and had figured out what you were up to? To try and take on such a task alone was foolish in the extreme."

The concern that marked his features filled Maura with hope. Surely he couldn't hate her if he could still look at her that way?

"I wasn't completely alone," she told him. "I had Violet."

"Miss Lafleur? Somehow I don't think she would have been much protection if you had run into serious trouble." He tilted his head, looking up at her questioningly. "I suppose she was your contact with the theater world?"

She nodded, remembering Violet's promise to do some investigating of her own. "Yes. And she told me before I left for Rosemont Hall that she would question some more of her acquaintances about the men in Mama's past. Maybe she has been able to come up with some other suspects. I could—"

Cutting her off with a sharp slashing motion of his free hand, he released her wrist. "No, Maura. I will speak with Miss Lafleur once we return to town. I told you that your involvement in all of this is at an end, and I meant it."

"But—"

"I said no!"

It was practically a shout, and his increase in volume had Maura flinching and casting an uneasy glance toward the wall that separated her room from her aunt's.

The unequivocal statement was also instantly punctuated by a faint scratching noise from out in the corridor just outside the door. They both froze, waiting with bated breath for a knock at the portal or a loud voice demanding to know what was going on.

When nothing happened, however, and they heard nothing further, Gabriel expelled a weary gust of air and reached up to pinch the bridge of his nose, continuing in a hushed tone. "Believe it or not, I do understand how you feel. I know guilt can be a very strong motivation for doing things you wouldn't normally do. But this isn't the answer. It has to stop now. You will not risk your life any further."

"You have no right—"

"I'm taking the right!" He shot up from the bed and seized her by the elbows, scowling down at her in obvious frustration. "Damn it, Maura, don't you think that's the least I deserve? A say in the rest of the investigation?"

When she said nothing, simply shrugged and looked away, he let her go and spun around, stalking back to the far side of the bed to stand with head bowed as he addressed her over his shoulder. "I knew you were up to something. Something dangerous. I don't know how I knew, but my instincts were screaming at me from the moment I found you lurking about Lord Lanscombe's masquerade. I kept telling myself that I had to find out what it was, no matter what it took. And it's a good thing I did, because you obviously were never going to tell me."

His words plucked at Maura's insecurities, rousing the suspicions she had so recently put to rest. She tried to tell herself that she was wrong to even have such doubts, but they rose up nonetheless, like vicious wraiths to taunt her. "Is that what this has all been about?"

At her quiet words, he looked over at her, a frown marring his brow. "What?"

"All of this. You and me. Together." Tugging the sheet higher against her chest in a self-protective gesture, she took a step back from him, her heart giving an anguished squeeze at even having to ask the question. "Did you make love to me just to find out what you needed to know?"

There was an icy silence, and his face went blank and still as they both stared at each other.

A small eternity seemed to pass by, and when he finally replied, his response held an underlying thread of gruff resignation. "That's the second time you've accused me of that, Maura, and I'm not going to bother to defend myself to you again. I told you I wouldn't do that. Apparently you didn't believe me."

She waved a hand at her traveling valise lying on its side on the floor, then at her mother's diary lying on the table with the letters alongside it. "How can I think anything else? You just said that you were determined to find out what I was up to, no matter what it took."

"And it never occurred to you that I felt that way because I just might give a damn what happens to you?" When the volume of his voice started to rise again, he snapped his mouth shut and visibly attempted to rein himself in before going on in stilted tones. "I'm not going to let you twist this around so that you can feel less guilty about not telling me, Maura."

"That's not why I—"

"Isn't it?" He eyed her scornfully. "You said that my shutting you out of the investigation was only part of the reason you didn't tell me what was going on. What was the other part?"

Tears blurred her vision and she turned away, not quite able to bring herself to meet his gaze. "I didn't know you, Gabriel. I had no idea how you would react. And I didn't know whether I could trust you."

"You didn't trust me. Yet you slept with me."

"I'd heard the stories about you for years! How could I trust you completely? You're very good at playing whatever role is convenient. I looked at you and saw what you wanted society to see. I saw—"

"You looked at me and saw the Devil's Own. Just like everyone else." With a shake of his head, he turned and strode for the door, pausing with his hand on the knob, speaking without looking back. "Prepare yourself, Maura. I will be paying your father a visit on Monday once we are back in London, and I will expect you to hand over the diary and the letters. Think whatever you like about me, but come what may, I'm clearing my father's name."

Without another word, he walked out of the room, closing the door with a soft snick behind him.

And Maura sank down onto the edge of her bed, her hopeless tears overflowing to spill down her cheeks.

# Chapter 21

*"Despite his predilection for hard liquor and his rather notorious reputation, Hawksley has become a very valued confidant. Next to Theodosia, he is the only one who truly seems to understand me. I know that all of London thinks that we are having an affair, and though I have let them continue to believe that, nothing could be further from the truth. We have shared with each other the scars that no one else can see, and I know the pain and sorrow he hides behind that devil-may-care façade."*

From the diary of Elise Marchand,
June 22, 1812

As he stepped out into the hallway, Gabriel barely restrained the urge to slam Maura's door behind him with a resounding bang. Such a display of temper might give him a temporary sense of satisfaction, but it would only succeed in waking the guests in the neighboring rooms and would do little to alleviate his anger and frustration.

Or his anguish.

In truth, he couldn't help but wonder if he would ever be able to get past the confusing welter of emotions that had his head reeling. His whole world had just been turned upside down with shocking abruptness, and nothing was what it had once seemed. Lady Albright hadn't been a whoring witch intent on seducing his father away from his family. And his father hadn't been a murderer.

He had been a man tormented. A man in love with someone he couldn't have.

Standing in the shadows of the corridor, Gabriel leaned against the wall for a moment, his shaking hand braced against the plaster for support as he attempted to make sense of it all. He suspected that a very large part of him was still in shock. He had no idea what to think or how to feel, but somehow he would have to find a way to come to grips with what he had just learned.

And while he was doing that, he also had to figure out how to accept the fact that the woman he had bared his soul to, the woman he had just been coming to believe might possibly be the woman he was destined to share his life with, obviously didn't feel the same. She couldn't possibly care for him and still accuse him of what she had just accused him of.

Gabriel felt a painful jab in the vicinity of his chest. After what they had shared today, after the way she had given herself to him, how could she once again accuse him of seducing her to gain information? He had been convinced that she cared for him, that she had finally come to see him for who he truly was. But her accusations had proven that wasn't the case after all. Just when he had started to let down his guard with her, to believe that they could have some sort of future together despite all that stood between them, she had thrown his feelings for her right back in his face as if they were of no consequence, and it had hurt like hell.

He would never admit that to her, however, and he couldn't let himself dwell on it. Not now. The wound she had dealt him was too new, too fresh, and he had other matters he needed to contend with. He had just been handed information that could possibly clear his father's name, and that was exactly what he planned on doing. For the time being, he would focus on that and do his best to put Maura from his mind.

"Well, well, what have we here?"

The feminine voice came from behind him, startling in the stillness, and he whirled to find Lady Lanscombe lounging in the open doorway of the room across the hall from Maura's, observing him with upraised brows. With her long blond hair loose and flowing and her lush figure draped in a filmy dressing gown that outlined her ripe curves, leaving little to the imagination, she was a vision that many a lustful male would have appreciated.

But she left him absolutely cold.

"Why, I wonder what the Lady Maura's auntie would think if she knew you were visiting her at this time of night, Lord Hawksley?" she went on in a silken purr, her narrowed eyes taking on a knowing gleam that he could see even in the darkness. "Or for that matter, what would she think if she knew that her charge had paid a visit to your room earlier this afternoon?"

Gabriel's fists clenched. Damn Stratton! He should have known that bastard couldn't keep his bloody mouth shut!

Abandoning her deliberately provocative pose, the viscountess moved forward into the corridor and sent a pointed look at the Lady Olivia's door before facing him with arms crossed beneath her breasts. Though her rosy lips were curved in a smile, there was a hardness in her expression, a calculating maliciousness that boded ill as to her intentions. "Shall I knock and find out?"

Spurred into action, Gabriel covered the distance between them with a few long-legged strides. She opened her mouth as if to protest, but before she could say anything further, he had seized her by the wrist, bundled her into her room, and shut the door behind them with a nudge of his boot heel.

For a brief instant, Lady Lanscombe looked non-plussed by the speed with which he had removed her from the hallway. But after a second, the knowing light reentered her eyes, and she pressed up against him, fluttering her lashes.

"How masterful of you, my lord," she cooed. "But if you wanted to be invited in, all you had to do was ask."

He gave a disgusted shake of his head and set her from him, then glanced about the spacious chamber. The room was dimly lit by a single lamp and devoid of any other occupant. "Where is your husband?"

"Who knows? When I left him in the ballroom, he had his hand halfway down the bodice of that cow Lady Kirkenwell. I doubt I will see him before dawn." She peered up at him, her tongue flicking out to wet her lips suggestively. "Why, darling? Were you hoping for a bit of sport before he returns? If so, I would be more than happy to accommodate you."

"I don't know what sort of game you are playing, my lady, but it stops now."

"No game. I simply hate to see you wasting yourself on that silly little chit across the hall when you could have any woman you wanted."

Gabriel leveled her with a look of contempt. "I suppose that includes you?"

"Of course, darling." The viscountess spoke in a low, sultry tone, reaching out to trace the deep vee of his shirt with one finger, the tip of her nail just brushing the skin of his chest. "I've made no secret of the fact. All you have to do is say the word."

Barely restraining the urge to recoil at her touch, he brushed her off and took a step back, needing to put some distance between them before he was tempted to throttle the woman. "I'm sorry, Lydia," he told her firmly, unequivocally, "but I'm afraid I'm not interested."

"Your loss, love. Though I'm certain I could please you much better than she ever could. If you'd just let me . . ."

Her words trailed off, and the next thing Gabriel knew, she had peeled back the edges of the dressing gown and let it fall to the polished floor with a shrug, baring her naked body before him. Then, lifting her chin, she trailed one hand languidly over her breasts and belly in an obvious attempt to draw his attention to the pale thatch of curls at the juncture of her thighs. "Do you like what you see?"

His gaze took in the soft pink flesh, the abundant curves, with an almost clinical detachment. On a level completely separate from his sexual urges, he could admit that she was a very attractive and enticing package. But he wasn't going to take her up on her offer. He felt not the slightest hint of desire for her, and in his mind's eye he kept picturing a smaller figure. A figure with creamier skin and curves that were slighter, but still filled his palms to perfection.

Bending over, he snatched the robe up off the floor and practically shoved it into Lady Lanscombe's hands. "That's enough," he grated harshly. "Put it on. Now."

"But—"

"I said, enough!"

Furious color flooding into her cheeks, the viscountess slid into the dressing gown and belted it closed with stiff, jerky motions. "My God, you are as obsessed with the little bitch as I'd feared," she hissed. "I knew it when I caught you gawping after her like some love-struck simpleton out on the terrace the other day, but I didn't want to believe it. Why on earth would you involve yourself with her? The daughter of the woman who led your father to ruin?"

"Whom I choose to involve myself with is none of your affair. And the marchioness wasn't—" He cut himself off, enraged that he was actually standing here making excuses. He owed her nothing. This vicious creature was more of a slut than Lady Albright had ever dreamed of being, yet she hid behind her highborn status and had the temerity to denounce people like Maura and her mother for crimes she was guilty of herself.

Taking a deep breath to rein in his increasing temper, he fixed the woman with an icy glare. "I am leaving, my lady," he informed her sternly. "And I would suggest that you give your actions a great deal of consideration before you go about slandering Lady Maura. I would be most displeased should I find out that you are spreading nasty and unfounded rumors."

"Un-unfounded?" she sputtered, her nostrils flaring in indignation. "How dare you imply that I would make up such falsehoods. You know they are nothing but the truth. And it is a good thing I had someone put a bug in Lord Waldron's ear as to the sort of behavior she is predisposed to. I'm not blind, and I saw her molding herself against you like a bitch in heat in the billiard room this morning. The daughter of that whore doesn't deserve to be a marchioness!"

Her bitter tirade had Gabriel seeing red. So it had been Lady Lanscombe who had made sure that the story of what had taken place in the billiard room had made the rounds and that it had eventually gotten back to Lord Waldron. Never mind that he had no liking for the man himself, especially after witnessing the way he had turned his back on Maura at the ball. That this vindictive witch would deliberately sabotage Maura's future in such a way when she didn't even know her was beyond all tolerance.

Knowing if he stayed there for another second he would be tempted to kill the woman, he pivoted and started for the door. Halfway there, however, a lady's satin slipper sailed through the air and hit the wall next to his head. It barely grazed his ear in flight, but as he turned to avoid being struck, his gaze fell on a slip of paper that lay on a nearby mahogany table.

*Dearest Lydia,*

*I cannot wait any longer. I must see you. Wait for me by the fountain in the garden at midnight and I will come to you as soon as I am able.*

Gabriel froze, every muscle tensing as he stared at the letter in disbelief. The handwriting was hauntingly familiar. In fact, he was almost sure he had seen that exact same handwriting less than an hour before, in a missive penned to the late Marchioness of Albright.

Sweeping the note off the table, he swung back around and advanced on Lady Lanscombe, brandishing it before him. "Where did this come from?" he gritted out, certain of what her reply would be, but nonetheless compelled to hear her say it.

When she only gaped at him, he caught her by the shoulders and shook her, his voice rising dangerously. "Goddamn it, who wrote this?"

As if determined to tempt his wrath further, she tossed her head, and a taunting smile curved her lips. "Why? Are you jealous, darling?"

"Do not play coy with me right now, my lady. I asked you who wrote this, and I expect you to tell me."

Something in either his tone or his tight expression must have alerted her to the fact that he was within a hair breadth of strangling her, for her eyes went wide and genuine fear crept over her features.

"I can't—" she began.

"You can and you will, or I will be forced to bring your husband into this!"

A pause. When she spoke again, it was as if the words were being dragged out of her, a syllable at a time. "Stratton. Lanscombe's son."

Gabriel released her, not even noticing when she stumbled out of his path as he began to pace furiously. Stratton? Was it possible? It wouldn't quite fit Maura's scenario of events, as the viscount's son would have been much too young to have been involved with the marchioness during her years as an actress. Eight or nine at the most. Yet he supposed Stratton could have learned the intimate details of that relationship from Lanscombe. And he certainly hadn't been too young five years ago, when Lady Albright had taken up with his father once again.

Stratton's voice from earlier that afternoon rang in his head, the words suddenly coming together to make a horrible sort of sense.

*The Devil's Own in love with the spawn of London's most notorious Jezebel. But then the women in that family do tend to have that effect. They lead a man into sin against his better judgment, tease*

*and torment him, then open their legs for the next*
*male in line like a common strumpet.*

Jezebel . . .

Facing Lady Lanscombe once again, Gabriel
struggled to keep his voice steady, even as his pulse
pounded in his ears. "Tell me. Has Stratton ever
showed any undue interest in the late Lady Albright?"

Something flashed in the depths of the viscountess's eyes, and she laughed bitterly. "Undue interest? In his own way, he is every bit as fascinated
with her as his father ever was. Never mind that
the woman has been dead for five years. He speaks
of her with a venomousness that borders on hatred. Yet, before we left London to come here, I
found a drawer full of old playbills that he was
hoarding in his room from her days with the theater." She shivered and wrapped her arms about
herself as if to ward off a sudden chill. "My God,
he has even called out her name when we are making love! That's part of the reason I threw him out
tonight and told him it was over between us. I am
tired of being little more than a replacement for
that harlot."

She glowered at Gabriel. "What is it about the
women in that family that turns men into fools?"

He wasn't about to attempt to answer that question, so he asked one of his own. "Where is Stratton?"

"I don't know. He stormed out of here an hour

ago, right after I told him I wanted to end our affair. He said something about returning to London, and he seemed angry enough that I doubt he will wait until morning."

Which meant if Gabriel hurried, he might be able to catch the man packing to leave.

A fierce sense of anticipation filled him, and for an instant he considered knocking on Maura's door and telling her what he had uncovered. However, he dismissed that notion almost immediately. She would insist on being involved, and he didn't want her anywhere near Stratton. If upon interrogating the man he found that his suspicions were correct, then he would take the information to her father and his friend, the Bow Street Runner. But for now, it was best if she stayed out of things. She had already placed herself in enough danger with her foolhardy investigation.

Whether or not they were able to patch things up between them, he couldn't stand the thought of any harm coming to her.

Moving back across the room, he returned the note to its original spot on the table before offering the viscountess a stilted bow. "Thank you, my lady. And I would advise you not to leave that letter lying about for your husband to discover." He arched a derisive brow. "Permissive he might be, but I doubt that even he would turn a blind eye to you fucking his son."

Lady Lanscombe's face flushed a dull red, but he

didn't wait around for her retort. With a muttered good evening, he flung open the door, prepared to head straight for Stratton's room.

Only to find himself staring across the hall into Maura's startled blue eyes.

For what seemed like a small eternity, he stood there, trapped by her stare as she peered at him through the crack in her door, her face pale. And when her gaze traveled to a spot over his shoulder, it was clear from the hurt etched into her stricken countenance that she had caught sight of the scantily clad Lady Lanscombe hovering in the chamber behind him.

Gabriel knew exactly how it must appear to her, what she must think he had been doing. But even as he opened his mouth to explain it all, to tell her she was wrong, something stopped him. Perhaps it was his pride or the pain that still twisted at his insides from her earlier denunciation. Whatever the reason, he refused to plead for her belief in him. If she could believe the things that she had accused him of, if she could believe that he would leave her and go directly to another female for physical comfort, then there really was no hope for them at all.

Feeling as if the heart that had so recently come to life and started to beat again was ripping apart inside his chest, he tore his gaze away from hers, closed the door, and stalked off down the corridor.

Without looking back.

# Chapter 22

*"This evening, at the Ralston dinner party, Philip stumbled upon me alone with Hawksley in a secluded alcove. The look on his face told me that he had misconstrued the situation, but instead of demanding explanations, he merely turned his back and walked away. It seems rather ironic. Time and again, I have deliberately flirted with other men, all in an effort to strike back at my husband and hurt him as his defection has hurt me. But now that I have finally succeeded without even trying, I find myself wanting to chase after him and profess my innocence. The entire incident has left me feeling cold and empty inside."*

From the diary of Elise Marchand,
October 1, 1812

**M**aura stared out through the parlor window at the foggy, rain-drenched world beyond the glass, thinking how well the dismal weather reflected her mood. The gray skies above had been weeping copious tears almost from the moment she and her aunt had returned from the country late the afternoon before, and it showed no signs of letting up.

Just like the pain in her heart.

With a frown, she pressed her forehead against the window frame and watched as the few intrepid souls who had been brave enough to venture out into the deluge sloshed through puddles and dodged raindrops on their way to whatever appointments they were intent on keeping. Despite the gloominess of the day, she couldn't help but savor the familiarity of her surroundings. After everything that had happened, it was good to be home, among the people who cared about her.

Upon arising on Sunday morning, Lady Olivia had remained resolute in her decision to leave Rosemont Hall immediately. Feeling lost and utterly devastated, Maura had seen no reason to argue. She certainly had no desire to stay, to be forced to put her social mask in place for the sake of the other guests and to pretend nothing was wrong while everyone whispered behind her back.

And more than that, she hadn't wanted to take a chance on running into Gabriel.

At the thought of him, all the anguish she had been trying so hard to keep at bay flooded through her in an almost overwhelming wave. It had been bad enough believing that he had made love to her for the sole purpose of gaining access to the secrets she hid. But opening her door, only to be greeted by the sight of him coming out of the Lady Lanscombe's chamber, had been a bit like dying on the inside.

Never could she remember being so miserable. How she longed to simply be able to put her trust in him and his protestations of innocence, longed to believe that the man she had fallen in love with truly existed and that there had been a perfectly logical reason for him to have gone to the viscountess's room, other than the obvious. But his jaded past kept rearing its ugly head to taunt her, filling her with doubt. It was so difficult to have faith, to stay optimistic, when life had a habit of disappointing her every time she allowed herself to hope.

As it had turned out, however, she hadn't needed to worry about coming face to face with Hawksley. According to Phoebe, who had heard the news from the two informative housemaids she had befriended during her time in the Hall's servants' quarters, the earl had departed sometime before dawn without any explanation. And while Maura was glad that she hadn't had to cope with seeing him again so soon after their strained parting, she also couldn't help but be troubled by the fact that he had left without telling her or even saying good-bye.

"Please, child, do come away from the window," a voice spoke up gently from behind her. "You have been standing there for almost an hour, and peering out at all that gloom will only serve to make you more melancholy."

Maura glanced back over her shoulder at the dowager duchess, who was ensconced in one of the brocade-padded settees on the far side of the room. The elderly lady had accompanied the Daventry women on their journey back to London, and Maura would be forever grateful for the dowager's presence on that interminable carriage ride. It had been the only thing that had prevented her aunt from haranguing her into exhaustion.

But it hadn't kept Olivia from towing her niece straight to the marquis's bedchamber the instant they had entered the Albright town house and filling his ear with a list of her transgressions.

As if reading her mind, Theodosia leaned forward in her seat, her gaze searching Maura's with probing intensity. "You have yet to tell me exactly what happened once you arrived here yesterday," she pointed out, her lined face full of concern. "I gather that Olivia made things difficult for you."

Maura flushed. That was certainly an understatement! Her aunt had been furious and had gone on and on at length, airing her grievances in minute detail. Being the target of the woman's invective had been an unaccustomed and less than pleasant experience for Maura. And the fact that it had all taken place in front of the recently returned Jillian and Connor, who had been visiting with Lord Albright in his chamber, had only added to her humiliation.

Crossing the room, she sank down onto the settee next to the elderly lady with a weary sigh. "She accused me of single-handedly ruining any chance this family had to redeem itself in the eyes of the ton. According to her, I am 'ungrateful, selfish, thoroughly spoiled, and deserve nothing less than the severest of punishments.' Those were her exact words, I believe." She shook her head, a wry smile curving her lips. "Thank goodness Papa is so understanding. He listened very calmly, then patted my hand and told me that he always thought Lord Waldron was a pontificating bore and he was thankful not to be forced to welcome him as a son-in-law."

"Aha! I'll bet that knocked the Queen of She-Beasts on her stiff-arsed rump!"

The delighted crow had Maura stifling a reluctant laugh. "That's one way of putting it, I suppose. In truth, I felt a bit sorry for her. Her face turned positively ashen, and I was sure she was going to swoon right there in front of us all. As it was, she wound up calling for Mrs. Bellows and the hartshorn and retiring to bed early."

Theodosia's eyes lit with fierce satisfaction. "How I wish I had been here to witness that."

"I'm afraid the rest of the conversation didn't go quite as well and wasn't nearly as entertaining."

At Maura's suddenly serious expression, the dowager sobered and reached out to lay a sympathetic hand on her arm. The elderly lady might not have been privy to all that had gone on over the weekend, but she was far from unobservant, and she was well aware that something momentous had occurred. Something that had caused Maura a great deal of pain and grief.

"Hawksley?" she queried softly.

"Yes. Papa didn't say much on the subject, but I could tell he couldn't understand why I would even deign to speak to the man."

"You didn't explain it to him?"

"I didn't know how. How could I possibly even begin to tell him what I've spent the past three weeks doing? Especially when it has all been for naught?" Maura glanced over at the window once again, following the moist trail of a raindrop with her gaze as it rolled slowly down the glass. "And it's not as if he won't know about everything before too much longer anyway. Hawksley said he intended to pay a call on Papa today, and that's one promise I have little doubt he will keep. He wants to see his father's name cleared as soon as possible, and I can't say that I blame him."

"Lord Hawksley is coming here?"

The anxious query had Maura and Theodosia both whipping their heads about to find Aimee hovering on the threshold of the parlor, her cheeks drained of color. She held an open book in one hand, but it dangled from her limp fingers as if forgotten, perilously close to sliding from her loosened grip.

She looked so distressed that for a brief instant Maura considered denying it. But it would do little good to lie. Her sister would know sooner or later, when the earl showed up at the door. "Yes, he is, sweetheart."

"But why?"

"It's nothing." Rising from her seat, Maura forced a reassuring smile to her lips and started toward the girl. "Why don't you take your book and—"

"Don't!"

The word escaped Aimee with such explosive force that Maura froze mid-stride, her mouth falling open in surprise.

For what seemed like a small eternity, all was silent. Then, straightening her shoulders and visibly reining in her composure, Aimee took a step into the room and set aside her book before facing her older sister with her fists clenched at her sides.

"I don't want you to send me off with a pat on the head," she said quietly, her voice ringing with a strength and authority that caught Maura even more off guard. "I thought we talked about this before you left. I want you to tell me the truth. What's really going on? Does it have something to do with the reason Aunt Olivia won't get out of bed this morning?"

Maura closed her eyes and lifted a hand to pinch the bridge of her nose as she debated with herself. Her sister was right. Aimee was no longer the fragile, timid creature she had once been, and it wasn't fair to continue keeping things from her, especially when it directly pertained to their family. It would be far better for her if she was prepared for the revelations that were to come.

After exchanging a long look with Theodosia, who nodded imperceptibly, she reached out and took her sister by the hand, leading her over to the settee and drawing her down onto the cushions next to her.

"Lord Hawksley is coming to speak to Papa—to all of us—about Mama," she began, choosing her words with care. Though she owed Aimee the truth, she had no wish to alarm her unduly. She got no further than that, however, before a rap at the door interrupted her.

"My lady?" It was the butler, Iverson. His usually impassive expression held just the tiniest hint of anxiety as Maura bade him to enter, and he came toward her with a silver tray bearing a folded note. "A street urchin delivered this to the back door and insisted that I make sure you received it at once."

Her brows knitting, she reached out to take the note, then dismissed the servant with a nod. "Thank you, Iverson."

He bowed stiffly and left the room, closing the door behind him.

The flowered stationery was instantly recognizable to Maura as Violet's, and she unfolded it with trembling fingers and made quick work of reading the contents.

*I have urgent news regarding your mother.
Please meet me at the costume shop at once!*

Doing her best to remain calm despite the excitement that had her stomach fluttering, she glanced up at Theodosia and Aimee. "It's from Violet."

The dowager's eyes widened. "Does she have news?"

"Apparently. She says it is urgent and wants me to come to the costume shop right away."

Heavens, but was it possible that Violet had stumbled across something during her quest for answers? Maura wondered. It must be of some import if her friend wanted her to come to the shop right now rather than meeting later. Of course, Gabriel had warned her to stay out of things from this point on, and he wouldn't be happy if he showed up to find her gone, but it wasn't as if she were doing anything dangerous. Surely he would understand if she came home with information that could be helpful to the investigation?

She got to her feet, stuffing the note into the pocket of her day gown. "I must go."

Theodosia rose as well, leaning heavily on her cane. "Then I'm going with you."

"But you came this morning in order to visit with Jillian. She and Connor should be here any minute, and—"

"You are not going alone, young lady, and that

is final." The dowager cut across Maura's protestations in a tone that brooked no refusal. "Between you and your elder sister, I have more than learned my lesson when it comes to allowing you to venture anywhere unattended."

From the stubborn angle of the woman's jaw, it was obvious there would be no arguing with her. "Very well. But we must hurry so we can make it back before Hawksley arrives."

Aimee spoke up from her spot on the settee, her amber eyes rife with trepidation. "What is going on? Who is Violet?"

Turning to place a hand on the girl's shoulder, Maura gave it a gentle squeeze. "Once Lord Hawksley gets here, you will know it all. I promise. But for now, I have to go." She leaned forward, her gaze holding her sister's unwaveringly. "If Papa needs me, the dowager duchess and I have gone to the costume shop on Bond Street. Can you remember that?"

"Of course."

"Good." Overcome by a rush of emotion and anticipation, Maura threw her arms around her sister in an exuberant hug. They were so close to the end of things. She could feel it! "Everything will be fine, Aimee. You'll see. And please, try not to worry. By the time I come back, I may have the answers that we've been searching for."

*And maybe then*, she added silently, *we can finally put Mama's tortured spirit to rest for good.*

\* \* \*

Gabriel climbed wearily down from his carriage in front of the Albright town house, frustrated and exhausted beyond measure. He had spent the past twenty-four hours trying to locate Stratton, who had managed to avoid being questioned by slipping away from Rosemont Hall without informing anyone of his departure, and who had remained elusive ever since. He didn't appear to be in residence at either Lanscombe Manor or at the family's abode on Berkeley Square, and if those among his usual circle of acquaintances had any hint as to his whereabouts, they weren't being forthcoming with it.

Ignoring the steady fall of rain, Gabriel swept off his hat and peered up at the red-brick façade of the building that loomed over him. He had hoped to have some more definitive answers regarding Stratton's possible involvement in the death of the marchioness before paying this visit to Maura's father, but it seemed that wasn't to be. Now he could only hope that conjecture alone was enough to convince the marquis that his suspicions were well founded.

From behind him came a soft splashing sound and a muffled curse as a booted foot trod in a puddle, drawing his attention to the fact that the Viscount Stonehurst had also alighted from the carriage. Having kept his promise to stay in town and keep an eye on Violet Lafleur, he had filled Gabriel in on the former actress's recent forays to the theater where she and Lady Albright had once performed, then had insisted on accompanying him on his search for Stratton.

Surly and withdrawn though he tended to be on occasion, the man was a far better friend than he would ever admit, Gabriel mused with a wry curve of his lips.

"Are you going to knock or do you plan on standing here until you are swept away by the flood tides?" the viscount grumbled as he came to stand at Gabriel's elbow.

"You meant that in jest, I'm sure, but that choice isn't quite as easy as you think. It's likely that Albright's first instinct will be to throw me out on my ear."

Stonehurst folded his arms and contemplated the large front entrance with lowered brows. "True. But once he learns what you are here for, simple curiosity should be enough to compel him to at least hear you out. After all, it's not as if you're planning on asking him for his daughter's hand in marriage or something else similarly guaranteed to give the man apoplexy." He paused, then leveled Gabriel with a ferociously disapproving scowl. "You aren't, are you?"

Now there was a question.

In truth, Gabriel hadn't the slightest idea what he planned on doing at this point. From the moment he had left Hampshire, he had vacillated between being furious with Maura for so quickly jumping to conclusions to being furious with himself for not continuing to try to convince her of his innocence, especially once she had seen him leaving Lady Lanscombe's room. But despite his anger, he ruefully acknowledged that he had to accept his share of the blame for their misunderstanding. For years he had deliberately cultivated an image of a profligate scoundrel who seduced and abandoned women on a regular basis. Could he really fault her for having trouble believing that a better man existed behind that façade?

Right now, all he knew was that he wasn't ready to give up on her. Not yet. The connection between them was simply too strong for him to just walk away. And after being parted from her for this long, he'd had more than ample opportunity to come to terms with what he felt for her. There was no longer any doubt that his emotions were well and truly involved.

He was in love with the infuriating minx. It was why her insistence on believing the worst of him had hurt so much. If he hadn't cared, it wouldn't have mattered what she thought of him. But he *did* care, and for that reason her opinion of him mattered more than anything in the world.

But he didn't bother to say any of this aloud. Instead he ascended the stairs to the front door with Stonehurst at his heels and pounded the brass knocker against the wood in a peremptory fashion.

There came the shuffle of footsteps from the other side of the portal, and after a minute or two, it swung open to reveal a balding, rail-thin butler who eyed both of them askance.

"May I help you, my lord?" he inquired, his tone coolly polite in spite of his wary expression.

Gabriel was well aware that he and his friend more than likely presented a disreputable picture, what with their dripping appearance and the scar marring Stonehurst's face, so he swiftly produced his card and handed it to the servant with what he hoped was an ingratiating smile. "Lords Hawksley and Stonehurst, to see Lord Albright."

The butler glanced at the card, wrinkled his beaked nose, and shook his head. "I am afraid His Lordship is indisposed and isn't receiving visitors at present."

"Yes, I was sorry to hear of the marquis's recent illness, but I'm certain that if you inform him that I am here about a matter of grave importance, he will make an exception in my case."

"I'm afraid that is highly unlikely, my lord. I shall tell him you called, of course, but it would be best if you came back at another time."

The door began to close, but Gabriel braced a hand against it, using his superior strength to force it the rest of the way open before brushing past the butler into the foyer of the house.

The servant's eyes widened and he shifted his slight weight nervously from one foot to the other, wringing his hands. "Now see here! You can't do that!"

"My good man, I believe I just did."

With that, he marched off along the short hall-way that led from the foyer, peeling off his soggy gloves as he went. Stonehurst followed, a formi-dable presence at his back, and the harried butler scurried along in their wake, protesting feebly.

Gabriel hadn't gone far when the murmur of voices alerted him to the presence of several people through an archway just up ahead on the left. He strode into the room to find himself in a luxuri-ously furnished parlor.

The voices instantly quieted.

"I am sorry, my lord." The butler hovered on the threshold, bobbing up and down like an agi-tated wren. "I tried to stop them."

Gabriel ignored the servant and took stock of the small group assembled before him. Lord Albright was seated in an armchair next to the marble fire-place, a bit pale and bundled in a heavy dressing gown against the slight chill, but looking healthier than Gabriel had expected the man to look. Across from him on a matching settee sat a tall, full-figured young woman with thick black hair and spectacles, who bore more than a passing resemblance to the late marchioness. From the description Maura had given him, he assumed that this was Lady Jillian. And the large, muscular, russet-haired fellow who shot to his feet and took up a protective stance in front of her and the marquis must be her husband, Connor Monroe.

Of Maura, there was no sign.

"How dare you barge your way into this house, you foul miscreant!"

That, of course, was the Lady Olivia.

Straightening from her position leaning against the arm of her brother's chair, she pointed a condemning finger at him, her eyes blazing with outraged indignation. "Haven't you caused this family enough pain, Lord Hawksley? Leave at once, before I have the servants fetch the watch!"

As difficult as it was to be civil to the bloody harridan after Maura had confided in him about the mistreatment she and her sisters had suffered at her aunt's hands, he nonetheless managed to offer her a stiff bow. "I apologize, my lady, but I can't do that. It's very important that I speak with Lord Albright at once."

"You arrogant jackanapes! He isn't interested in anything you might have to say, so get out and take your horrid beast of a companion with—"

"Olivia, that is enough."

Though the marquis did not raise his voice in any way, his firm reprimand had Lady Olivia subsiding with a glower.

Steepling his fingers together under his chin, Lord Albright then calmly surveyed Gabriel for several long seconds before motioning to Monroe to retake his seat and waving the butler on his way. "It's all right, Iverson. That will be all."

With one last leery glance at Stonehurst, who

had moved to stand just inside the room, the servant acceded to his master's wishes and hurried off.

"Now, Hawksley, after the tales that have been related to me regarding certain events that took place at the Maitland house party over the weekend, perhaps you would care to explain why I shouldn't do exactly as my sister suggested and have you tossed out?"

Gabriel hesitated. He was loath to go into the matter without Maura's presence. It seemed a bit too much like a betrayal to discuss her recent actions behind her back. But it wasn't as if she hadn't known he intended on coming here today. Perhaps she had deliberately made herself scarce so as to avoid her father's displeasure, and if that were the case, waiting for her to make an appearance would be useless.

So he took a deep breath and stepped forward. "As I said, I apologize for forcing my way into your home like this, but I believe you will understand when you hear what I have to say. It is regarding your wife. And your daughter."

He then proceeded to tell the marquis everything, from Maura's discovery of his wife's diary and the threatening letters, to her exploits in the last several weeks, to his own suspicions of Lord Stratton. Of course, there were certain aspects he kept to himself. He doubted that Albright would appreciate hearing that his former rival's son had slept with his daughter. Until he and Maura had a chance to talk and come to some kind of accord, he intended to save for later any revelations regarding his feelings for her.

When he was done, a hush settled over the room, and the atmosphere hummed with a tension so thick it could have been cut with a knife.

"I don't understand," Lord Albright murmured, his countenance stricken. "Maura never said a word. Not a word."

Lady Jillian reached over to cover her father's hand with her own. "You heard Lord Hawksley, Papa. You were so ill, and she didn't want to worry you. And I've known for some time how guilty she felt for doubting Mama. I suppose this was her way of making up for it."

Gabriel nodded, remembering the wistful glow in Maura's eyes when she had talked about being the one to finally make things right for her family. "Your daughter is right, my lord. Lady Maura wanted only to make amends for believing the worst of her mother all these years."

"Nonsense!"

The icy exclamation came from Lady Olivia, who began to pace in front of the fireplace, her cheeks suffused with angry color.

"I told you, Philip," she continued, her tone shrill as she addressed her brother. "The child has changed. Why, she has ruined us all with this scandalous behavior. She could have been the making of us, and instead she will destroy us for good. It is only a matter of time before word of this gets around, you know." She sent Gabriel a contemptuous glare. "And if you believe anything this . . . this vile cad just told you, then you—"

"Hush, Olivia!"

This time the marquis did raise his voice. In fact, it was so loud in volume that Lady Olivia jumped and came to an abrupt halt, her outburst ceasing.

Lord Albright lurched to his feet. Wobbling precariously for a second before gaining his footing, he then crossed the parlor toward the door with halting, unsteady footsteps. "Maura! Where is Maura?"

"Papa, please wait," Lady Jillian called out, unable to hide her concern. "Let someone help you."

But he didn't wait. He pushed past Gabriel and a stoic Stonehurst and made it out into the hallway before Connor Monroe caught up to him and assisted him with a hand at his elbow. The other members of the group trailed behind.

Once he had reached the foot of the main staircase, the marquis freed himself from Monroe's grip and came to a stop, shouting for his middle daughter in an authoritative bellow. "Maura, come down here at once!"

Despite the strain of the moment, Gabriel found himself unexpectedly eager to catch a glimpse of the woman he now knew held his heart. Whether she was still angry with him or not, it had been a full day since he had last seen her, and he had missed her beyond bearing. More than he had thought possible.

But it wasn't Maura who came into view at the top of the stairs. It was a tiny slip of a girl with golden-brown hair that hung down her back in braids and an elfin face that reflected a wealth of tentative uncertainty.

This must be the youngest sister, Aimee.

As all eyes remained on her, she descended toward them, her small, pearly white teeth gnawing at her lower lip. But just as she reached the bottom, Lord Stonehurst suddenly shifted in the shadows next to the banister, and the light from a nearby lamp fell over his scarred visage. The sight must have startled the girl, for she gave a gasp and faltered as if her slippered toe had caught on a stair tread. Teetering off balance, she toppled forward.

Only to be rescued when the viscount lunged forward and seized her by the arms, steadying her.

There was an instant of stunned silence. Then one corner of Stonehurst's mouth twisted in cynical amusement as he set her back on the step and released her. "Careful, little mouse," he said gruffly.

Her expression arrested, she stared up at him for a dazed moment, then seemed to recover her composure and lifted her chin before moving away from him and approaching her father with hands clasped tightly before her.

"I'm sorry, Papa, but Maura isn't here."

Lord Albright looked nonplussed as he settled his hands gently on his youngest daughter's shoulders. "No? But where is she?"

"She left with the dowager duchess almost an hour ago. She said something about a lady named Violet and a costume shop on Bond Street."

The girl's words had Gabriel's heart skipping a beat. "Violet? Miss Lafleur?"

In addition to everything else, he had filled Albright in on Maura's association with the former actress, and the marquis glanced over at him now with worried eyes. "Do you think the woman may have discovered something?"

"It's possible."

For some reason, Gabriel had a very bad feeling about this. He and Stonehurst had attempted to pay a call on Miss Lafleur earlier to ascertain what, if anything, she had found out during her questioning of her theater acquaintances, but the woman had been out at the time. Only something of the utmost urgency would have sent Maura out into the rain to Violet's costume shop, especially after he had made her promise to leave the rest of the investigating up to him. And the fact that Stratton was still unaccounted for only made things that much worse.

What had Violet uncovered in her snooping? Was it something that could have put both her and Maura in danger?

"Well, at least she took Theodosia with her this

time, Papa," Lady Jillian was saying, wrapping a comforting arm around her father. "I suppose that's something, at any rate."

Somehow Gabriel doubted that the dowager would be much help should circumstances become desperate, but he didn't wish to alarm the marquis, so he didn't bother to point out that fact.

"Stonehurst and I will head over there and collect them," he said instead, doing his best to keep his calm mask in place. "Whatever information Miss Lafleur has stumbled upon, it is vital that we all hear it as well."

Connor Monroe moved to stand at his side. "I'll go with you," he murmured. And though his voice was quiet and held no overt threat, the determination etched into his craggy features told Gabriel that there would be no swaying him. Not that he had any intention of attempting to do so. Monroe struck him as a man who could more than handle himself, who had seen the rough side of life on more than one occasion and lived to tell about it. If things went badly, Gabriel would more than likely be glad to have such a person in his corner.

He turned his head to meet the marquis's gaze. "Don't worry, my lord," he said. "I'm sure she's just fine."

But even as he said it, he wasn't so sure. His instincts were screaming at him that the woman he loved was in trouble, and he could only pray that he was wrong.

# Chapter 23

"*I came out of my room after an argument with Philip this evening to find Maura lurking in the hall. I am certain she heard everything, and there was so much hatred in her eyes for me that I was rocked by it. I have been so closed off for so long, I never noticed the way the girls have drawn back from me. Is this what I have wrought with my childish bids for my husband's attention? How could I forget that in hurting their father, I am hurting my daughters as well? Philip tried to tell me this, though I didn't want to believe it. But now that I have seen for myself, it is time to reassess things. Please don't let me be too late. I cannot lose my daughters' love . . .*"

From the diary of Elise Marchand,
August 10, 1813

**T**he bell over the glass door tinkled as Maura and Theodosia stepped over the threshold into Violet's darkened shop.

All was ominously still. The racks of colorful costumes hung unattended, and no shopgirls came hurrying from the back to ask if they could help them with anything.

"Where is everyone?" The dowager duchess whispered the question in Maura's ear, her expression curious.

"I don't know," Maura whispered back. A sudden chill of foreboding raced up her spine. This was decidedly odd. The shop was usually bustling with activity, especially during the Season, when there were so many masquerade balls that required fitting for costumes.

"Violet?" she called out, removing her soaked bonnet as she let her penetrating gaze travel from one end of the room to the other. "Violet, are you here?"

The silence was deafening, and with every second that passed without her friend appearing, she grew more and more concerned. What could have happened?

Pressing Theodosia's hands, she spoke in a low murmur. "Wait here, Your Grace."

The elderly lady started to protest, but Maura whirled before she could get the words out and advanced farther into the shop. "Violet, I received your note. You said you needed to speak to me about something important, so I came at once."

Still no answer, and the tingle at the nape of her neck was growing more insistent. Reaching the counter, she peered through the archway into the back room, but could make out nothing except boxes stacked one on top of the other, more costume racks, and shadows.

"I don't understand," she began, but just as she turned to face the dowager duchess once more, she caught sight of something sticking out from behind the counter.

A slippered foot.

With a cry, she hurried forward. Violet was lying dangerously still on the planked floor, her skin as pale as death. Blood seeped from a large gash on her forehead, but she appeared to still be breathing. The rise and fall of her chest was shallow, but steady.

"Your Grace, please!" Maura cried over her shoulder, pushing aside terrible images of her mother lying in a similar position as she bent to feel for her friend's thready pulse. Unlike the marchioness, Violet was still alive, but there was no telling for how much longer if they didn't act quickly. "You must send your driver for help! Hurry!"

"I'm sorry, Lady Maura, but I'm afraid I can't let you do that."

The unexpected male voice had her whipping about, her heart flying into her throat, just in time to see Theodosia slump to the floor, as pale and still as Violet.

Lord Stratton stood next to where the elderly lady had fallen, his mouth set in a grim line. With his clothes torn and stained and his hair a limp, greasy, snarled mass about his face, he looked as if he had been through a war.

And he held the pistol that he had slammed into the dowager's temple aimed at Maura's heart.

Maura swallowed convulsively, and one hand flew to her throat in horrified dismay. "Lord Stratton. What are you doing here?"

"Cleaning up a bit of a mess, it would seem. But then, that's nothing new. I'm good at cleaning up messes."

Maura's heart skipped a beat at his words. Could it be? Had Lord Lanscombe been the culprit after all?

"For your father?" she prompted, her voice shaking in spite of herself. "He murdered my mother, didn't he? And you've known all along. You're covering his tracks."

He shook his head with a derisive curl of his lips. "My father knows nothing about this. I'm afraid I'm covering my own tracks, as it were."

"Your own . . . ?" The wild light in those narrowed eyes struck a chord inside Maura, and suddenly she knew. Their numerous encounters over the last few years came together like puzzle pieces as she recalled all the times he had called her "Jezebel" in that venom-laced tone, the times he had accused her of being just like her mother.

"You killed my mother?" she choked. The world

swam around her and she staggered against the counter, bracing her palms on its polished surface for balance. "But . . . but that's not possible. You . . . You're too young. You couldn't have been involved with her twenty-five years ago."

His weapon wavered in his hand, and he took a menacing step toward her. "You stupid chit! I was never involved with her. Not like that. But I stood by and watched her seduce my father away from my mother. Some common actress who wasn't fit to wipe my mother's shoes." Ice-cold fury vibrated off him in waves so intense that it was almost palpable. "He'd had his affairs before, but once he met Elise, he was blinded to all else. It was as if she put some sort of spell on him."

He paused, then went on, his words holding such a confused mixture of reverence and hatred that Maura could no longer doubt that he had been the one who had written those letters to Lady Albright. "He used to take me with him to visit her when I was a boy, you know. I was nine, and the first time I saw her on stage I thought she was some exotic Gypsy princess. And she was kind to me, unlike the others. So I thought . . . I thought she was different." His fingers tightened on the pistol until his knuckles turned white. "But she wasn't different at all. She seduced my father and threw him aside for the next man who came along. Just as she did with Lord Bedford and Lord Cunnington."

Maura felt ill. "You behave as if your father

was some innocent victim, but he—"

"He was! She was a blight upon my family. My father couldn't forget her. I . . . couldn't forget her. And several years later, she was back. Married and a marchioness, but the same slut she'd always been. Taunting and teasing my father, leading him on. Then along came Hawksley's father, and she abandoned him once again."

A faraway look came over Stratton's face. "Oh, I wanted her. I admit it. What man wouldn't? And I was a man now, wasn't I? I was sure she'd be glad to welcome me between her legs, slut that she was. But when I approached her, do you know what she did? She laughed at me. Told me that she had never thought of me that way." His own laughter was incredulous and vaguely maniacal. "Can you believe it? That whore would fuck a drunken sot like the earl, but turn *me* away?"

Struggling to remain calm, Maura watched him closely. He was clearly coming undone, and that frightened her more than ever. A glance over his shoulder at the front door of the shop showed that while she had been busy assessing Violet's condition, he had managed to flip the closed sign around and lower the shades over the glass, so there would be no customers wandering in to come to her aid. That meant she was on her own. At least until someone at home started to wonder where she was and thought to ask Aimee. Who knew how much longer that would be?

Somehow she would have to figure out a way to stall him. But she would have to be careful. If she pushed him too hard or made him any angrier, there was no telling what he would do.

Taking a deep breath, she spoke in a low, soothing tone, as if she were trying to comfort a wounded animal. "I'm sure Mama didn't mean to be cruel."

Stratton scowled at her. "Of course, she did. That was her nature. She enjoyed having men at her whim, ruining them. And I knew she was going to be the ruination of many more if she wasn't stopped. I had to make her stop."

"So you killed her."

"It was so simple. I was at the Briarwood ball, you see. I forged a note from the late Lord Hawksley and had one of Lady Briarwood's servants deliver it to her." The smile that spread over Stratton's face was full of malicious glee. "And a second letter was delivered to the earl, signed 'Your Loving Elise.' It sent him racing to her side, eager to run away with his beloved."

Maura closed her eyes for a second. More than likely, the poor man had been confused and wondering what on earth was going on. He had to have known that something was wrong after reading that letter. Had to have known that her mother hadn't written it. So he had come to the Albright town house with the sole purpose of getting to the bottom of things. Only he had been too late to save her mother.

Or himself.

Stratton was still speaking, oblivious to her preoccupation. "All I had to do was show up at the door that night and your mother let me in, thinking I was him. Then I waited around to dispose of Hawksley. It was a perfectly executed crime. I rid London of a faithless whore, and I had a dupe to pin it all on."

"But it wasn't perfectly executed, was it?" Maura said quietly. "You made mistakes. People started to suspect that something was off, didn't they?"

"Not until your bloody sister and that Bow Street Runner began poking around," he snarled at her. "And then you came along and had to start sticking your nose in things as well. I overheard you and Hawksley in your room at Rosemont Hall the other night as I was leaving my stepmother's chambers. You were discussing everything, and I heard you mention that your friend over there would be questioning people at the theater." He indicated Violet with a jerk of his head. "I've paid more than my share of visits there over the last few years. I liked going there, spending time in Elise's old dressing room, recalling the days when Father and I used to visit her there. I knew if Miss Lafleur asked the right person, she would find out about me. And she did."

At that moment, out of the corner of her eye, Maura caught sight of a slight blur of motion off to her right, a shift in the shadows of the back room, and her mouth went dry. Was someone in there? Had someone finally come to their rescue?

If so, she had to continue to keep Stratton occupied.

She licked her lips and took a step away from the counter, moving a bit to the left to draw the man's gaze away from the entrance to the back room. "Lord Stratton, you must see you can never get away with this. Perhaps you could have gotten rid of Violet and myself without too many questions being asked. But the Dowager Duchess of Maitland?" She looked down at Theodosia. From this distance, she couldn't even tell if her friend was still breathing, and her heart clenched. "Her death will not be brushed off so easily."

He lifted a shoulder in a shrug. "She's a rather unexpected complication, but it can't be avoided. It shouldn't be too difficult to explain, however. A robbery attempt, gone tragically wrong. These things happen all the time." As he moved toward Maura, his lascivious stare trailed over her in a way that left her feeling as if he had physically touched her. The sensation was far from pleasant, and she had to stifle the urge to retch. "Perhaps I could even take a bit of time to sate myself with you. I promise, I'd make it good. But in the end, you all must die. You have to be stopped. Just like your whore of a mother."

"But you were wrong about Lady Albright, Stratton."

Maura recognized the voice immediately, and she felt a wave of relief and gladness wash over her as Gabriel appeared in the archway to the back room. He carried no weapon, but stood with his arms hanging casually at his sides, tall and strong and gloriously heroic.

Her guardian angel.

"You were wrong," he said again, his gaze never wavering from Stratton. "And so was I."

The other man stiffened and blinked, the tip of the pistol shaking slightly as he lifted it so it was on a level with Maura's head. "What are you doing here, Hawksley?" he grated. "And what the bloody hell are you blathering about?"

"Lady Albright never had an affair with my father. And though she may have been involved with him in the past, she never let your father touch her when she returned to London as the Marchioness of Albright."

"That's a lie!" The words exploded from Stratton, and a muscle jumped in his jaw. "She—she slept with him. She was a whore. She let him—"

"No, it's not a lie." Hawksley's green eyes were steady and solemn. But even as he kept his stare trained on the other man, he shifted closer to Maura, the move so subtle that he almost hadn't seemed to move at all. "She was in love with Lord Albright. And because she was full of hurt and disillusionment due to her estrangement from him, she let him and the rest of society believe some things that were not true. But once she was married, she was faithful to her husband."

"You—you can't know this."

"I do, Stratton. I know because I've read her diary."

The pistol shook once again and swung briefly in Hawksley's direction as confusion marked Stratton's features. "But I killed her. I had to." He sounded like a small child, trying to convince himself of what he was saying. "He told me. I had to kill her because she was a whore and I hated her."

Hawksley shook his head and eased forward even more, until he stood in front of Maura, his body shielding hers. "You loved her. And that's why the thought of her with other men hurt you so much. But you must see that she wasn't who you thought she was. When you love someone, Stratton, you see who they really are. You see through their façade to the real person underneath it all."

His words resonated through Maura with powerful intensity. It was almost as if he were speaking to her. And perhaps he was.

Stratton was shifting his weight nervously, his eyes glazing over. "I— You— He said— No! It's a lie! I killed her! I stopped her from hurting anyone else!"

He leveled the pistol over Hawksley's shoulder, straight at Maura's face.

"Damn you, you bitch!" he yelled, his breath coming in such heaving pants that they sounded like sobs. And maybe they were, for tears started to spill from his eyes and flow down his cheeks in torrents. "All my life you've tormented me. Why couldn't you want me? You have to die!"

He took a single step. And in that instant, several things happened at once.

The front windows of the shop shattered, and several people came pouring into the building. And Theodosia's eyes snapped open as she swung out with her cane from her position on the floor, striking Stratton in the legs and sending him stumbling forward.

His pistol went off.

Hawksley turned and flung himself at Maura, knocking her over backward and covering her with his body as the sound of the shot reverberated in the small room. It was followed by several more shots. Then all was quiet.

It took Maura's hearing what seemed like a small eternity to return to normal. Through the buzzing in her ears, she could barely make out what sounded like Tolliver and her brother-in-law, Connor, shouting at each other, accompanied by Theodosia's excited babbling.

And then she realized that Hawksley was still sprawled atop her, his body a dead weight.

Fear seized her. With a panicked cry, she wrapped her arms around him, smoothing her palms over his broad back, checking him for injuries as she spoke with hoarse urgency close to his ear. "Gabriel! Gabriel, can you hear me?"

There was no reply, and when her hands came away from him wet and sticky with blood, the room spun sickeningly around her.

"Help!" she screamed, forcing the cry past her constricted throat, trying to make herself heard over the melee. "Someone help! Lord Hawksley's been shot!"

She shoved at his shoulders in an attempt to roll him off her, and she felt several other hands reach for him, guiding him carefully over and onto his back. She shot to a sitting position, and a hasty inspection quickly revealed where the blood was coming from. It was pouring from a wound in his right side in a sluggish tide, rapidly staining his coat and the floor beneath him.

Her heart seemed to stop beating in her chest and she cradled him to her, stunned and shaken and rapidly descending into shock. Dear God, his face was so white, and he was barely breathing!

And that was when she knew. As she sat there with his head in her lap and the blood he had shed for her staining her hands, she knew that she loved him no matter what. No matter what anyone else thought, no matter who or what he was underneath his façade, devil or angel, she wanted him in her life. Had to be with him.

Tears fogging her vision, she looked pleadingly up into the faces clustered over her. They were little more than a blur, but surely one of them could help her save him.

"Please," she whispered to them. "Please don't let him die."

# Chapter 24

❦

*"In the midst of everything else, I am also trying to cope with a most shocking letter that I received from Hawksley at the ball this evening. Its contents astonished me, for I never suspected that his feelings for me had taken a turn in this direction. I had honestly believed his heart would always belong to his past love. So now I must meet him shortly and somehow make him understand that there can be nothing between us. Despite all of the anger and pain we have caused each other, I still love my husband. And my daughters are all that I live for. I could never, ever leave them. Not for anything or anyone."*

From the diary of Elise Marchand,
August 10, 1813

Gabriel's eyes drifted open to a dim room and the feel of a soft bed beneath him. His mouth was dry and he ached all over, as if someone had taken to beating him with a club while he was asleep.

With a groan, he started to sit up. But a gentle hand against his chest—along with a sharp, wrenching pain in his right side—stopped him.

"Don't try to move."

Even without looking, he would have recognized her voice. It was Maura, and she sat in a chair next to the bed, studying him with beautiful blue eyes full of concern.

"How are you feeling?" she asked quietly.

"As if I'd fallen under the wheels of a carriage." He squinted up at her, unable to recall how he had gotten here or what she was doing at his bedside. "What happened?"

"Lord Stratton shot you. You've been in and out of consciousness for two days now."

Stratton!

The alarming memory almost sent him arrowing upward in bed again. The pistol. The crazed look on the man's face . . .

Capturing Maura's hand on his chest, he threaded his fingers through hers and held her gaze with unwavering intensity, trying to read the truth in her expression. "Are you all right?"

"I'm fine, thanks to you." Her angelic smile warmed him all over, like a soothing balm to his soul. "So is Violet. And Theodosia, though she has a nasty bruise on her temple. And by the way, you may want to thank her the next time you see her. When she struck him with her cane, it knocked his aim off, so the bullet only grazed your side. A few inches over and—"

She stumbled to a halt, but she didn't need to finish. Gabriel had sensed how close he had come to death. And he could only thank God that it had been he instead of she. If he had lost her . . .

Shoving away the untenable thought, he glanced around the room, attempting to get his bearings. Nothing looked familiar to him, however, so he turned back to Maura. "Where am I?"

"At my family's town house," she replied, easing her hand from his and reaching up to smooth a strand of hair from his forehead. "And before you say a word, my father insisted upon it. You did save my life after all. And it's not as if you had anyone else to look after you at home."

He raised a brow at her. "I'll wager your aunt has loved that."

She moved to sit next to him on the edge of the mattress, lifting a shoulder in a shrug as she did so. "I could care less what my aunt thinks about anything anymore." A twinkle suddenly entered her eyes, and she gave a low, melodious laugh. "In fact, I do believe my sisters would like to personally shake your hand. Ever since the day they carried you in here, Aunt Olivia has stayed locked in her room with her vinaigrette, bemoaning her fate in private. We've all been much happier."

He laughed with her, but after a second their eyes locked and they both sobered.

"So Stratton killed my father and your mother," he ventured after a short span of silence. "I had come to suspect that, but I wasn't certain until I saw him holding that pistol on you. Was he arrested?"

Maura shook her head and glanced away. "No. He is dead. He was shot during the skirmish when Mr. Tolliver, Connor, and Lord Stonehurst burst into the shop."

"And?"

"And I suppose that is punishment enough. But I can't help thinking about all the years that my family has suffered because of him." Her chin lifted at a militant angle. "He deserved to suffer before he died. To suffer for what he put us through."

Gabriel reached out to take her hand again, enfolding her cold, trembling fingers tenderly. "In his own way, I'd say he did suffer. He was quite mad, you know."

"I know. But still . . ." Pursing her lips, she blew out a weary breath. "In any case, it is finally over. That will have to be enough for me. And it has helped to stay busy." She cast him a sly look from beneath lowered lashes. "You needed a personal nursemaid, after all."

"And your father has allowed you to do that?"

"Her father didn't have a choice."

The deep voice drifted from the direction of the door, and they both jerked their heads around to find the Marquis of Albright standing in the open archway, watching them with an unreadable expression.

Advancing into the chamber, the man came to stand at the foot of the bed, his shrewd gaze taking in how close Maura sat next to Gabriel, as well as their entwined hands. But he didn't comment. "My daughter wouldn't hear of letting anyone else do it," he said with a hint of amusement. "And I wasn't about to argue with her. She was most fierce. And rather frightening."

The flush that stained Maura's cheeks at Lord Albright's words delighted Gabriel, but he wouldn't prod her about it in front of her father. Instead he inclined his head to the marquis in grateful acknowledgment. "I thank you for your generosity in allowing me to recuperate here, my lord."

"Nonsense. You saved my daughter's life, and put your own life in jeopardy in the process." Albright paused, then tilted his head in consideration. "You must care for her a great deal."

"Papa—" Maura started to protest.

But the man cut her off with an upraised hand. "It's all right, dearest. I'm not going to press him. I'm certain when he is ready to ask me for your hand, he will do so." One corner of his mouth curved wryly as his knowing eyes rested on their linked hands once again. "Though he does appear to be clinging to it rather tenaciously already."

Maura let out a gasp and tried to pull away from Gabriel's hold, but he stubbornly hung on, his stare never wavering from Albright's. Something almost imperceptible passed between them, an unspoken message that told Gabriel that the marquis knew exactly what he felt for Maura and approved.

As if in confirmation of his impression, the older man gave him a subtle nod before facing Maura and placing a hand on her shoulder. "I have finished reading the diary."

She looked up at him, her features drawn into a mask of worry. "Are you all right, Papa?"

"I'm fine. Angry with myself for being blind to so many things. And for being so weak." The marquis heaved a sigh. "I never should have closed your mother out the way I did, but I suppose I wasn't nearly as strong as I had thought myself to be. I was so sure that I would be able to stand at her side, to turn my nose up at society no matter what they thought of my marriage to her. And that was easy to do when we were hiding away in Dorset. But the moment we were back in London, the moment our love was put to the true test, I abandoned her."

He lifted the book he held in his free hand. His wife's journal. "It has helped to know she was faithful to me, that she loved me until the end. And now that we know what really happened, who the real killer was, maybe we can all have some peace."

Letting his eyes drift closed for a brief instant,

Gabriel pictured a better future. One with Maura by his side. "I hope so, my lord."

Several silent moments ticked by as they all reflected on what had been and what had yet to be. Then the marquis cleared his throat and looked at Gabriel. "Yes, well, you've had a visitor this morning. Lord Stonehurst. Actually, he has been by several times in the last couple of days."

Gabriel winced at the viscount's name. "I'm sorry."

Lord Albright chuckled. "Don't be. He may seem a bit grim and gruff on the outside, but he was a great deal of help to us in the aftermath of what happened with Stratton."

"I don't know what we would have done without him," Maura agreed, squeezing Gabriel's hand, her eyes lighting with evident fondness. "He has been very worried about you, you know. I can tell, even though he never says much. And Aimee seems fascinated with him, which surprises me. She's usually so very timid around strange males, and he's so . . . well, big. Bigger even than Connor. But he's been most patient with her trailing after him."

Gabriel was surprised, but thankful for the Daventry family's ready acceptance of his withdrawn friend. His heart swelling with gratitude, he lifted Maura's fingers to his lips for a brief caress. "Yes. Stonehurst is a good friend."

There was the sound of a gruffly cleared throat. "Well, as I have several estate matters to see to that have been neglected since my illness, I suppose I shall leave the two of you alone." The marquis pressed a kiss to his daughter's cheek and started for the door. But he hesitated before departing the room and glanced back over his shoulder, his countenance serious as he met Gabriel's gaze. "For what's its worth, Hawksley, I apologize for believing the worst of your father. For letting my attitude toward you through the years be colored by my judgment of him. You're a good man."

"Thank you, my lord."

Once the marquis had disappeared out the door, Maura turned to Gabriel, her manner suddenly tentative and uncertain. "He's not the only one who needs to apologize."

"Maura, sweetheart, don't—"

"I have to. Although I don't know how I shall ever forgive myself, even if you can forgive me. I thought so badly of my mother for so long, and then found out I was wrong about her. You would think I would have learned not to judge a person by what you see on the outside." She blinked rapidly and lifted a hand to dash at a drop of moisture that had spilled over to trickle down her cheek, then took a deep breath to steady herself before continuing. "What about you? Now that you know that your father was innocent, will you be able to forgive him?"

"Perhaps I can begin to come to terms with my memories of him, if not precisely forgive. My situation was a bit different from yours, love. Innocent or not, my father was so bitter and disillusioned by what he lost that he had no room for love in his heart. He never loved me or my mother. And I didn't love him. But you . . ." Gabriel lifted a hand to cup her cheek, his thumb brushing at the wet spot left behind by her stray tear. "Your mother loved you, sweetheart. And she wouldn't want you to keep blaming yourself."

He drew her into his arms, holding her close against his chest.

They might have stayed that way forever, content to bask in the pure joy of their togetherness, if he hadn't been seized by a sudden fit of coughing. He winced as his side gave him another painful reminder of his injury, and Maura got to her feet, crossed the room to pour him a glass of water from the pitcher on the nearby stand, and brought it back to him. Once he had finished greedily downing the contents with her help, she set the glass aside and settled onto the bed next to him again, her gaze downcast.

He peered up at her, trying to guess the direction of her thoughts. "I haven't told you how sorry I am that I didn't tell you about my suspicions regarding Stratton," he murmured. "But it happened that last night at the Hall and—"

"We argued. I know." She bit her lip, her features marred by anxiety. "I'm so sorry for that, Gabriel. I never should have doubted you or accused you of such vile things."

"It was just as much my fault. You had no reason to trust me and—"

"Hush." Maura placed a finger over his lips, silencing him. "I had every reason. You'd come to my rescue time and again. Shown me the man behind the mask. I just didn't want to admit I could be wrong about so many things. You. Me. Your father. My mother." She stroked his lower lip with her thumb, and he had to restrain the urge to catch it between his teeth. "And most of all, what I wanted."

"And what do you want?"

"You. And me. Together. I love you, Gabriel."

Gabriel's heart leaped and his breath seized in his chest at the words it seemed he had been waiting an eternity to hear. It took every bit of willpower he possessed to keep his tone calm and even when he responded. "Are you sure about that?"

"That's the one thing I am sure of."

Tilting his head on the pillow, he craned his neck so he could look directly into her eyes. "I love you too."

"I know. I think I've known it for a long time. But I was scared of what you made me feel."

"I want you to know I never touched Lady Lanscombe that night," he rushed to assure her. "I was talking to her about Stratton, and that's all. I wouldn't—"

But she halted him once again. "It's all right. You don't have to explain to me. I trust you."

His brow lifted as he surveyed her thoughtfully. "And what do you think society will make of our match?"

"I find that matters very little to me anymore. Those who love me will understand. Theodosia is singing your praises, and so are Aimee and Jilly. And I'm sure you can tell that my father approves. As for the rest . . . well, we can do anything if we face them together."

"And Lord Waldron?"

"Believe it or not, he actually came to see me when he heard about what had happened. Papa showed him the door with little ado." She laughed, an enchanting, carefree sound that he didn't think he had ever heard from her before. "I can't believe that I actually thought of marrying him. That I believed love and passion were things to be avoided. That's all I want now."

"Me too. With you."

There was another pause as she leaned over him, looking down at him with sad eyes. "Your parents. My parents. So many people whose lives were ruined, simply because they let society dictate their decisions. I don't want that to happen to me, Gabriel."

"Nor do I."

"I want to live my life for me now. Not for Aunt Olivia, Or Mama. Or even Papa. Though somehow I think he may be happy to hear that, rather than disappointed."

Smoothing a wisp of hair back from her cheek, Gabriel slid his palm around the nape of her neck to draw her closer, until their lips were just inches apart. "Your father wants you to be happy, Maura. That's what makes him happy. And that's what makes me happy."

He captured her mouth in a thorough kiss.

When they broke apart, they were both breathing heavily.

"I know what else would make me happy," he said with a grin. "To see you again in that dress you wore to the Lanscombe masquerade. That was most becoming, love. And very eye-opening.

A slight stain of pink appeared on her high cheekbones, though her mouth curved in a seductive smile. "That was Violet's. But perhaps I could borrow it if you are a very good boy."

He skimmed his lips once more over hers before whispering, "That would be nice. But I would like it even better if you were wearing nothing."

"Ah, well, once you are fully recovered and we are properly wed, I'll see what I can do about that, my devilish love. Until then, you shall have to take me fully clothed."

And with a soft growl, her devilish love proceeded to show her that he was delighted to take her any way at all.

# Epilogue

In a darkened room, before an empty hearth, a lone figure sat slumped in the corner of an elegant settee, a copy of the *London Times* clutched in bloodless hands.

So it was finally over. Stratton had taken the fall alone and was now dead, and no one would ever know that someone else had been involved in the Marchioness of Albright's death.

A heavy sigh drifted on the chilly air in the still chamber. Everything would be all right.

As long as the youngest girl never remembered a thing . . .

*Next month, don't miss these exciting new love stories only from Avon Books*

## The Viscount in Her Bedroom by Gayle Callen

**An Avon Romantic Treasure**

Simon, Viscount Wade, leads an orderly life. Then he meets the vivacious, witty, and beautiful Louisa Shelby and everything is turned upside down. Suddenly, Simon finds himself drawn into the mystery of Louisa's past . . . and dreaming of a future in her arms.

## At the Edge by Cait London

**An Avon Contemporary Romance**

A powerful empath, Claire Brown has learned it's much easier to live in solitude than constantly be exposed to the pain of others. But when a desperate man moves in next door, she finds herself powerless against his pleas for help—and unable to stop him from breaching her carefully erected walls.

## The Templar's Seduction by Mary Reed McCall

**An Avon Romance**

Spared a death sentence, Sir Alexander must impersonate an earl if he wishes to stay on the king's good side. But his task is made all the more complicated by the earl's lovely—and suspicious—wife, who is starting to believe that the miraculous return of her husband is not all that it seems.

## A Dangerous Beauty by Sophia Nash

**An Avon Romance**

Rosamunde Baird has sworn off adventure and temptation. That's what makes the mysterious Duke of Helston so dangerous—and compelling. And now, to hold on to the love he never expected, the duke must reveal a past he has so desperately kept hidden.